"DATA! ARE YOU ALL RIGHT?"

"Yes, I am all right," he replied. "Merely chagrined. I came here to rescue you."

"Yes, well there is some question as to whether or not I require rescue," Tasha told him. She did not appear to be held prisoner. She was wearing a long, loose dress of a softer gold color than her uniform.

She turned to the man standing behind her near the fire, leaning on the mantelpiece. "Data, may I present Adrian Dareau, better known as—"

"—better known as former Starfleet Commander Darryl Adin," Data supplied, the most wanted criminal in the Federation."

Ignoring the four weapons still covering him, Data stepped forward.

"As an authorized representative of Starfleet, I arrest you, sir, on twenty-one counts of murder, two counts of conspiracy, and three counts of treason against the United Federation of Planets."

Tasha gasped.

Darryl Adin simply stared at him, dumbfounded, for a moment.

Then he threw back his head, and laughed out loud.

Look for STAR TREK Fiction from Pocket Books

#4

SURVIVORS

JEAN LORRAH

POCKET BOOKS
New York   London   Toronto   Sydney   Tokyo

An *Original* Publication of POCKET BOOKS

POCKET BOOKS, a division of Simon & Schuster Inc.
1230 Avenue of the Americas, New York, NY 10020

ISBN: 0-671-67438-2

First Pocket Books printing January 1989

10 9 8 7 6 5 4 3 2 1

POCKET and colophon are trademarks of
Simon & Schuster Inc.

Printed in the U.S.A.

Foreword

I would like to thank Gene Roddenberry, the creator of *Star Trek,* which has been such an important influence in my life; Joseph Stafano and Hannah Louise Shearer, the authors of "Skin of Evil," a major influence on this novel; and Dave Stern, editor at Pocket Books, who gave me strong support in bringing this book into existence. I have been a *Star Trek* fan since 1966, when the first Classic Trek episodes appeared. I learned to write through fanzines, and have made many wonderful friends through Trekfandom. And now, incredibly, Mr. Roddenberry has given us Trekfen [sic] a whole new world and a whole new group of characters to love in *Star Trek: The Next Generation.*

You may be familiar with my Classic Trek novels, *The Vulcan Academy Murders* and *The IDIC Epidemic.* If you wonder how I can write about the new characters and the new ship after spending so many years with the originals, the answer is that the new episodes are a continuation, not a replacement. The spirit of Trek is as much alive as ever—as I hope you can feel in this novel.

Most of the action of *Survivors* occurs late in the first season of *Star Trek: The Next Generation,* between the episodes "The Arsenal of Freedom" and "Symbiosis." By that time the crew of the new *Enterprise* know one another pretty well, and Lt. Commander Data, who is one of the main characters in this book, has had experiences that have led him a little farther along the path to understanding the human spirit than where he was at the opening of the series. Lt. Tasha Yar, the other protagonist, is succeeding in her career, and has no expectations of the fate in store for her. She seems far more contented and serene than in earlier episodes—and this book will suggest why.

If you have been a *Star Trek* fan for years, you may already know about fandom. If you have just joined us via the new series, welcome! Paramount sponsors a fan club with a bimonthly newsletter to tell you all the latest news about the movies, the TV series, the actors and creators:

The Official *Star Trek* Fan Club
P.O. Box 111000
Aurora, CO 80011

But Trekfandom is not limited to the fan club. If you write or draw or make music or costumes or want to interact with other fans, you want the original fandom: friends and letters and crafts and fanzines and trivia and costumes and art-work and filksongs [sic] and posters and buttons and games and conventions—something for everybody.

The way to that fandom is not through me, or any other author of *Star Trek* novels. You want that wonderful organization, *The Star Trek Welcommittee*. Be *sure* to include a stamped, self-addressed envelope, as this is a purely volunteer organization of people who love *Star Trek* and are willing to answer your questions and put you in touch with other fans. The current address:

The Star Trek Welcommittee
P.O Drawer 12
Saranac, MI 48881

In both Trekwriting and my other professional science fiction, I have a strong belief in the interaction between authors and fans. Authors want your constructive comments. They cannot collaborate with you, write the stories you want to tell (you'll have to do that yourself), or critique your novels, (they're busy writing their own). They have lives, families, jobs, too—for example, I am Professor of English at Murray State University. After teaching all week I want to spend my weekend working on the next novel I am writing for you to read, not writing letters about how to write novels. You can't learn to write that way anyway; you must learn by doing. Get involved in fanzines and develop your skills as so many of us did. Writing workshops can be a great help, too—the authors conducting them have set that time aside specifically for that purpose, and will welcome you.

All authors are happy to receive comments about their books, and most will answer questions. Did you know that almost everyone who writes Trek novels also writes other science fiction novels? If Trek novels by a particular author appeal to you, you might very well enjoy that author's other work. Chances are, the themes he or she chooses to develop in Trek are the same ones he or she treats in other books. Ask at your booksellers for other science fiction books by your favorite *Star Trek* authors.

If you would like to comment on this or any of my other books, you may write to me in care of my publishers, or at P.O. Box 625, Murray, KY 42071–0625. If your letter requires an answer, please enclose a stamped, self-addressed envelope.

Keep on Trekkin'!

Jean Lorrah
Murray, Kentucky

SURVIVORS

Chapter One

THE PLANET WAS CALLED New Paris, for the emigrants from Earth who sought refuge in space after the Post-Atomic Horror meant their new world to be a planet of light. They intended to found a society where people could be free, healthy, and happy, where the arts would flourish, where love would grow and hate wither.

Unfortunately, when New Paris was rediscovered by the United Federation of Planets in the Twenty-fourth Century, it was far more like the Paris portrayed by Victor Hugo than that depicted by Toulouse-Lautrec. The dream had died generations since; in the struggle first for survival and then for dominion, the inhabitants of New Paris had brought upon themselves the very fate their ancestors had risked their lives in fragile sub-light ships to escape.

In a city that had once been a model of the union of form and function to produce beauty and comfort, a fifteen-year-old girl huddled in the ruins left by The Last War. There were no more wars on New Paris that could destroy on that scale; today's ganglords held power by the strength of their bodies, their numbers, their fighting skills, or their control over food and drug supplies.

Ragged and filthy, the girl held in her arms the one

11

comfort in her life, a ginger cat with whom she shared what food she could find or steal, who in turn kept the rats away from her while she slept—in fact allowed her to sleep, knowing the cat would wake her if anyone or anything came near. One time it had even sprung, yowling, on the neck of a man who was trying to kill the girl for the roasted fowl she had pilfered. It gave her the chance to get her knife out, and while the cat kept the attacker occupied, dispatch him. Needless to say, the cat shared generously in the girl's stolen feast that day.

But the cat, which she had never named because she knew nothing of the Earth custom of keeping pets and giving them names, could not help her now. She had been spotted by one of the rape gangs—and she was only too aware that this time they would not give up their pursuit.

The one and only time they had caught her, she had been barely twelve. That time, they had used her for their own amusement, then laughed at her and let her go. She was too young, too skinny, too hungry.

"We're throwin' ya back, gel. Grow up and get some bazooms! Then it'll be worth it t'feed yer hungry belly, 'cause there's allus geezers'll pay high fer fresh meat—an' you'll get nice clothes and lotsa pretties, and plenty o' joy dust t'keep ya happy."

That was when the girl learned to fight. There were girls in the gangs; in fact some gangs were made up of women and girls. But, as she had not been born into a gang, they would not have her while she was small and skinny, weak and hungry. The only way to join a gang was to prove your worth—and she had no worth, as the rape gang had just demonstrated. Well, she certainly didn't want to become valuable in their way! The only alternative was to become strong and skilled, so she could join the warrior women, and never worry about rape gangs again. She turned her shock and fear into anger, her anger into determination.

But determination was one thing; training was another. The girl had no connections with any of the gangs. Her mother had deserted her when she was only five, and the old woman who had taken pity on the starving child was a derelict who had outlived the rest of her own gang. She saw in the child someone to do petty thieving for her, and huddle with her against the cold at night. And perhaps most of all, someone to talk to. She had taught the girl the tricks of a cutpurse, simple lock-picking, and the very important skill of finding the way through the labyrinth of ruined buildings.

She taught the girl to read a little, to be able to decipher the occasional sign still legible in the cellars and tunnels that had survived the holocaust. To the street people of New Paris—the vast majority of the population—avoiding radioactive zones or finding the way through endless miles of identical corridors was the only use for understanding letters. There were no books in their world; any that might have survived had been burned many winters ago for whatever warmth they might provide. Newspapers were unheard of, for the wealthy druglords who lived high above the ruins exchanged their messages by runners or communications consoles. In those few tall buildings left standing, they kept some measure of leftover technology. None of the comcons in the streets below worked, nor electricity, nor plumbing. Such luxuries were only for the powerful few.

So at age twelve, the girl had no skills worth the trouble of a gang to feed and protect her—and so she set out to learn to protect herself. She had a weapon, the old woman's knife that was all her legacy, "And more than ever I got o' me own mother!" the girl had said upon finding her companion dead when she awoke one morning. She had not been able to make herself take her clothes, but had gone through the pockets. The old woman would have expected it. After all, she had no more use for the two coins, the scrap of bread, the three pins, and that all-purpose knife, the blade honed to half its original width, left from her gang days.

But the day the rape gang found the girl, just two days after the old woman's death, the knife did her little good. Perhaps sorrow had made her careless, inattentive to the movements in the shadows. The knife was wrenched out of her hand by a laughing man who used it to force her to submit.

They had tied a hood over her head, so she could not see to fight, could not bite, could not see what was happening as she nearly suffocated while they took their turns at her. And then, when it was over, the leader pulled the hood off and scornfully tossed her knife down beside her, knowing she was too weak and terrified to use it.

She had learned from that experience. Care for a dead woman had let her be caught, so she would not think about anyone else, ever again. She made no attempt to befriend the packs of urchins who scorned her as "The ol' witch's slavey." She was no match for a man if he once got his hands on her, so she would learn to throw the knife, to kill from a distance. That she could teach herself, and did; within weeks she could hit a fixed target every time, and more and more often she skewered the rats she aimed at, even when they scurried in the dimness.

Some two years later, when she rescued the cat from a pack of wild children intent on setting its tail afire, it eased her loneliness a little. She didn't really care about the animal, she told herself, except that it was useful. Like her knife. That made it all right to feed the cat, stroke it, be comforted by its purring when she woke from restless dreams.

The way the children had scattered, despite the fact that they could have taken her by virtue of their sheer numbers, gave her confidence. The added wariness she had developed after her painful experience stood her in good stead as she picked locks and crept into the market at night to help herself to the best food, instead of trying to filch whatever she could, along with all the other urchins, in the daytime.

The rape gangs never took her again, although they pursued her. Twice, when she had eluded the bulk of them, one member continued to dog her. She doubled back and lay in ambush, killing silently with her knife, tossing the body down the bottomless shafts that were just another danger in the ruins. She grew bigger and stronger—and then her body betrayed her by blossoming a woman's curves, even though she remained thin and wiry.

It was time, she decided. She would approach one of the

women's gangs, show them her skill with a knife, tell them of killing two rape gang members—offer to show them how she did it, for of course the women's gangs and the rape gangs were deadliest of enemies.

She set her sights on the Hellcats, who controlled four blocks of ruins and had electricity working in the building they lived in and guarded like a fortress. Surely, like all the buildings in the ruins, that fortress had rats. She planned to offer the cat along with herself, as a parcel, for in the rat-infested ruins a cat was a most valuable commodity. That was probably why the children had been so terrified when she caught them torturing it: she might have been part of a gang that would have punished them severely. Careful-ly, she rehearsed her speech: how appropriate the cat would be as mascot for the Hellcats, how she herself had learned catlike stealth, how she could strike and kill her enemies—

As she lay on her side with the cat perched on her shoulder, purring contentedly, the girl thought happily about tomorrow night. Instead of this pile of rags, she might have a real bed in the Hellcats' fortress. She wondered if they ate hot food every day. Her stomach rumbled and her mouth watered at the thought.

No, she mustn't think about food. Pickings had been lean lately. Even in the market, there wasn't much—so little of some items that she dared not take any, as there would not be enough left to rearrange to hide her pilfering.

So she thought about warm clothes to replace the ones falling off her growing body. She had had to tie front and back of the top of her garment together with bits of string, and it kept slipping down in front, barely covering the "bazooms" which now made her a valuable commodity to the rape gangs.

Some men had seen her today, and eyed her greedily, but she had slipped away, hoping they were not rape gang members. When they did not follow her, she assumed they were not. Still, being drooled over that way brought back the memory of being caught—

She turned over, spilling the cat off her shoulder. It came back quietly as soon as she settled in a new position, purring again. The girl rubbed its head, taking comfort in its warmth, its softness, the way it pushed against her hand as if to say it would take care of her.

Suddenly the cat arched, sat up, then leaped off the girl, hissing and spitting.

She sat up—and saw a glimmer of light down the twisting corridor.

But she was not trapped; she had learned never to be without a bolt-hole.

She picked up the cat and scurried into an adjoining tunnel where she knelt, trembling. She tried to calm the cat, fearing it would run toward their hunters and be killed. When she felt secure that it would come with her out the other direction, she set it down headed the way she meant to go, whispering, "Now run! This place isn't safe at all." She took one final glance toward the corridor where she could see the lights, hear the men calling, taunting her—

The ruins were a deathtrap at night, but there was no choice. She had to run, risk falling into one of the bottom-less shafts—

A hand closed on her shoulder.

She turned by reflex, shock seizing her gut as she recognized the leader of the rape gang, come in the back way—

The cat leaped on him!

The man yelled, and the others came pounding in as the girl slashed her attacker's shoulder.

Instantly, she realized her mistake. She should have run out past him; she might have had a chance in the tunnels in the dark.

Revenge had cost her her chance—two men grabbed her from behind, while their leader captured the cat in a hammy hand, then wrested the knife from the girl and before her eyes gutted the only living being who cared for her.

She shrieked, struggled, bit, but it was no use. Again a hood was slipped over her head, drawn tight about her throat. Her hands were forced behind her back and mana-cled together, and she heard the man in front of her say, "We been watchin' you, girl. You growed up nice an' purty. You'll fetch a good price, oncet we've had our own fun!"

Then she was picked up, slung over somebody's shoulder, as he continued, "Let's get outta here. Gotta get this cut fixed afore I do my playin'—an' don't you go gittin' no ideas 'bout havin' her first!"

Struggling was hopeless. Her only chance was to go limp, let them think she had passed out. Save her strength. It wasn't all easy going—eventually her captor had to put her down and rest a moment. Even manacled and hooded, she jumped up and ran, barking her shins on something, hitting her head—

Pain didn't matter! If she fell down a bottomless shaft, even death would be better than joy dust and a life of being used against her will. Enough joy dust, and she wouldn't care. Wouldn't care about anything, not even her own child—like her mother.

Although in her heart she knew it was hopeless, the girl used rage to keep fear at bay.

A foot was thrust into her path. She fell headlong, unable to catch herself. She turned her face sideways, but her cheek still impacted painfully with solid rock and she came to being partly carried, partly dragged up into the night air, chill against her skin. The man carrying her was swearing and sweating with the exertion, but it did nothing to warm her. Despite her best intentions, shock and fear took her. She shivered uncontrollably.

"Let's rest here," she heard the leader's voice. "Damn— I'm still bleedin'!"

The girl was dumped to the ground, but did not see the kick coming and so could not avoid it. It caught her in the ribs. She cried out in pain, and felt her trembling increase.

"Wassamatter girl—you cold? Good! You made me suffer, *you* suffer. Shunta kicked ya—don't want no marks t'spoil yer price. But no reason you should be comfortable."

The girl felt the knife at her throat, but it didn't cut her skin. Instead, the strings holding the top of her garment were severed, and it dropped off. Then the knife was at her waistband, slitting the rest of her clothes, peeling them off as if he were skinning her, while the other men murmured approvingly. The memory of former pain and humiliation refused to be denied. The girl lost contact with her anger and shivered more and more violently—

"What's going on here? What do you men think you're doing?" an authoritative voice rang out.

"Who're you?" the rape gang leader responded. Even through her shock and despair the girl heard astonishment and a hint of fear in his voice.

"My God!" said another voice, this one female. "They're raping her! Dare—stop them!"

"She's mine!" exclaimed the gang leader. "You got yer own woman!"

"Let her go," said the authoritative voice again. "She can tell us whether she's yours or not."

The strange voices were hard to understand; the girl had never heard anyone who spoke just like them before, even though they were speaking her language.

"Lookit!" said one of the gang members. "They got a purty woman, jewelry, an' technic stuff! There's only three of 'em—"

"Shut up! You want druglords' revenge?"

"Drop 'em down the pits. No one'll know. It's only *three,* Hafe! Look, man, that's *gold* they're wearin'!"

With her head covered, the girl could not tell exactly what happened, but she could guess that greed overcame fear, and the gang rushed the newcomers, intending to rob and kill them.

Grasping the unexpected chance, she began worming away from the sounds of the fight.

She heard a strange, high-pitched whirring sound, like nothing she had ever heard before, and thuds of bodies dropping, followed by gasps of fear and footsteps running . . . away.

Hands touched her. She squirmed and kicked in terror.

"Hey—it's all right!" said the female voice. "We're not going to hurt you. You're safe now."

The hands were untying the hood, so the girl lay still, desperate to be free of it. "Oh, my God—it's just a little girl!" said the woman. "Honey, you're safe," she repeated. "We won't let them hurt you anymore."

There was light, not torch beams but some strange bright electric light that brought tears to the girl's eyes as she peered up at her new captors.

The woman was at her side, but the girl's eyes traveled past without taking her in, looking up, up long black-clad legs, past some sort of yellow-green pattern on his chest to the face of her new possessor.

To the terrified girl, it seemed a cruel face, staring into hers with eyes as dark and cold as the winter sky. Then the full lips parted, and compassion she assumed was false warmed his features as he squatted down beside her. "Poor little thing! Margie, can't you get her hands untied?"

"They're not tied," said the woman. "They're hand-cuffed."

"Can you talk?" the man asked. "Can you understand us?"

"I . . . understand," the girl ventured warily. As her eyes got used to the light, she could see the bodies of at least four members of the rape gang lying sprawled within her range of vision. These were obviously very dangerous people. Had to be druglords.

"Good," the man said with warm approval. "We'll get those things off your hands, and then— But you're cold!" he said as a new wave of shivering coursed through the girl's body. He looked around, picked up the remains of her clothing and dropped it at once, dusting his hand against his thigh. Then he touched a glittering gold brooch on his chest. It made a chittering noise, and the girl jumped.

The man gave her a reassuring smile, but what he said was not to her or to anybody there with them. "Adin here. I need a metal cutter and a blanket to these coordinates—and hurry. And send down a medic—preferably female. We've got a little girl here, assault case."

"Yes, sir," the brooch answered him.

"It's . . . a comcon!" the girl said. "Innat teeny thing!"

"Yes, that's right," the man said. "And you know the word for it."

"Yah. But where's the wire?"

"Wire?"

"The wire the sound travels through," she explained. Did he think her so stupid she didn't know how comcons worked?

His lips parted again, this time as if he had suddenly discovered something. "So *that's* why we couldn't get a response on any frequency! They don't have wireless communications." He looked past the girl to the woman, a question in his eyes.

She lifted the technic thing hung over her shoulder and pointed it at the girl. It made a whirring sound, and something on it lit up. "Reads human," she said, "and the translator didn't kick in. That's why what these people say sounds strange: it's our language, changed just enough to sound different to us." She glanced meaningfully at the ruins around them. "Obviously, they once had a much higher level of technology, too. Dare, I think we've found a lost Earth colony."

"Thank God," he said. "That means we can take this poor child out of here."

"Dare, you can't—" the woman began, but was interrupted by yet another peculiar sound. A glittering glow appeared a small distance away, and the girl sat up in utter astonishment as out of nothingness coalesced a blanket with another technic thing on top of it.

The third member of this very strange gang brought both over, and the woman did something with the technic thing behind the girl's back. Suddenly her hands were free. Then the woman gently wrapped the blanket around her. It was wonderfully soft, clean, whole. The girl pulled it tight just as the glittering glow appeared again—and this time turned into another woman!

"I'm Dr. Munson," she introduced herself. "We won't hurt you, child." She held up a small silver thing. "This instrument will tell me how badly you've been hurt."

The girl backed off, wondering where the woman meant to stick the thing, but she only pointed it. It made a soft whirring as she held it near different parts of the girl's body. Then the woman looked at it and said, "A slight concussion, one broken rib, contusions, and shock are her immediate

20

problems. But Mr. Adin, you were right to call me, She's malnourished, needs extensive dental work, and is suffering from both internal and external parasites. Please note that the latter means we all go through full decontamination when we beam up."

"No protest on that, Doctor," replied the man that, confusingly, this woman addressed as "Mr. Adin," but the other woman called "Dare." It must mean, the girl reasoned, that one was his name and the other his title; he must be the leader of this gang. He rubbed his hand against his clothes again as he asked, "Is it all right for me to ask her some questions before you take her to sickbay?"

"Take her to—?" The woman's eyes widened, her tone of voice a protest.

The other woman said, "The girl and the men we chased off speak a variant of our language. It's an Earth colony, Doctor."

Doctor looked around. Dawn was just breaking, revealing the ruined city. "I can see why your first instinct is to beam the child up, Mr. Adin, but we'll have to have the Captain's permission, and also that of her parents."

Silently, the girl absorbed that. So Mr. Adin/Dare was not the gang leader; he answered to someone else. She had to leave off puzzling that out as Doctor turned to her. "Do your parents know where you are, child? They must be worried sick."

"Parents?" the girl asked.

"Mother. Father. Your family."

"Got no family," the girl replied sullenly. Actually, she had no idea whether her mother was even alive, although she doubted it. Hooked on joy dust, she probably didn't survive more than a year after abandoning her child.

"Who takes care of you?" asked Mr. Adin.

"Take care o' myself!"

He studied her, obviously wanting to ask something else but saying instead, "My name is Darryl Adin. My friends call me Dare. What's your name?"

"Tasha," the girl replied. It sounded strange; no one had spoken her name since the old woman died.

"Tasha," said Darryl Adin. "Pretty name for a pretty girl."

"Don't wanta be pretty!" the girl told him angrily. "'Tracts the rape gangs!"

"Rape gangs!" exclaimed Doctor. "What sort of place *is* this?"

"Not exactly the ideal planet for shore leave," Darryl Adin replied. Then he returned to his questioning. "Tasha, do you have another name?"

Tasha thought rapidly. This was a very, very powerful gang. It had more technic things than she had ever seen, and this man, obviously important in gang ranking even if he wasn't the leader, wanted to take her with him. She knew what that meant, had known the moment he said she was pretty.

How was she to escape, when they had weapons to defeat a whole rape gang without any of them so much as being cut? Tasha was exhausted, and still cold despite the blanket. She couldn't fight them, so the best thing was to cooperate. For now.

There were women in this gang, and they appeared to be treated with respect. Maybe she could gain the same respect.

Doctor had said things that suggested Tasha's injuries would be cared for. And Darryl Adin had told her to take the girl to someplace called Sickbay. Maybe he didn't want her with a black eye and broken rib—she remembered what the rape gang leader had said about not marking her. Druglords were particular about their women.

That made up Tasha's mind. She was weak, tired, injured. Healing would take a few days, and in the meantime they might feed her and give her new clothes. Druglords had plenty of food and clothing—they had plenty of everything. She would take what they gave her, regain her strength— and then, as soon as she was well and Darryl Adin expected her to be delivered to his bed, she would escape.

Perhaps escape would be impossible. Perhaps they would catch her and force her to submit, or kill her if she refused.

But they would certainly kill her if she did not cooperate with them now, for she had no strength left. For the time being it was best to be very cooperative, try to fit in. Be sweet to Doctor Munson while she was in this Sickbay place, maybe learn how women got to be gang members instead of just men's playthings. The two women were dressed like the two men, except for different colored patterns on the tops of their clothes. It had to mean they were actual gang members. The way Doctor Munson talked back to Darryl Adin, it was certain *she* was!

Darryl Adin had asked if she had another name. He had two names. Doctor Munson had two names. Probably the other gang members had two names, as well. She didn't remember her mother's name—and if she had, would not have wanted to be known by it. So she took one more legacy from the old woman who had taken in a frightened, starving five-year-old and shared what little she had with her. "Yar," she replied boldly. "My name is Tasha Yar!"

Chapter Two

STARFLEET LIEUTENANT TASHA YAR, Security Chief of the U.S.S. *Enterprise,* beamed aboard from the planet Minos with a sense of profound relief. For a time, as an uncontrolled weapon relentlessly pursued them, she had feared that she and the people she was responsible for would all perish—but once again the smooth cooperation of an *Enterprise* away team had brought them through.

Nonetheless, after she had logged her report and gone off duty, Yar found herself on edge and unable to relax.

She tried a book-tape and soft music, hoping to lull herself to sleep. . . .

The door buzzed. "Come in," called Yar. Not surprisingly, it was her close friend, Ship's Counselor Deanna Troi.

"You are troubled, Tasha," said Troi without preamble.

"Are you here as my friend or my counselor?" Yar asked warily.

"Either," Troi replied with her serene smile. "Or neither, if you wish me to leave."

"No, no—if I'm broadcasting emotions, then I suppose I need help in dealing with them," Yar admitted.

"And you detest asking for help," her friend responded gently. "Why don't we just talk? You probably don't really need my professional skills."

Yar studied her beautiful friend. Also off duty, Troi was wearing a robe of soft blue, green, and violet, and her hair was loosened into a riot of curls. It made her look younger than her usual severe upsweep, as did the fact that the loose robe concealed her voluptuous figure as her form-fitting uniform did not.

Yar noticed Troi notice what she was wearing as well: plain blue tailored pajamas under a short, untrimmed coat of darker blue.

Oh, damn.

Seeing Troi's smile tilt her lips again, Yar said, "Don't look so smug. Yes, I see what I've done. I'm hiding my femininity again, and you don't think that's normal when I have to wear a unisex uniform all the time I'm on duty."

"Tasha, the term 'normal' is meaningless, as you very well know. Wearing plain nightwear is nothing to be concerned about. However, being unable to sleep is, especially after the day you've had."

"Maybe I'm overtired."

"Perhaps. Or perhaps feeling helpless down on the planet triggered your worst memories. The ones you try to keep hidden, even from yourself."

Was that it? Did she fear to sleep lest her old nightmares about the rape gangs resurface? They had once before on this mission, when she was almost forced to stand by and watch the execution of Wesley Crusher, who was the same age Yar had been when Starfleet rescued her.

"I know I hate to lose control of a situation," she told Deanna. "The Captain and Dr. Crusher were in trouble, and we couldn't even *find* them." She heard the tension in her voice, could not stop it. "And that . . . that weapon kept appearing, stronger and faster every time—I couldn't stop it."

"You speak as if it were your responsibility alone, Tasha. Will Riker was in command of the away team, and Data was—"

"Security is *my* job! I was there to protect them, not the other way around. If I cannot trust myself—"

Troi merely sat in silence.

Yar got up, paced. "There it is again. I can't trust anyone but myself." She shook her head. "But I do, every day. I delegate responsibility. I trust the other members of an away team to guard my back, as I guard theirs."

"Yes, you do. By habit, by practice. But could it be that inside you still fear that any one of them could let you down?"

"They're only human. Except Data, of course."

"Interesting you should mention Data," Troi said invitingly.

"Forget it!" Yar snapped. "That is private territory that I don't discuss even with you. It has nothing to do with my current concerns."

"Are you sure?" Troi asked.

"Positive."

"Even though Data is everything you wish you were?"

"What?" Yar asked, completely puzzled. She had thought Troi was referring to the time she had seduced their android colleague—which, since it had happened in the privacy of her own quarters, and since Data had adhered as scrupulously as she to her instruction that "It never happened," was absolutely nowhere in the records. Not even the Ship's Counselor knew. *Oh, damn. I just told her by my reaction that there's something unresolved between Data and me.*

But Troi was pursuing a different train of thought. "Tasha, you have made an incredibly successful recovery from the terrible traumas of your childhood. It is little wonder that you have trouble relying on other people, that you expect far too much of yourself. Do you envy Data his strength, his quickness, his knowledge?"

"Doesn't everyone?" Yar asked. "If he weren't programmed with humility, he would be a regular pain in the—"

"It's not programmed humility, Tasha," said Troi. "Data envies *us.*"

"That's ridiculous. He has everything humans have, and more. What could he possibly envy us?"

26

"I am not revealing a confidence, for he has said it openly. You've heard him: he wishes he were human."

Yar frowned. She had never given that particular aberration of her android colleague much thought. "Does *Data* come to you for counseling?"

"He is a member of this crew. He has the same right as the rest of you."

"But he's a *machine*," Yar protested. "He can't really have . . . feelings?"

"He can and he does. Look up the records of his entrance examination for Starfleet Academy. There was no question of his intelligence, of course, or his physical stamina, but one of the entry requirements is that one be sentient. Not only sapient, but sentient, Tasha. Self-aware. That implies feelings. Computers and robots are not admitted to Starfleet Academy. Data was."

Is she feeling guilt from me now? Yar wondered. *This means I hurt him—at the least I confused him. And it's been so long now. How do I apologize?*

Troi's huge dark eyes studied Yar. "You will sleep untroubled tonight, I think."

"You do?" Yar asked, startled. "Why? I've just discovered another problem."

"Yes—but it has to do with someone else, not yourself. And you are very good at caring for others, Tasha. Your problems all come when you demand too much of yourself. I will say good night now. But one more thing."

"Yes?"

"Talk to Data." Before Yar could protest the apparent invasion of privacy, Troi continued. "It would be good for both of you. Tasha, you want to be the iron woman, able to defeat all enemies with any weapon or your bare hands, all pertinent facts ready at hand. Data has the physical strength and wide-ranging knowledge you envy, and yet he would give it all up to be human. Talk with him; I think you will learn a great deal from one another."

"Is that a prescription, Counselor?"

"It's a suggestion, friend."

And after Troi had gone, Yar discovered—in the morning, when her wakeup sounded—that she did indeed sleep well, untroubled by worrisome dreams.

Lieutenant Commander Data was at his usual post on the bridge when the message arrived from Treva. Instantly, he accessed all available information on the planet: Class M, humanoid culture of undetermined origin, technological level comparable to pre-atomic mid-twentieth-century Earth, no space travel, but space trade with non-Federation cultures before contact by the Federation. Preliminary petition for Federation membership presented to the Federation Council some fifteen Standard Years ago. A Starfleet survey team's report had approved a full-scale investigation which could lead to eventual membership with the approval of the citizenry. But Treva had never tendered the formal request for that investigation, and so the planet's potential for Federation membership remained in limbo.

Somewhat to Data's disappointment, Captain Jean-Luc Picard did not ask him for information on Treva. Frustration was one human experience the android was only too familiar with: designed to operate as the perfect information retrieval system, time and again he was denied the opportunity to fully demonstrate that function.

Instead, the Captain had the message played on the viewscreen. It showed a woman who identified herself as Nalavia, President of Treva. With a rapid cross-check of the files, Data verified her identity between one word and the next.

He had no trouble recording what she was saying at the same time that he studied her image, intending to ask Commander William Riker at some later time whether he thought the woman beautiful. To Data all humans—all living beings—were beautiful, each in a different way. It was only recently that he had become intrigued by standards of beauty, after discovering that while seascapes, sunsets, or starfields were almost universally agreed upon, there were widely varying opinions of what constituted beauty in sapient beings. Realizing that it was futile to compare

Human, Vulcan, Klingon, or Andorian aesthetic preferences with one another, he was for the moment trying to comprehend beauty in human form—the image in which he himself had been created.

Data recognized nothing about Nalavia to make humans consider her *not* beautiful. While height was impossible to judge in a viewscreen image, he could see that she was neither thin nor fat, and that her body was proportioned within the range generally considered pleasing. She had no scars, no squint, no frown lines to detract from her acceptibility, nor did she appear to be of that age after which, for reasons Data could not fathom, human men determined that women be accorded intellectual respect rather than physical admiration.

Judging by all known criteria, Data would have said that Nalavia was beautiful, yet he had discovered that humans perceived things he could not, and contradicted one another and even themselves so often that he had not yet been able to discover what factors unquestionably defined beauty.

The woman on the screen had black hair and pale skin. Her most distinctive feature was a pair of large round eyes of a strange green color—but then, Data could not be certain that its strangeness was not a result of the transmission. He had seen green eyes in humans before, and could not put a finger on what made this particular green seem . . . unnatural.

Deciding to consult Riker later, Data focused his attention on what the woman was saying.

"The planet Treva is experiencing grave political difficulties. The duly elected democratic government is threatened by self-appointed warlords seeking to destroy government by the people and reinstitute the ancient rule of the sword. They have killed three members of the Legislative Council, and threaten all of us.

"As President of Treva, I ask military aid of the United Federation of Planets. The Legislative Council desires membership in the Federation—but our efforts are thwarted by these attacks. In the name of the duly elected government of

Treva, I request that you send a starship to put down this insurrection of warlords, so that Treva may take its place in the Federation."

"Message ends," Data reported.

Captain Picard said, "Obviously they have little notion on Treva of what the Federation is about. Lieutenant Yar, send a message to President Nalavia, acknowledging her request and informing her that it is being forwarded to both Starfleet Command and the Federation Council. Then make it so."

"Aye, Captain," the Security Chief replied with her usual efficiency, and Data read the outgoing messages on the periphery of his attention, as he did all data generated on the Enterprise bridge. His interest, though, was in the captain's response.

Data turned so that he could see his commanding officer, who as usual had come forward from the command chair to view the message on the screen. It was one of those human idiosyncrasies that he noted without comprehending: there was nothing wrong with the Captain's vision or hearing, and approaching the screen would not make him more imposing to a recorded image. Nalavia would, in fact, never see him at all; she would receive an audio message in Tasha Yar's voice.

The android did not ponder the Captain's habit now, though; he simply counted on it to bring Picard to his shoulder, so that he could ask, "Will the Federation send aid to Treva?"

"Would you, Commander?" Picard responded. The use of title rather than name told him the Captain saw this as a learning experience for him. The sudden swing from commanding officer to teacher could be aimed at anyone on the bridge, from William Riker to Wesley Crusher. Data never minded it, although he knew that some of the others occasionally did.

It took less than the time to tilt his head for him to realize, "There is insufficient information on which to base such a decision."

"And from the information we *do* have, what do you think will happen?" the Captain pursued.

"A call for help cannot be ignored. The Council will wish more information, and Starfleet will send someone to investigate. As the *Enterprise* is the closest starship to Treva, we should be prepared to divert from our present assignment.

"However," he added, "our assignment is to deliver a consignment of Droghenian wheat to Brentis VI. Droghenian wheat is resistant to the Fulgian rust that has destroyed their crops two years in a row, but it must be planted within the next seventeen point three days. We are scheduled to arrive in five point two days. Diverting to Treva would dangerously reduce the time available for planting the seed once it arrives. The *Enterprise* cannot be diverted until after we have offloaded our cargo at Brentis VI."

"Correct," said Picard approvingly. "However—" he invited.

"—if what President Nalavia says is true," Data continued, "these 'warlords' are murdering innocent people. Starfleet records give no information on Treva's own police or armed forces; we do not know why they cannot contain the insurrection without Federation help."

Picard turned from Data then. "Lieutenant Worf, what should Starfleet do?"

"Dispatch a scout to investigate, sir," the Klingon officer answered. "Commander Data, are there any Starfleet scoutships as close to Treva as the *Enterprise*?"

"Negative," Data supplied.

"Then," Worf continued, "I predict that Starfleet will direct the *Enterprise* to send an away team to investigate the situation on Treva, and determine whether it constitutes a true emergency."

Lieutenant Yar looked over at Worf with a congratulatory grin, then said, "Message from Starfleet, Captain. We are to send a shuttle to investigate events on Treva, and notify Starfleet at once if the situation warrants our taking action."

"Tell them we will do so immediately," the Captain told her. But he was not through with the lesson. "Acting Ensign Crusher."

"You want me to go, sir?"

"No, Ensign." Data saw Picard control annoyance once again at the boy on his bridge. "I want you to tell me how the Prime Directive applies to this situation."

Wesley blushed. He had 'put his foot in it,' as the peculiar human saying had it. "Uh, I don't know, Captain. What is Treva's status?" He looked desperately at Data, but did not ask directly as Worf had.

When the silence threatened to stretch forever, Data volunteered, "Treva has applied for Federation membership, but only the preliminary survey has been completed."

"Um, if the report was not negative," Wesley groped for an answer, "then at the request of the duly elected leadership we may provide appropriate aid."

"Very well," said the Captain. "And next time, Ensign, do not hesitate to request information of either Commander Data or the computer. The computer will never volunteer it, and you should not expect your fellow crew members to do so, either. Had we been in the midst of a crisis, the delay you caused might have been crucial."

"Yes, sir," the boy said, caught between pleasure at having given the correct answer and embarrassment at not having gone about it in the right way.

Meanwhile, Captain Picard was saying, "Commander Data, Lieutenant Yar, take Shuttle 11 and proceed to Treva. Nalavia's message was notable mostly for its *lack* of useful information. Find out what the hell's really going on there."

Tasha Yar considered: several days alone with Data in the confines of a shuttlecraft would give her the opportunity to talk with him as Deanna Troi had suggested. An unconscionably long time had passed. If she *had* caused Data pain, his attitudes suggested that he was over it by now. In fact, his lack of reaction, even soon after the event, made her wonder if her command, "It never happened," had actually erased the event from his memory banks.

That possibility was worse than the idea that she had hurt him. Still, although she badly wanted to know, Yar was not certain her curiosity would be appreciated since they had discovered Lore—since Data had learned he was not unique, and had in fact been created deliberately less human than his prototype.

Still, fate—and Captain Picard's orders—had cast them together with nothing to do but stare out at the stars once the *Enterprise* had warped into nothingness. Capable of speeds no faster than warp one, the shuttle's movement was imperceptible from minute to minute unless they were within a star system. Yar glanced at the control console.

"We will reach full impulse within seven minutes," Data said without looking up.

"Have you added telepathy to your abilities?" Yar asked.

That brought a startled glance of his golden eyes. "It . . . was a logical assumption that you wished to know, Lieutenant," he replied. "Of course you could have deduced it yourself from the information on the console screen."

"Not so quickly, though," she said. "You have begun frequently volunteering information, Data."

"Yes. I must learn when it is appropriate and when it is not. I should not have done so for Wesley, on the bridge."

"He asked you."

"Not directly. I recognized a learning situation, and should have waited, giving him the opportunity to act in an appropriate manner for a Starfleet officer-in-training."

"I, on the other hand," Yar assured him, "learned that particular lesson years ago. Besides, on this bridge, you are in command."

Data gave his slight, pleasant smile. "You are one officer who has never challenged my rank."

"Why should I? You've earned it, or you wouldn't have it. Starfleet is hardly prodigal with promotions."

"There are many who think it was prodigal with mine," the android replied. At her questioning frown, he added, "It is a matter of record. The question of whether to promote me beyond Lieutenant was actually brought before a meeting of Starfleet Command. Nor was the final decision unanimous. There are those who feel that an android has no place as a line officer frequently placed in charge of a starship and with the potential one day to command one."

"Is that what you hope to do, eventually?" Yar asked, fascinated by the turn in the conversation.

"No," Data replied. "That is Commander Riker's dream, not mine. I was not designed to command humans." He sat back in his chair, with the characteristic slightly mechanical movement of his head that, paradoxically, indicated that he was as confused as any human. "I do not understand the desire for power, Tasha. All my life, since I first came to consciousness, I had assumed an android could not experience such a drive: we are designed to serve, not to rule. And then . . . we found Lore."

"Lore was a mistake," said Yar. "You're an improvement on him, Data."

"Perhaps. But what if my design flaws are simply not so immediately obvious?"

"Then you'd be just like the rest of us," Yar told him, "striving to overcome our flaws and make ourselves better." At his look of surprise, she laughed. "I know you want to be human, Data—"

"No," he said.

"No? But I thought you had said—?"

"Commander Riker said it that way, and at the time it was not appropriate to challenge his terminology. I *wish* I were human," Data corrected. "To *want* the impossible is self-defeating and can end only in frustration. To *wish* for an unattainable goal, however, may mean achieving possible ones that one might not otherwise consider."

Yar nodded. "I like that—I'll remember it, Data, because you've voiced something I've learned myself, only I never could put it into words. I've sometimes questioned my own goal of becoming . . . the ideal Starfleet officer. Perfect. Never a wrong decision or a breach of honor. There is no such thing, but at one time I thought there was."

Data again gave her his smile, this time teasing, "Nobody's . . . perfect?"

"No, not even you," she laughed. He did not; light humor, especially irony or even whimsy, was within the android's range of emotions, but the indefinable humor that caused people to laugh was still beyond him. Yar had no doubt, though, that one day experience would bring Data the gift of laughter . . . and then he would be more human than just about anyone else she knew.

Data appreciated the company of Tasha Yar. For a considerable time—ever since the event which "never happened"—he had wondered if she was deliberately avoiding his company. He understood that humans sometimes experienced a disagreeable feeling called "embarrassment" concerning sexual activity, but it was another of those emotions he could only observe without participation or comprehension.

However, Tasha seemed at ease with him here, so he decided their lack of interesting discussions before now was due simply to the fact that their varied duties kept them out of one another's paths except on the bridge and a few busy away team assignments.

After a while Tasha grew hungry and dialed up a menu of what was available from the shuttle's provisions console. "What *is* this?" she demanded. "Aldebaran wine? Quetzi ramekins? Oysters?!"

Data was concerned to recognize anger in her voice. He turned, explaining, "All the standard programs are there as well. I simply added those because they are foods I knew you liked."

She stared at him for a moment, anger and astonishment warring with her careful control. Then, suddenly, amusement won over both, and she laughed. "Of course, Data— you couldn't know the implications of those foods."

"Implications?" he asked blankly.

Tasha blushed, but plunged on. "You installed the programs for the items I had in my room the time I . . . invited you in. You had no way of knowing that they all have the reputation of being . . . aphrodisiacs."

If Data could have blushed in turn, he would have. "I—I'm sorry," he stumbled.

"It's all right," Tasha said. "Do *you* like any of this?"

"I do not know. I never got the chance—" Data stopped again, dismayed. This, he suddenly recognized, was embarrassment. Perhaps later he would feel pleasure at comprehending another human trait. For now, he had absolutely no programming to cope with a sensation that was disagreeable indeed. All he could think to do was parrot what he had once overheard William Riker say, to himself rather than to the woman in question, in a somewhat similar situation: "Oh, damn."

Tasha stared at him for a moment, and then burst into giggles. Quickly, though, she forced herself sober, and assured him, "It's all right. All my fault." She took a deep breath. "What shall I program up for you?"

"Any combination of proteins, carbohydrates, and electrolytes suitable for humans can be made use of by my nutritive fluids."

"But don't you have a preference?" Tasha persisted.

"A chicken sandwich, an apple, and a glass of milk," he replied, falling back on the combination he had learned to dial up years ago at Starfleet Academy, so as not to draw stares or comments from his fellow students.

"Mm-hmm," said Tasha. "Standard Starfleet misfit camouflage."

"What?"

"When you're as strange as you or me, you learn every way possible to avoid calling attention to yourself," she replied.

"Now *you* are practicing telepathy," he observed. "But," he added, "you are not strange, Tasha."

"I was then," she explained. "When I entered Starfleet Academy I was eighteen years old, but only three years civilized. Barely. It was a very thin veneer. I'd crammed a whole education into those three years, with no time for social graces."

Data blinked at her. "Why?" he asked. "I mean, I know your records, that you were rescued from New Paris when you were fifteen—but why did you feel you had to push so hard at education?"

"Starfleet," she replied. "It was all I wanted, Data. Surely you know the feeling. You were also rescued by Starfleet;

36

you must have wanted to become a part of it as much as I did."

"Starfleet is the only place I can function to my full capacity," he told her.

"Yes," Tasha agreed with a nod, but Data sensed that she meant something far more profound than he did. Therefore he kept silent, waiting for a further response.

The food dispenser pinged, and Tasha removed from it a tray covered with small containers. No wonder it had taken so long to complete the program; this was definitely not a chicken sandwich, an apple, and a glass of milk!

"I decided to try some new items," said Tasha. "How about you?" She frowned. "It's not all the same to you, is it, Data?"

"Oh, I can distinguish the various tastes, textures, and aromas," he replied, "probably better than you can. However, I do not have inborn likes or dislikes. I simply seek to balance the nutrients."

"Oh." Data saw that Tasha was disappointed, but trying to hide it.

So he added, "I have found, though, that over time I have come to associate certain foods with certain events. Stimulating lessons, intriguing problems, pleasant company. When I later encounter similar flavors, I find that I have developed a preference for them." He smiled. "I expect I will develop a liking for all these foods."

Tasha gave him an acknowledging grin, and began to eat.

But to Data's disappointment she dropped the topic of their individual choices of Starfleet, to speak in general of the sector of space they were traveling through. Out here, that was the equivalent of "talking about the weather" on a planet: a neutral topic of conversation that would not stir any strong emotions to disturb digestion.

Intriguing. Data let his attention wander as he nibbled at the food. He required few calories to maintain the organic nutrients that served him in lieu of blood, but he understood meals as social interaction.

Data had no strong emotions regarding his choice of

Starfleet or his years at the Academy—although if he had been as aware of human sarcasm then as he was now, he might have developed some. Obviously Tasha had. Data had thought her experiences completely positive. She always spoke of being rescued by Starfleet, and her loyalty to its ideals resembled the devotion of a true believer to a deeply satisfying religion.

Curiosity was Data's great failing. When he had first become conscious, it had been indiscriminating—records of four centuries of baseball statistics had held the same fascination as the history of a star about to go nova.

Eventually, though, he had learned to place priorities on what he learned—and recently a personal priority had become the understanding of those people he had come to call his friends. He sensed now that there was something he had never guessed concerning Tasha Yar and Starfleet—and instantly he wanted to know it.

So when they had finished eating, as he gathered the containers and put them in the disposer he said, "Although it was quite nutritionally sound, a meal like that would draw stares for both of us in the Academy mess hall."

"It wouldn't bother me today," Tasha replied comfortably. "I was a wild thing when I was admitted, Data. It was only a probationary appointment, and as I think back I really don't know how I managed not to get shipped out that first year. I failed the Ethics and Moral Principles course—I simply could not accept, even as a hypothesis on which to base a reasoned argument, the belief that *Life is sacred. Everywhere.*"

Data stared, tilting his head. "I also failed that course in my first attempt," he replied. "I found it impossible to *challenge* that tenet, even when the instructor assigned me to take the opposite position in debate."

Tasha frowned. "You learned to challenge it?"

"To challenge it, yes—for each challenge met merely strengthens its truth. Only after I understood that was I able to pass the course."

Tasha nodded. "It met my challenges—as soon as I started questioning instead of assuming. Where I grew up, life certainly wasn't considered sacred. It's hard to give up the beliefs instilled by childhood experiences."

"I would not know. I was simply programmed with the belief." Data frowned. "As my brother was not. Lore thought . . . that made him more human than I."

"He was wrong!" Tasha said vehemently. "When I was rescued from New Paris, right through my first term at the Academy, I was less human than you are, Data. If it weren't for Darryl Adin—" She stopped, grimacing slightly, her skin paling. Her fists clenched. "I still can't accept—"

But her words trailed off, and Data recognized that she did not intend to go on.

However, he had accessed the records of the entire crew the moment he came aboard the *Enterprise,* and so he knew, "Darryl Adin, Security Chief of the U.S.S. *Cochrane,* exploratory vessel which rediscovered the lost Earth colony of New Paris. He headed the away team that rescued you. He returned you to Earth, and arranged for your care and education while he was assigned to other missions. You were in your final term at Starfleet Academy, when Adin returned to Earth for a course in the latest developments in starship security. You—"

He stopped, as the raw data suddenly coalesced into meaning, a tragedy of love and betrayal, made even more profoundly sad by the fact that its chief player was the woman before him, a person he regarded as a friend.

Inwardly, he damned his eager memory banks, turning up information with no regard for its emotional impact. For, all unwitting, he had accessed and blurted out facts that could not help but stir up painful memories for Tasha Yar.

When she had changed the subject, why had he not respected her obvious wishes and let well enough alone? Or at least kept silent until he had accessed the entire file on her relationship with Adin? Then he would have known better than to say anything.

Now he could do nothing except stop, with a mumbled apology.

Tasha was blinking, fighting tears. "It's not your fault, Data. I should have realized you had all the records anyway.

Now you know why I don't talk much about my days at Starfleet Academy. It was so wonderful there, learning to live the ideal I hadn't dreamed possible—safely breaking out of the shell of cynicism and disillusionment I had grown to survive on New Paris. And then it all came to an end, when the very person who had made me want Starfleet—the man who *meant* Starfleet to me—betrayed everything I had learned to believe in."

She fell silent. Data looked over at her, and saw her staring out at the stars . . . but he could tell she was seeing something else. Something from long ago.

Chapter Three

STARFLEET CADET TASHA YAR lay on her belly in the mud, beside a rushing river. A few meters away she could see something that ought not to be there: a boat. Not a primitive dugout or bark canoe, but a large, modern lightweight synthetic craft with a powerful automatic propulsion system.

No such contrivance should exist on Priam IV; its presence was in direct conflict with the Prime Directive.

Which meant it did not belong to Starfleet—but by order of the Federation Council only well-briefed and carefully disguised scientific observers were allowed on Priam IV. Permissible visitors, in fact, did not include one battered, exhausted, hungry, insect-bitten cadet, but Yar was not here of her own choice.

When the scoutship U.S.S. *Threnody* broke up in an ion storm, she had survived with two other cadets in an escape pod—but when its navigational sensors failed they had crash-landed more than a hundred kilometers from the legal landing site where—if their last frantic message was received—Starfleet would look for them.

T'Pelak and Forbus died in the crash of the escape pod. Only Yar survived—and tried to find her way to the site where Starfleet would look for survivors. To add to her isolation, the crash beacon had not survived the crash either, nor had any of the other electronic equipment. The final explosion that had thrown Yar free cracked the main storage battery. Forbus was crushed, T'Pelak electrocuted, and their phasers, communicators, tricorders, radio, and all the mechanized survival equipment turned to useless junk by that final power surge. Yar was alone and unarmed except for a machete . . . but she was far from helpless.

The environment was changed, but her position was little different from what she had known on New Paris. Yar had little doubt she would survive; it was whether she survived as a member of Starfleet that concerned her. Without a communicator, her only chance of being picked up was to reach the landing site. If she missed the search vehicle, she would miss continuing with her class into her final term of study.

She'd have to seek out the Federation scientists "gone native" on Priam IV. She knew the radio frequency that would silently place her message on the hidden console they were supposed to check daily—but the frequency did her no good without a working radio! So she'd have to identify them some other way, and arrange to be picked up with them, possibly years from now.

And in the meantime she would have to live as they did, among jungle primitives—the same strength-over-all, might-makes-right existence she had left New Paris to escape.

No. She was determined to reach the landing site, a desert area never visited by the natives because of high levels of natural radiation harmful to them but, at least for a few days of exposure, not to humans.

But her determination wavered as each day threw more obstacles in her path, and after six of the planet's days had passed she found herself only half-way to her destination. What if the search vessel had already come and gone? She had lost hours to hiding from stalking animals, two days to throwing up her guts when despite routine inoculations her body reacted to the planet's bacteria, and she could not say

42

how much time was lost to physical weakness after that attack.

Finally, she reached the river that would lead her to the landing site. But there were native settlements along the water, and the Prime Directive said that a lithe blonde human female could not be glimpsed in her true form by the green-haired, chalk-white-skinned natives. Besides, Prime Directive or no, they were at a level of culture at which they were most likely simply to kill such a strange-looking being on sight.

So she had spent the past two days resting while the local insects tried to eat her alive, and the nights creeping past the villages, cursing her luck that the river was at flood stage, not navigable by any vessel short of the technological marvel she now stared at . . . and lusted after.

Who could it be but Starfleet personnel looking for survivors?

No. If Starfleet sent a rescue party, they would be disguised as natives. But far more likely than risk exposure, they would contact the Federation scientists gone native here, asking them to look for survivors.

So whose boat was that?

Yar crawled through the mud, so covered by it that if she saw anyone in the pale light of dawn she could surely "disappear" simply by holding still, another mound of mud on the river bank. Slowly, slowly, she crept nearer the side of the boat away from the cluster of native huts, and pulled herself up and over the side, beneath the sun canopy.

The controls were of the sort found in any Federation ground craft. There was a small on-board computer, which booted to a chart of the river. The landing site was clearly marked—but the few words were not in English or other familiar language. There were three menus, presumably saying the same thing. One script looked vaguely Vulcan, one some system she did not recognize at all—and one menu was in Klingonaase.

Well, the Klingons were members of the Federation now.

Recent members. This craft, or its computer program, could predate the alliance.

And the Klingons used to be allies with—

Yar suddenly had more than her own survival at stake. This was not just some free trader defying the warning beacon; it was an invasion by non-Federation personnel. Starfleet had to be warned! Now she had even more reason to reach the landing site in time—and her best hope of doing so was in this boat.

After all, the local natives had already seen it.

"Computer—" she whispered.

There was no response. Yet she recognized the voice-activator grille. What the hell?

Oh, damn—of course. Her universal translator had shorted out, right along with her communicator and all the other electronic equipment. This computer would respond only to one of the three languages displayed on its screen. The not-quite-Vulcan script must really be Romulan, and even her Vulcan pronunciation was execrable at best. Breathing a prayer to the spirit of the inventor of the universal translator, she tried to call up enough sleep-taught Klingonaase to make herself understood.

It took three tries before the computer responded with what she hoped was Klingonaase for "Working."

"Not so—" Oh, hell, what was the word for "loud"?

And while she racked her brain for it, the computer repeated itself—louder.

"Shhh!" Yar said—

—and was rewarded with a klaxon and flashing lights!

The huts on shore erupted with white-skinned, green-haired natives!

"Khest!" Yar exclaimed, as fluently and inaccurately as any Klingon—that expletive was one Klingon term every cadet knew, and used daily. "Give me manual control!" she demanded, getting no response as she spoke those words in English.

Spears thudded against the canopy and the sides of the boat.

"Stop, you idiots! You'll hole it!" somebody shouted in guttural, sibilant tones.

The hissing in the voice told Yar where she'd gone wrong:

the language she had not recognized was Orion, and the Orion signal for danger was to hiss like a snake!

Adrenaline stimulated her thinking—suddenly she remembered the Klingon term for "Manual override!" She hit the starter, and the engines came alive.

The lightweight craft rose nearly out of the water, wonderfully responsive to her touch—but it swung in an arc, moored to a post on shore!

Yar grasped her machete and crawled forward beneath the canopy—

—as the boat's owner reached her and swung aboard!

He was a huge Orion male, gray-skinned reptilian face looming, yellow eyes glaring from beneath his flat headgear. He grabbed Yar's legs and pulled her back before she could cut through the lanyard.

Yar twisted in his grip, trying to swing the machete into position to slash at him.

But for all his size he was fast. He jerked her toward him, and an iron hand clasped over her wrist. It squeezed.

Yar twisted one leg free of his grip and knocked the breath out of him with a kick to his solar plexus.

But he did not let go! As he fell backward, he maintained his grasp on her one calf and the opposite wrist—and in a flash of blinding pain she felt her wrist break in the sheer strength of his hand. The machete fell to the deck with a dull clatter.

She had made the fatal error of a small combatant against a larger, stronger opponent: she had let him get a grip on her.

But in the close confines of the boat—

No. No excuses. She had lost this round, but the fight was not necessarily over. She must simply make the Orion think it was.

She moaned, and pretended to pass out, collapsing on his chest.

It didn't fool him, or else he was taking no chances. Before he let go of her broken wrist, he transferred his other hand to her good arm. Then he snapped a manacle about her good wrist, fastened it to one of many rings set into the hull of the boat—a slaver's vessel—and only then let go of her.

45

"Computer," he growled, "dock the boat and turn the bloody motor off!"

Yar understood his words—*his* universal translator was working.

The Orion poured a bucket of water over Yar's head, and with a splutter she was forced to acknowledge consciousness.

"What's this then?" he was asking. "A human? What're you doing on Priam IV, woman?"

She was so covered with mud that her uniform must be unrecognizable. "I'm a free trader. My ship crashed here," she replied. "When I saw your boat, I thought you might help me."

"So you decided to steal it?"

"When I saw it belonged to an Orion slaver."

He nodded. "Smart move. Too bad you couldn't carry it out—too bad for you, that is. For me, you'll make a nice extra." He grasped her chin and turned her face this way and that. "You'll clean up pretty enough, and you're stronger than you look or you wouldn't have survived. Some lonely dilithium miner will pay a pretty penny for a woman who's a looker and also has a strong back."

He got out a medical kit, scanned her wrist, hauled the bones back into alignment with no care for her cry of pain, and put a regen brace on it. The pain began to recede.

By this time the boat was back to its mooring, and three curious natives peered in at them. "Oh, my God," said one of them. "One of the cadets *did* survive!"

"Shut up!" growled a second—but it was too late.

So was Yar's second thought. In her pain and shock she blurted out, "You're Federation!"

Oh damn, damn, damn—why hadn't she had the sense to pretend to be unconscious or uncomprehending?

"Kill her!" said the first "native," raising his spear.

The Orion shoved him back. "Leave it! I'll sell her where she'll never see the Federation again—don't you worry. I don't want Starfleet finding out about our deal any more than you do."

"It's safer to kill her," said the second native.

46

"Touch her, I'll kill *you*," said the Orion. "She's worth as much as the whole boatload of Priamites."

"But you said——"

"I said we'd try 'em out as workslaves. They're strong, stupid, complacent, and prolific . . . here on their home planet. If they don't shrivel up and die in another environment, we'll be back for as many as you can provide. Let you know in maybe a year. Then, you keep the Federation off our backs, and Orion will make you rich. Now I must move—you're certain that Federation patrol won't be back?"

"We told them the cadets were dead—we thought they all were. That pod couldn't hold more than three, and we found two bodies. Don't worry; no more are going to show up now, and Starfleet won't send another ship for three years. By that time, we'll make enough from trading with you to retire in luxury."

Yar's heart sank. The Starfleet rescue ship *had* come and gone without her. She was forced to watch helplessly as the boat was loaded with manacled natives, and the Orion piloted it down the river toward the landing site—where, presumably, his shuttle waited to carry her along with the Priamites into a life of slavery.

Even with the powerful boat, it would take two days. Yar tried to talk to the Priamites, but without a working translator could not make herself understood. They did not talk among themselves much either, just slumped defeatedly in the bottom of the boat.

When night fell, the Orion slaver moored the boat and fed his captives some tasteless gruel. Yar lay down with the others, uncomfortable with one wrist fastened to the hull, the other aching and itching as it healed. She was hungry, bruised, and covered with dried mud.

Despite her exhaustion, she could not sleep. So when the Orion appeared to do so, she sat up quietly, and examined the manacle that bound her to the hull of the boat. Without its magnetic key, there was no hope of opening it.

In futile frustration, she gave it a jerk—and the loop fastening her to the boat hull came out of its socket!

She sat there, stunned.

Luck. Sheer, stupid, blind luck.

Somehow, the bolt holding her loop had been driven in crooked; it did not go through the metal bar under the hull laminate—and when she pulled hard enough, the light-weight hull material had given.

Before her luck could turn again, Yar slid silently over the side, back into the mud, and crawled off into the forest.

And into a dilemma.

There was no immediate escape—the Federation search vessel had come and gone. The Federation scientists would kill her on sight. If she did nothing but try to survive, the Orion traders would be back in a year, taking more passive Priamites into slavery.

But if she approached the Priamites—who upon closer acquaintance did not seem likely to kill her—she would break the Prime Directive. As she learned their language, she would undoubtedly let slip facts about the world she came from. Could she resist showing them improvements, even something as simple as the bow and arrow? She would have to make weapons for herself; the Orion slaver would certainly notify the traitorous Federation scientists of her escape, and they would be searching for her.

Her very existence here violated the Prime Directive, passively. She would actively violate it if she contacted the Priamites.

But if she did not do so, did not learn to communicate with them, how could she warn them of the Orion slavers?

Three years, the scientists had said. Possibly she could survive on her own in the jungle for three years. It would be much harder for the traitors to find her there than among the natives. She could follow them to the landing site when they were picked up, and report them to the Starfleet away team that came for them.

But in three years how many Priamites would be sold into Orion slavery? Strong backs and passivity—perfect slaves. She would not put it past the Orions even to exploit their sensitivity to radiation, use them as living detectors—

She felt sick.

The Prime Directive balanced against the lives of sentient, sapient beings—

Which was worse, interfering in the development of an entire culture, or allowing some members of that culture to be carried off into slavery? Starfleet wisdom claimed that historically every attempt to interfere with undeveloped races had resulted in disaster—hence the Prime Directive in the first place.

What if her benign interference led to the Priamites developing a dependence on other races? What if discovering how they had been betrayed by people who seemed just like themselves led to war among a people who heretofore had had no reason to invent it? What if, once the Prime Directive was breached, business interests moved in and began exploiting Priam IV's natural resources?

Furthermore, Yar's wide-spectrum inoculations had not prevented her from becoming ill on Priam IV. The Federation scientists had undergone total decontamination before landing here, but she had not. What if she carried bacteria and viruses deadly to the Priamites? What if in trying to save them, she ended up killing them?

All of those tragic scenarios had happened, more than once, in the history of the Federation.

But if she saved only herself, hundreds, maybe thousands, of peaceful people could be carried into slavery before the Federation even had a chance to know and stop the Orions—

Better to stop one definite horror now than worry about possible horrors in the future.

And if as a result Priam IV was exploited, its native culture destroyed? If the natives died of some disease benign to humans? Through her interference?

But the Orions were interfering.

Two wrongs didn't make a right—and the slavers were carefully *not* spreading their influence, so the tribes farther from the landing site would not be forewarned.

Deep in the forest, Tasha Yar sat in misery, her wounded

wrist aching, her mind in turmoil, wondering why she had ever wanted to join Starfleet.

In front of her weary eyes, the jungle shimmered into an odd pattern of small colored squares. That, in turn, dissolved into two large metal doors which pulled back to reveal a corridor and three people: a Vulcan woman and a human man in the garb of Starfleet medical personnel—and the Orion slave trader!

Yar stared in numb disbelief. This could not be happening!

"Tasha," the Vulcan woman said, "it is over. Come out of it now. The word is 'exercise,' Tasha. You are now awake and aware of reality."

Around Yar, the jungle of Priam IV dissolved into an empty holodeck.

She was sitting on the floor in her cadet fatigues, uninjured, merely sweating, heart pounding from exertion and emotional stress.

Slowly, rubbing her actually uninjured wrist, Yar remembered that it was all a test, and had taken place in an Academy holodeck. The human doctor kneeling beside her, running a scanner over her, was Dr. Forbus. The Vulcan healer was T'Pelak. Through hypnosis they had created in Yar the absolute belief that everything was really happening, making her incapable of thinking, "Oh, this is just a training exercise that seems real because of the holodeck." The doctor and the· healer had eased her into the illusion, appearing in it as her fellow cadets, killed in the crash of the escape pod.

But—the Orion? There were no Orions in Starfleet. Orion was not a member of the Federation, and never would be unless its people changed their entire way of life.

Yar flinched as the Orion squatted down beside her, saying, "You've really followed your dream, kitten."

That voice!

It stopped her reflex to attack, for it was not the sibilant voice of the Orion trader from her test. It was a voice from the past—

He stripped off the reptilian mask to reveal laughing brown eyes, an unmistakable large, straight nose, and a sensuous mouth quirking with delight at her surprise.

"Dare!" Yar exclaimed, surging onto her knees to throw her arms about him. "Darryl Adin! Why didn't you tell me you were here?"

Only at her enthusiastic hug did his arms come around her. "I just arrived this morning. When I found out you were in test, I pulled rank to find out how you were doing, and got drafted to participate." He drew her to her feet, saying, "You're all grown up! I'm so proud of you, Tasha."

To have her mentor, the man who had changed her whole life, proud of her warmed Yar's heart—and yet, "I still couldn't win against you, even when I was armed and you weren't."

"That wasn't what the test was about, Tasha," said T'Pelak. "It was programmed into the scenario that the Orion would attack when you were in an indefensible position."

"You fought splendidly," said Dare. "But then, you always did. *This* test, though, was about what you did after you finally won."

"Won?" Yar asked. "I didn't win—I escaped by sheer luck. That was a really stupid scenario, come to think of it. One coincidence after another."

Dr. Forbus laughed. "Cadet Yar, we had to stack everything we could think of against you to strand you in that situation."

"And then," said T'Pelak, raising one eyebrow in the closest expression Vulcans had to a wry smile, "my esteemed colleagues found that they had . . . 'written themselves into a corner' is, I believe, the human term. They had made it virtually impossible for you to escape."

"And when the Counselor pointed that out," said Dare, "I suggested that a scenario with a few screws loose might be resolved with a . . . loose screw?"

Yar greeted his grin with the appropriate groan. Oh, it was so wonderful to see him again, this strong, tough man with

51

the outrageous sense of humor. It was as if they had never parted . . . and yet as if she were seeing him for the first time.

It was seven years since she had last seen Darryl Adin, and over that time she could count the communications she had had from him on the fingers of one hand. But . . . he had not forgotten her, it seemed.

She could certainly never forget him! After he had rescued her from New Paris—for Yar always thought of him as her rescuer, discounting the rest of the away team—he had taken responsibility for civilizing her on the trip to Earth.

It was her good fortune that the *Cochrane* had been ready to return from its mission, for that meant she spent nearly two months aboard instead of being dropped off at the nearest starbase. In that time she had learned that Darryl Adin not only had no designs on her body, but was greatly interested in her mind.

At first she had distrusted everything and everyone aboard the starship, but living clean, with a full belly, a soft bed, and a whole crew to encourage her to learn and discover, she had slowly developed chinks in her emotional armor . . . especially where Darryl Adin was concerned.

From fear and distrust, she shifted to hero-worship. If Dare wanted her to learn to read more than a dozen words, and to write, she determined to do so. If he wanted her to use strange implements to feed herself, she would master them. And if he wanted her to spend many hours telling the story of her life into a tricorder, and then discuss it with the ship's Counselor, she would do it despite the pain her memories so often invoked.

In return, he took her into every area of the ship that was not restricted, explained its workings, taught her to swim, and, at her insistence, gave her lessons in the hand-to-hand combat he assured her she would not need as a civilized citizen of the Federation.

But the Federation was too big and diverse a concept to mean much to a fifteen-year-old girl with little knowledge of galactic history. Starfleet was what captured Tasha Yar's imagination—and by the end of their journey to Earth she had found her life's direction. Never before had she known people to work together without the basic motivation of sheer survival. And never before had she dreamed that loyalty could be built upon something more than mutual need, or greed.

By the time they reached Earth, Yar knew that her future lay in Starfleet—and her dream was one day to be the Chief of Security of a starship . . . exactly like Darryl Adin.

Dare had listened to her dreams and plans, encouraging her to try for whatever she wanted, insisting that a good education was the foundation for entry into Starfleet Academy as well as for any other future she might desire. He arranged to have her intelligence and aptitudes tested, and enrolled her in the specialized school that would attempt to compensate for the lost years of her life.

And then he was assigned to new missions with the starship *Copeland,* and later the *Seeker,* and Yar did not see him again until the day of her testing for degree candidate. In her delight at his sudden reappearance, she forgot for the moment that how she had performed would determine whether she was sent off to some other institution to complete a university degree, or whether she would be privileged to complete her final term at the Academy, and graduate as a Starfleet Officer.

Dr. Forbus said, "You must both be tired and hungry. Why don't you go eat, catch up on old times, and then get a good night's sleep? Cadet Yar, your interview will be tomorrow morning at 0900."

"Yes, Doctor," she replied, a sinking feeling in her gut. She had never reached a decision about Priam IV. They must have allowed her the allotted time, and then wakened her. Did that mean she had failed? Was she too indecisive? But what was the right answer? How could any human being decide between letting intelligent beings be carried away into slavery or breaking the Prime Directive?

There would be no answers tonight. If Dare knew them, she knew he wouldn't tell her. She might as well forget the test, and enjoy his company while she could.

Dare shed the rest of his Orion disguise, emerging in

Starfleet uniform. The first thing Yar noticed was that he was now a full commander, the solid third pip new and shiny. "Congratulations, Commander Adin," she said, then laughed at the incongruity of Dare's playing an Orion. His promotion was due to the role he had played in the *Seeker*'s breaking up an Orion cartel operating secretly on several outer Federation worlds.

He pulled off the heavy boots of the Orion trader.

And was suddenly short!

No—not short, but just above medium height for a human male, still well above Yar's petite stature.

But she remembered him as a giant of a man.

She had grown taller in seven years, she realized. Her hero was no longer larger than life . . . but he was still her hero.

"What are you doing here?" she asked. "Leave between missions?"

"Refresher course," he replied. "Whilst I've been out on the other side of the galaxy, Starfleet have been developing new security techniques. So, I'm here to learn all the latest before being given a new assignment. I'll be on campus all term." He smiled, that wonderful warm smile that turned his potentially threatening features not just handsome, but beautiful. "I'll be here to see my protégé graduate. I'm so proud of what you've done with your life, Tasha."

Yar felt herself blush. "Don't speak too soon," she warned. "I might have failed the Priam IV test."

"What makes you think that?" he asked curiously.

"I didn't know what to do!" she said in frustration. "Dare, I couldn't make up my mind. Some Starfleet officer I'd be, unable to make a decision—"

"Hush," he said. "Leave it for now—we'll talk about it in the interview tomorrow morning. And stop worrying. If you're still the little workaholic I used to know, you got this far by hard study—and that means you were ready for everything Starfleet could think of to throw at you."

He was right, as it turned out. The next morning Yar found out that her ethical dilemma was precisely what the Priam IV test was intended to induce. After she recounted her thinking after her escape from the Orion slaver, Counselor T'Pelak said, "You considered every clue, even down to your own illness. Cadet Yar, you have fully assimilated the philosophy courses which once troubled you so, and incorporated them into the practical applications at which you have always excelled."

"I don't understand," Yar said blankly, looking toward Dare, who was in on the interview because he had been part of the scenario. The men who had played the traitorous Federation scientists were there, too. "I didn't do anything. I couldn't decide what I ought to do."

"You could not, in the time we gave you, with the information you had," T'Pelak assured her. "You would have failed, Cadet, if you had been certain that you knew the right course to take."

"You mean any decision would have been wrong?" she asked in amazement.

"No, not any decision," replied Commander Erdman, one of the "scientists." "Only a hasty decision, an uninformed one, or one which you made without strong reservations. Had the situation been real, you would of course have had to make a decision eventually—but your instincts told you not to do so while you were injured and exhausted. We stopped the scenario at that point because we had all the information we needed. You passed, with a rating of excellent. Cadet Yar, you are now officially admitted to the graduating class."

The interview broke up as the others congratulated her, but Yar was still dazed as she left the conference room. Dare followed her. "That was the last test," he said. "What are you going to do now?"

"I have a week's leave before the term begins. I think maybe I'll sleep for most of it."

He laughed. "Not much rest last night, eh? I'm sorry, Tasha—I wish I could have told you you'd passed the moment you said you couldn't make up your mind. But you had to tell exactly what you felt this morning—and T'Pelak would've had my hide if she'd sensed I'd reassured you."

"It's not you I'm confused about," said Yar. "Of course you couldn't tell me. What I don't understand is the test. What good is a security officer who can't act?"

"The same good as one who goes off half-cocked, which I expect you've done a few times in your training?"

She nodded ruefully. "Oh, yes—my most frequent mistake."

"Well, now—in most situations you can correct for such an error even after it's made. What you have just proved, Tasha, is that when there is no chance to change things once you've acted, you *don't* jump the gun. You think it out."

"But what if it had been real?"

"What if it had been?" he threw the question back at her.

Finally, under the penetrating gaze of those warm brown eyes, she was able to think past the frustration of sitting there in the jungle, mud-covered and in pain, unable to make a move. Had it been real . . .

"I guess . . . no, I know, I'd find food and shelter, and think about it some more while my wrist healed and I kept out of the way of the traitors, who'd be trying to kill me. If they didn't succeed, I'd probably watch the natives for a while, and then make up my mind."

"That's my clever girl," he told her. "Survive, survey, and only then act. Now do you understand why I'm so proud to have had a hand in bringing you into Starfleet?"

As her final term proceeded, what Tasha Yar sensed from Darryl Adin was a paternal pride in her achievements. It pleased her for a time, but then slowly she began to find it disturbing.

They had two classes together, Advanced Security Techniques, seminar and practicum. In the classroom Yar was, as usual, the star pupil. Dare took notes, provided information from personal experience when the instructor requested, but did not volunteer. Yar was astonished to discover at midterm that she was still first in the class. Darryl Adin was second.

"Why?" she asked. "No one would mind if you spoke up in class more. And you know I enjoy it when you challenge me—you certainly do in the practicum!"

Dare explained, "That's not it, Tasha. You young people need to discuss the theories until you understand them thoroughly. Commander Zarsh knows I've been through that part; I can learn the new material without taking up time you cadets need."

"Then why is my average three points higher than yours?" she demanded. "You're the experienced officer; you ought to outscore *any* cadet."

He laughed. "I could if all the tests were objective. It's the essays, Tasha—I simply can't write as well as you do. Which I suppose I ought to be ashamed of," he added with a twinkle that showed he hadn't a bit of shame about it, "as I had a proper education and you didn't. But B+ is good enough for me on the essays—when it's averaged with the objective part I still end up with an A. In security it's the practical applications that count, not the mellifluous prose in which you turn in reports."

"Is that why you go all out in the practicum?" In that class, their positions were reversed—the first time Yar had not led the class when it came to physical activity.

"I have to, if this old body is going to keep up with all the young ones."

"Dare! You're not old!"

"I'm over thirty," he said.

"By less than two years."

He shook his head with a rueful smile. "In our business, age encroaches very quickly if you don't keep up every moment. My reflexes are as good as yours, Tasha, and I can still outshoot you—"

"I'm practicing!"

"—but even with modern medicine the injuries inherent in security work take their toll. I'll never be as flexible as I used to be, because my back was broken on Twenginian."

"What? You never told me—"

He shrugged. "The spinal cord wasn't severed. They got me to sickbay, and in a month I was back on duty. I can pass all the medical tests, well within tolerances. But *I* know I can't meet my old standards. And unless I keep up daily practice, against the strongest, sharpest opponents available, my abilities will degenerate." He stared blankly for a moment, at something not in the room with them. "I've seen it happen. I won't let it happen to me."

Although Dare quickly changed the subject, Yar later took advantage of her security clearance as a final-term cadet to look up Starfleet records of what had happened to Dare on Twenginian. Everybody knew about the *Seeker*'s routing the secret nest of Orions from that Federation planet, but the details were classified.

Although he had been Chief of Security of the *Cochrane,* a small scouting vessel, Dare had been Assistant Chief on his next two missions, on progressively larger ships. In each succeeding mission he had been in charge of more personnel, with more responsibility; the assignments, despite the title, were promotions.

On Twenginian the away team had been headed by Chief of Security Venton Scoggins, a man with over twenty years of experience in Starfleet. The record showed flatly that when trouble broke out he did not reach the scene in time to prevent his assistant from being injured. There was no reprimand, nothing to indicate that the man had been remiss in any way.

The *Seeker* continued its mission against the Orions. By the time they reached Conquiidor Dare was on his feet again—and Scoggins assigned him to lead the away team that freed over two hundred Federation citizens from Orion slavery and made Darryl Adin a hero. When the mission ended, Scoggins tendered his resignation and retired from Starfleet with full honors.

Yar read between the lines: Scoggins felt responsible for Dare's injury, and resigned before anyone else got hurt under his command.

But Yar was too young to worry about failing reflexes. As for Dare—well, any man who could beat a whole class of senior Starfleet cadets in the toughest security practicum ever devised certainly had nothing to worry about!

Yet the subject of age kept coming up in Dare's speech. "You young people," he called his classmates until one day when they were working together on a homework assignment in tactical theory, Yar retaliated.

"All right, oh wise old man—show me from your vast experience how to take that hill with seventeen aggressive and well-armed Mercaptan warriors guarding it, when you have only three security personnel!"

There was no such thing as a Mercaptan warrior; the unrepentantly hostile beings were totally imaginary creatures who increased in ferocity and eccentricity as each new class of cadets passing through the Academy added to their characteristics. Currently, they stood three meters tall, had scales, fur, claws, fangs, and hand-held photon torpedoes.

"Treat it like chess," Dare replied to Yar's outburst.

"Like chess?" she asked, confused. She didn't particularly like chess, while Dare was proficient at virtually every game ever invented, and played them all to win. There was even a story, which she had never been able to verify, that he had once won a *klin zha* tournament in which all the other players were Klingon.

"We don't have to take all their personnel to win," Dare explained. "All we have to do is trap their king."

"Mercaptans don't have a king," said Yar.

"But they *do* have something very similar, Tasha," he said.

"Oh, all right," she said grudgingly, admitting the analogy. "They follow the commands of the Troop Controller. But they also protect him at all costs."

"So how do we get at him?"

"I have the feeling you know," she replied. "But I don't. He is surrounded on every side by warriors, and has a personal force field as well. There's no way to get to him."

"We don't have to get to him," Dare said. "We only have to trap him."

"But how—?"

"Think, Tasha. Without the guidance of their Troop Controller—"

"Mercaptan warriors turn berserker—as if they weren't bad enough in the first place!"

"That's right. And what do they attack?"

"Anything that gets in their way, including one another. That's an old trick, Dare—but we don't have enough troops to decoy them into a circle or two lines facing each other, and even if we did, we don't have the firepower to destroy their Troop Commander so they'll attack each other."

"You weren't listening, Tasha. I said we'd trap him."

She looked from the glowing screen to Dare's face. "How? With what? I don't see any mine shafts to topple him into."

"At least you're on the right track," he said. "We want him cut off from his warriors—but first, we want them positioned so when the Troop Controller's commands are cut off, their nearest targets will be one another."

Yar looked back at the screen. What could Dare have in mind? Only three Starfleet security personnel to work with. How could they possibly—?

Suddenly her hand leaped to the board, and she punched up the descriptions of the security people. She grinned. "Thonis, an Andorian—but a graduate of the Vulcan Academy of Sciences. There it is: graduate-level classes in computer technology, taught by Sarek of Vulcan. Top student in every class. With *those* qualifications, Thonis can inveigle any computer ever built—including the Mercaptan Troop Controller's. All he needs is a tricorder . . . yes, there it is, in his equipment inventory. So we have Thonis patch into the computer, order the troops into the position we want, and then short out the Troop Controller's modem circuits before he can counteract the order!"

"You've got it," Dare said smugly.

"You've had this assignment before!" Yar accused.

Dare shook his head. "No. I simply know how important it is to determine the special abilities of all away team personnel. Remember that, Tasha—security people aren't Mercaptan warriors. They are not faceless disposable beings armed with phasers."

"I know that," she said. "I'm one of them, remember?"

"Yet how much do you know of your fellow students' special abilities, beyond their performance in the classes specifically designed for security trainees? What musical instrument does Johnson play?"

"Uh, I don't know," Yar admitted.

"Piano," Dare supplied. "And Pringle—why is she so proficient at word processing?"

"She is?"

Dare smiled. "She writes articles, Tasha—in fact, she has had half a dozen published in various horticultural journals while she's been here at the Academy."

"Horticulture? Well, no wonder I didn't know," said Yar. "I've never had any interest in gardening."

"But if you were on an away team with Pringle, and had run out of food concentrate?"

Yar nodded. "Or if there were flesh-eating plants around —yes, Dare, I see your point. Do you know these things about the whole class?"

"T'Keris is an expert on architecture. Jessamin's discipline and grace come from a lifetime of ballet. Wokonski sculpts. Por-prenicle is an archaeologist. Verne—"

"Stop!" Yar protested. "You've shamed me enough. I've known these people for three years, and never thought to find out what they do when they're not working on Academy assignments or going out with the gang. You're absolutely right, Dare; I will be sure to find out as much as I can about my fellow crew members *before* we are put on an away team where some unexpected skill might save the day."

He smiled reassuringly. "Don't feel bad. You're still young, Tasha. With time—"

"Stop that!" she said angrily.

He frowned in puzzlement. "Stop what?"

"Stop talking like you're an old man. You're not my father, Dare!"

"No," he said softly, "I am not your father, Tasha." He looked into her eyes, the glow from the computer screen reflected in his. "And I can't keep up the pretense that my feelings for you are paternal for much longer."

Something stirred inside her, a weird combination of pain and pleasure. "I'm all grown up now, Dare," she said, deliberately stepping closer. She didn't tell him it was the first time she had ever acted upon the unsettling stirrings of desire which—after her brutal introduction to sexuality—had only surfaced after years of therapy with Starfleet's Counselors.

Her heart pounded as she entered his personal space. He could not mistake her intent, nor did he pretend to. "Tasha," he whispered as his arms came naturally and easily about her.

She lifted her face, instinct telling her what she wanted. He smiled the wonderful smile that took all the sternness from the rugged features nature had given him, tilted his head slightly so their noses would not bump, and kissed her.

With Dare it was easy, natural—and then stirring as the kiss intensified. She went from the warm, sweet sense of homecoming she had felt when she had first set foot in Starfleet Academy to a whole new world of feelings, a completion she had never known before.

And when their lips parted he did not release her, but held her gently against his chest as he whispered into her hair, "Oh, yes, Tasha—you certainly are all grown up."

Chapter Four

"TASHA?" Lieutenant Commander Data was concerned. His companion had been sitting staring out at the stars for too long. But when Tasha turned, there was the remnant of a smile on her lips. Whatever her thoughts, they must have been pleasant ones. He was glad his clumsy "snooping" had not brought only sad memories.

"I'm all right, Data," she said. "Time heals all wounds."

"That sounds like—"

"An aphorism. Yes. But comments become aphorisms by being repeated, and that happens because they are true. I can never forgive Darryl Adin for betraying Starfleet . . . but he was not all evil, Data. Nobody is, you know. I can remember him now the way he was when I first knew him, strong and brave and clever."

"And handsome?" Data asked. "A knight in shining armor?"

She laughed. "Hardly. Actually, he looked rather like you." Then, "Oh! That didn't come out right!"

Data was puzzled by her reaction. "So far as I can determine, my appearance is an approximation of the human male norm—stature, facial structure, hair coloring a composite of the many human races. In purely organic beings, of course, no one meets that norm. And obviously I was not designed to fool anyone into thinking me human—my skin color is simply the most efficient for absorption of energy, and my eyes are clearly—" He stopped. "Forgive me. I am babbling."

But Tasha was smiling at him. "You're not so much average as ideal," she said. "Or maybe I just feel that way because you do look something like the . . . first man I ever loved. First love is never forgotten, Data."

He had the distinct impression that she had begun to say "only" instead of "first." But that was too near a topic he could not reopen. So he said, "I am not handsome."

"Conventionally? No—but that doesn't bother you a bit, does it?"

"Handsome is as handsome does," he replied. "Beauty is only skin deep. Beauty is in the eye of—"

He stopped when, as he hoped, Tasha chuckled. When he had first discovered that accessing his memory banks for a list of definitions or examples provoked laughter in humans—unless the situation was tense, in which case it elicited annoyance—he had turned to studies on humor and for once found an analysis he could comprehend: repetition of a pattern soon became amusing to humans, familiarity causing reassurance and relaxation. Once Data understood that, he frequently used the technique to defuse an uncomfortable situation.

This time, however, it did not distract Tasha. She continued on the same topic: "Why should it bother you not to be designed like a Starfleet recruiting poster, when more women throw themselves at you than at Will Riker?"

"Women do not—"

"Come on, Data—don't pretend you don't notice!"

Not knowing how to handle this turn of the conversation, he said, "I do not think women judge men by appearance so much as men judge women."

"As usual," said Tasha, "your observations are quite accurate—at least for humans. Remember what you said about how associating certain foods with pleasant occasions

64

causes you to like those flavors when you encounter them again?"

"Yes," Data said uncertainly, trying to make connections, food/aphrodisiacs/beauty, that didn't seem logical. Then Tasha continued, and he saw that she meant something quite different.

"That's something like how women see men. We think those men are handsome who look like the men we've loved. Psychologists say most women like men who resemble their fathers. Well, I didn't have a father, so I suppose I will always find attractive anyone who looks like the first man who was ever good to me." She grinned impishly. "I'm afraid that you'll have to put up with me thinking you're handsome, Data."

"I . . . will consider it a compliment," he replied, and grasped the opportunity to discuss his current topic of study. "Among humans there are more generally agreed-upon standards for female than for male beauty."

"That's right," she told him.

"You are beautiful," he said.

She seemed startled. "Some people think so."

"It is generally agreed upon among the bridge crew. Yet you are quite different in appearance from Counselor Troi, who is also universally admired. Captain Picard thinks that Dr. Crusher is beautiful, while her son finds that fact both incomprehensible and disturbing."

"Data—what have you been doing?" Tasha asked in dismay. "Taking a poll?"

"Yes," he replied honestly. "I wish to comprehend human ideals of beauty."

"You really do believe in wishing for the impossible, don't you?"

He tilted his head. "Is it impossible? I realize that there can never be total agreement in matters of esthetic judgment, but surely there is a formula by which I can determine that, say, a majority of humans would consider a particular person beautiful. I find Commander Riker a most useful barometer of feminine beauty; thus far I have never found the majority, or even a significant minority, disagreeing with his assessment. Unfortunately, I did not have the opportunity to ask him about President Nalavia."

Tasha laughed. "Oh, I can tell you what he'd say about *her*, Data—and if you surveyed the entire complement of the *Enterprise*, you would find a significant minority indeed disagreeing with him!"

"I do not understand," said Data.

"Every man aboard would say she is beautiful, and every woman would say she is not. Furthermore, all the women would be lying!"

"Tasha, you are confusing me," Data objected.

"Nalavia is the kind of woman," Tasha explained, "who by her nature attracts the attention of human males. She's . . . practically an archetypal figure of the Earth-mother, but young and unmarked by strife or care. And she exploits it. That's the difference between Nalavia and Deanna, who has a similar physical beauty. Deanna combines the no-nonsense attitude of a Starfleet officer with the motherly sentiment that is part of her job as Counselor. Together they defuse the threat of her physical beauty."

"Threat?" Data questioned.

"Deanna is almost *too* beautiful," Tasha explained. "It could make men afraid to approach her. She handles it by being friendly and efficient. That's why the women on board like and trust her as much as the men do. Nalavia, though . . . right through the viewscreen she was issuing an invitation to every human male on the *Enterprise* bridge."

Data replayed the scene in his mind. Yes—the human men had all come to a sort of stunned attention. "Still, no one accepted it," he pointed out.

"Starfleet trains its officers, male or female, never to think with their hormones. But have you ever before known Wesley Crusher to become that flustered in a non-crisis situation? Poor kid—he hasn't had that training, and he's in the middle of puberty. He didn't stand a chance."

"Ah," said Data, intrigued. "Now I understand. I have never known Wesley to make as unlikely an assumption as that the Captain would send him on an away team to an unfamiliar planet."

"Oh, Wesley wanted to go!" said Tasha. "He just didn't know why—but all the other men on the bridge did, and Captain Picard really shouldn't have been so hard on him. Wesley will be a fine man one day—if he just manages to live to grow up."

Data caught himself before protesting that Captain Picard would never send their Acting Ensign into danger, recognizing that Tasha spoke jokingly. He took time to analyze it, relishing this opportunity to discuss human feelings with a female friend. "You mean that his combination of youth and intellect is resented, and that therefore some person or persons aboard might consider disposing of him out of annoyance. However, you make the suggestion facetiously."

"Exactly right, Data," she said, "but analyzing it spoils the joke, which wasn't very funny to begin with."

He nodded. "Humor is difficult enough, without trying to distinguish degrees of funniness."

Tasha smiled. "You'll learn, Data," she said. "Through experience, like anyone else. Now, how long before we can begin to monitor transmissions from Treva?"

"Not for more than sixteen hours, unless they send us a subspace message." He frowned. "What do you suspect, Tasha?"

"Nothing specific. Call it intuition. I don't think Nalavia told us the whole truth."

"Obviously she could not in such a brief message."

"No—that's not what I mean. I'd call it female intuition, except that Captain Picard noticed as well. There is something about Nalavia which inspires distrust."

"Can you delineate what it is?" Data asked.

"Expecting Starfleet to do her bidding without a full investigation, for one thing."

"Trevan culture is fairly primitive," said Data. "Warlords protesting the advance to a representative form of government. Even a seasoned politician on such a planet may be unsophisticated by our standards. Or we may be missing a piece of information—there are cultures in which a cry for help from the weak impels the strong to protect them."

"Camelot," said Tasha with a nod, referring to a planet founded upon the ideals of a chivalry which, to the best of historical knowledge, had never before been widely practiced outside of legend. "Yes, it could be that we are unaware of some basic Trevan assumption, but if you did not find it in the reports of the Federation Survey Team, Data, I cannot imagine what it would be."

Unable to learn anything more for sixteen hours, Tasha exercised, slept, and ate another meal. Data had no need for further organic nutrients yet. Sometimes they talked, and sometimes there were companionable silences. The shuttlecraft proceeded on course. Every twelve hours, Data sent the routine "proceeding as scheduled" message to the *Enterprise.*

Finally, they came into the extreme range at which Data could monitor Treva's radio transmissions. Such sound transmissions over the entire main continent were a well-established technology here. What was new was the transmission of pictures along with sound, and when Data tested frequencies and configurations he quickly discovered, "They are using the Ferengi broadcast technique!"

"The Ferengi trade everywhere," Tasha reminded him. "Until they join the Federation, there is no reason for the Trevans not to do business with them."

"But if they trade with both the Federation and the Ferengi, what if they have asked both for help?"

Data saw Tasha set her jaw. "We'll deal with whatever situation we discover, once we get there. The Ferengi probably see no profit in helping the Trevans with their internal affairs. If barriers to trade with the Ferengi and other non-Federation cultures were the reason Treva hesitated to proceed with their application for membership, they may be more amenable if we help them solve their problems."

"Diplomacy is not one of my stronger areas of programming," said Data.

"It's definitely not one of mine!" Tasha replied. "Come to think of it, we're rather an odd away team for this mission."

"I have never known Captain Picard not to choose judiciously," said Data.

"Neither have I. Let's take a look at those broadcasts. Perhaps they'll give us some clues as to what is going on."

They did.

The occupants of the shuttlecraft spent the next two hours ignoring the glory of the starfield about them, eyes fixed on the steadily-improving image on the shuttle's central viewscreen.

At first there were only entertainment broadcasts: a dance performance, an athletic event, and some dramas which made little sense taken in brief snatches out of context. All were interrupted from time to time by announcers urging viewers to purchase various products. Data recognized the "free enterprise" system by which advertisers "sponsored" programming, paying the cost of preparing and broadcasting it in exchange for the right to lard it with promotions of their goods for sale.

"It is something like the transmission from Minos—" he began to explain.

Tasha nodded, cutting him off impatiently. "They probably got it from the Ferengi along with the broadcast equipment," she said.

Data tried various frequencies, but found only more of the same until the end of the athletic competition. At that point there was interminable advertising of intoxicants, weapons, cosmetics, clothing, and private transportation. Then more intoxicants: beverages, inhalants, tablets, all promising instant happiness. Data noticed Tasha's sudden silence and looked over to see her frowning. "This disturbs you?"

She took her attention from the screen. "Is life here that bad? Data, I understand how it *can* be. My own mother took drugs because her life was so harsh and hopeless. These people, though—they have honest work, enough to eat, homes and families. Drugs can only ruin those things."

"Widespread chemical dependency was not in the report of the Federation Survey Team," Data pointed out, putting Tasha's statement about her mother together with the fact that she had abandoned her five-year-old child.

But Tasha clearly did not want to discuss her past. "Here comes a news broadcast, finally," she said, and turned her attention back to the screen.

The feature story was the arrival the next day of representatives of the Federation, to aid in putting down the rebel insurrection.

"Rebel insurrection?" questioned Data.

"What happened to the warlords?" asked Tasha.

There was no mention of warlords in the broadcast—but there were some scenes showing "Starfleet in action": a starship of the old Constitution class blasting a planet, personnel in uniforms from a century ago using ground weapons against Klingons, an ancient shot from the first war with the Romulans of a Federation battle cruiser blasting a Bird of Prey out of existence.

"They're making us look like aggressors," Tasha exclaimed. "Bullies. Murderers!"

"It is all quite real," Data assured her, "but long out of date as well as edited to make Starfleet appear to be a war fleet."

The announcer's voice continued, "This is the power that will come to our aid if we persuade their representatives that we are worthy. We urge you to make the Federation welcome. The chief representatives in their delegation are Starfleet Commander Data and Security Chief Yar."

"We're the *only* representatives," Tasha murmured. "And did you hear how they gave our titles, Data? It sounds as if we're part of Starfleet Command." She gasped suddenly. "Where did they get *that?*"

On the screen a younger version of Tasha Yar was shown on a ship's bridge, phaser in hand, holding off an attacker too close to the camera to be seen clearly.

"That was the *Starbound*," Tasha whispered. "My training cruise. Good God, where did they get that scene?"

"For young Tasha Yar," the announcer's voice was saying,

"her very first assignment became an opportunity for heroism when she saved fellow crew members after their ship was attacked and boarded by a ruthless enemy."

Phaser fire exploded around her, but Tasha stood her ground with grim determination, no hint of fear in the young eyes. The attacker lunged toward her, she fired, and the scene ended in a flare of camera-overload.

"They don't show the rest of the *Starbound* bridge crew falling around me," Tasha said grimly. "Saved fellow crew members, indeed. It was Dare who—"

She stopped abruptly, and Data stored the comment for future consideration as he let his attention remain with the Trevan news broadcast.

Tasha was next shown in recent records, in her duties aboard the *Enterprise*.

Then the scene shifted to Data—in a test made at Starfleet Academy. He was shown lifting three, four, and then five of his classmates, looking bewildered as to why such a demonstration was asked of him. He remembered: he *had* been bewildered at the unscientific experiment, having already been through tests which accurately measured his strength and resiliency. Later he learned that the scene became part of the information Starfleet released about him to non-scientists, especially to schools. One of his early assignments, before he was assigned to serve aboard a starship, had been as Starfleet Education Representative to schools all over the solar system.

"At least I know where they got this information," he told Tasha. "Starfleet probably still sends it out to anyone who asks about me. It is also years out of date, and . . . I am not sure why seeing it again now . . . disturbs me."

"Because it treats you like an object rather than a person," Tasha responded instantly. "And by the way, Starfleet does *not* provide this stuff in your dossier today. I've never seen it before; I'm sure it's buried in the archives as an embarrassment Starfleet Command would rather forget. You're a valued officer now, not a curious piece of equipment they're not sure how to use."

But the rest of the broadcast on Data was no better than

that about Tasha. He, too, was shown fighting, shooting—each time appearing to be aggressive and very, very dangerous.

"With the help of Starfleet," the announcer continued, "we will rid our peaceful planet of the rebels who oppose our way of life and attempt to take power over us all. In Tongaruca only today, rebels attacked villagers gathered for the weekly market—"

The scene showed a crowded marketplace devastated when an explosion suddenly went up in its midst. People fled, screaming, right into a circle of well-armed men and women who seemed to take great pleasure in clubbing and stabbing the unarmed citizens, phasering those with the fortitude to fight back.

Data frowned. "These 'rebels' have phasers. Why does Nalavia not have an armed force of her own, to protect her people from such attacks?"

"Just one of the things we need to find out," replied Tasha. "Such as how warlords have metamorphosed into rebels. What do you suppose they are rebelling *against?*"

There was no answer to her question, but there was to Data's as well-armed soldiers in ground vehicles arrived at the devastated marketplace and drove off the rebels. None of their shots seemed to connect, however; the original attackers escaped, and the soldiers turned to aiding the survivors.

Data turned away from the broadcast. "If these local news stories are as carefully edited as the ones about you and me—"

"The terms you're looking for," Tasha said grimly, "are 'slanted' and 'biased.' I wonder whether Treva has a free press."

"They claim to," Data told her. "Do you think the journalists oppose Starfleet's aid, and are therefore trying to portray us as representatives of a military force?"

"Perhaps," said Tasha, "whoever prepared those reports thinks the audience *wants* someone to come in and smash their enemies." She shrugged. "Possibly they do. Their own soldiers seem remarkably ineffective."

"But their journalists remarkably effective," Data observed. "They were prepared to record that attack before it began."

Tasha's eyes widened. "You're right! Data, it just doesn't make sense—unless, of course, the journalist sides with the rebels and is trying to show that they are invincible . . . no. He wouldn't want to show them as terrorists, then. But attempting to show *us* as little better would make sense." She sighed. "I can't figure it out."

"Neither can I. Insufficient information." He turned back to the viewscreen, but the broadcast had turned to a weather forecast, which was followed by another program of musical entertainment. Other frequencies brought more of the same, except that a lesson in botany was added to the assortment. He turned the viewscreen off. "I do not think we will learn much more until we land on Treva."

The next day, when they neared Treva, Lieutenant Tasha Yar called up the broadcasts onto the viewscreen again. There was the same entertainment fare; only the news programs were different. Everything was prepared for their arrival. Tight security measures were in force, as the enemies of the people might attempt to attack the Starfleet representatives.

"That is interesting," Data observed. "Not warlords now, and not rebels. Enemies of the people."

Furthermore, when the old records of Data and Yar were replayed, this time instead of segueing into the two in battle they faded into recent records from Starbase 74, showing Yar excelling in the game of Parrises Squares.

Data was shown demonstrating, with inhuman patience, the operation of the *Enterprise* educational computer to four young children from the ship's families.

"Now this stuff," said Yar, "is what Starfleet probably provided on us. Quite a different picture from yesterday."

"Indeed," Data replied. "Either they did not expect us to be monitoring them yesterday—"

"—or they didn't think we were capable," Yar mused.

"The shuttle isn't," Data confirmed. "Not the weak

signals Treva's broadcast system puts out. I enhanced them. At our present distance, though, they expect us to be watching." He looked over at her with puzzled innocence. "Why would Treva's press present a distorted picture of us yesterday, but an accurate if incomplete one today?"

"A free press likely wouldn't," Yar replied. "It's evidence, although not absolute proof, that Nalavia controls what is broadcast."

Data gave one of his mechanical nods, indicating that he was storing information he had not yet analyzed, and turned back to the screen. Watching him in profile, Yar saw again the resemblance to her former mentor—but until the moment yesterday when she had blurted it out she had not been conscious of it. Even if Data's skin were flesh-colored, no one would take him for Dare—but they were the same type: medium height, slender build, with striking similarities of feature. Both had the sharp brow bone, heavy-lidded eyes, large straight nose, and firm jaw, although Data's chin was not as strong as Dare's. Their mouths were completely different, Dare's his saving grace, the full, curving lips producing a smile so devastating no woman could resist . . . but when he was angry a snarl that made brave men search for cover.

Data had neither of those expressions. His lips were pale and thin—although Yar knew from experience that they could be exquisitely sensuous when applied topically. But the android never smiled broadly, never grinned. Life experience had not yet taught him the feelings to provoke those expressions. Likewise, she had never seen Data more than mildly angry—perhaps no more than annoyed. No one would ever look into Data's face and see it as frightening, threatening. Darryl Adin's anger was both—and the memory of that expression was seared into Yar's memory, for he had worn it both the first time she had ever seen him, and the last. The first time his anger had been directed at the rape gang on New Paris. The last time, it had been at her.

Data turned, looking puzzled, and Yar realized she had been staring intently at him. His wide light-gold eyes with

their large pupils were his least human feature. She wondered if, as he fumbled toward humanity, they would
eventually lose their rather flat appearance, develop the
depth of the brown eyes that still occasionally haunted her
dreams. Was it possible for an android to rise to such
emotional heights, to crash to such devastating depths? She
sighed. His programming probably prevented it—to keep
him from becoming dangerous, treacherous, devious and
untrustworthy . . . like his "brother."

Like Darryl Adin.

"Tasha?"

"Yes? Do you have our ETA calculated?"

"One hour, seventeen point three minutes." He paused,
then added, "You are concerned. Should we send a message
to the *Enterprise* about what we have observed?"

"Definitely," she replied, glad he had misinterpreted her
introspection. They were not due to report to the *Enterprise*
again until after they had landed . . . but right now they had
the time to compose a detailed message. Data included the
two news broadcasts, and they both tried to explain their
misgivings.

When they were satisfied, Data dispatched the message.
The *Enterprise* had been warping away from them all this
time, so each message would take longer to reach the
starship. Thus far they had received two routine "message
received" signals to their first progress reports. It would
probably take another day before they had a reply to this
one, and since they would not be aboard the shuttle by then,
the flight computer would simply store it until one of them
came aboard.

Then it was time to communicate with the spaceport in
Treva's capital city, and bring the shuttle down. It was
quickly directed into a hangar, where Data and Yar emerged
to find themselves surrounded by men and women in
uniforms of black with large areas of red, blue, or greenish
gold. They were not exact attempts to copy Starfleet
uniforms—but at a distance, Yar realized, these people
would give the impression of a platoon of Starfleet person-

nel. Were the natives so stupid as to believe they had all come out of one small shuttle?

There was a crowd of people, held back by soldiers, at the edge of the tarmac. Data and Yar, however, were hurried past them at some distance, into a waiting groundcar. They drove through streets from which traffic had obviously been cleared, followed by other vehicles carrying the people who had met the shuttle. Behind barricades, people lined up to stare at the visitors.

The Presidential Palace was a short distance outside the city, set in beautiful parklike grounds. Their groundcar was passed quickly through the security perimeter. Yar automatically took note of the design, one she knew half a dozen ways to circumvent. To her surprise, no one asked for their phasers, either there or when they entered the palace.

Nalavia was waiting for them in a reception room, extending a hand to each in the human manner . . . before a battery of cameras. It was a showpiece, Yar recognized. She searched her mind for rules of protocol, which had never been of much interest to her except for the military protocol of Starfleet. The Trevans were in transition from a sort of benevolent tyranny to a parliamentary democracy, the change begun two generations ago. As a result, class distinctions were blurring, and so were customs. There was no neat set of rules by which to interpret Nalavia's behavior.

Except one: hereditary or elected ruler, this woman was the head of her planet's government. Yet she had been waiting for them, rather than having them ushered into the reception room and then making an entrance. She met them as equals, which they were not. That meant she wanted her people to *think* they were.

Treva's President wore a wine-red form-fitting outfit that sketched a tribute to being a military uniform by sporting epaulets and a cluster of gold brooches on the left bodice. It was two-piece, the top tightly belted over a skirt split to well above the knee. With it Nalavia wore knee-length boots with tall, thin heels that brought her to Data's height but made Yar wonder how she managed not to fall off them.

On a wide ribbon, she wore about her neck a golden badge, the symbol of the Presidency . . . but the length of the ribbon caused it to dangle precisely between breasts whose lush inner curve was exposed by the deep cleavage of her bodice, beneath which she wore neither blouse nor shirt.

The color, Yar noted, suited Nalavia's pale skin and black hair, but was wrong with her eyes. Oddly flat green eyes, yet although "reptilian" sprang to mind, it was the wrong description. Cat's eyes they were certainly not; no wide-eyed clarity here. Something about those eyes nagged at Yar, but she could not decide what was wrong with them.

The meeting was brief and very formal. Nalavia had a prepared greeting; Data had a prepared response. Yar was glad he outranked her and therefore had to handle this part of the proceedings; she hated public speaking. It also gave her the opportunity to note something in Nalavia that just might be frustration. Now what could cause . . . ?

Then she realized what Captain Picard had done: to face a woman so voluptuous that her sensuality reached through a recorded message to trigger every male hormone on the *Enterprise* bridge, he had sent a woman and an android! Yar smothered a grin at her captain's perspicacity.

When the public meeting was over, Data and Yar were shown to their quarters. Each had a suite of two rooms and a bath, on opposite sides of a wide corridor sporting paintings, statues, and well-armed guards.

Yar found that her belongings had already been put in the drawers, closet, and bathroom cabinet. *And probably thoroughly searched in the process.* But there was nothing to find. She carried her phaser, tricorder, and combadge.

Dinner with Nalavia was scheduled in an hour and a half, so Yar bathed and put on her dress uniform, taking the time to put on makeup in deference to the formal occasion. She was glad she didn't have to wear a formal gown, although she was certain Nalavia would.

A few minutes before they were due, Data appeared at her door to escort her to the private dining room where they hoped they would learn more of what was really happening on Treva. The android was also in dress uniform. "I suppose it is safe to leave our phasers in our rooms," he said.

"You seem as uncomfortable without it as I do," Yar observed. "Have you checked your room for listening devices?"

"There are none. However, I wish Counselor Troi were with us," he replied. "Even I sense that we are not being told the truth—and neither are the people of Treva. What do you sense, Tasha?"

"The same. And that you frustrated Nalavia today."

"Frustrated?"

"You didn't react to her charms. Hmmm. Data, do you know how to flirt?"

"I am programmed in a broad variety of pleasuring techniques. Among them are 234 forms of flirtation."

"Then I suggest you try a few of them on Nalavia. Give her a bit of her own medicine, and see what happens."

"What happens? Tasha, if I do so, she will undoubtedly expect—"

"No!" Yar said sharply. Then, "I mean, not tonight. If you give her what she wants immediately, there will be no reason for her to give you what *you* want."

"Which is?"

"The truth. What's really happening on Treva. You do understand that we can't ask her directly?"

"Yes, Tasha," he replied with his slight smile. "Even I am not that naive. I *have* lived among humans for twenty-six years."

Yar could not resist. "You've been around the block a few times, you weren't born yesterday, you're no longer wet behind the ears—" And she had the delight of seeing Data's smile widen.

"Please do not steal my act," he said softly. "So far, it is the only one I have."

"Oh, no, it isn't," she said, and kissed his cheek. He was designed to be nice to touch, as she well remembered: warm, soft, with underlying strength. Up to now, Yar had regretted her seduction of Data under the influence of the uninhibiting virus. Perhaps what she ought to regret, though, was her instruction that "It never happened."

When their mission was over, after all, there would be another long journey in the shuttlecraft, just the two of them, alone together. . . .

She put such thoughts out of her mind, and settled down to the business of dinner with the President of Treva. Nalavia met them in a small salon, offering wine and cocktails. Yar accepted a glass of wine; Data did not. That was odd; alcohol had little or no effect on him.

"Now that we are alone," said Nalavia, "we can speak as friends. My planet is in great trouble. I am sure you know that the saddest of all wars is that which sets people against their own brothers. That is happening on Treva."

"Civil war," said Yar. She knew only too well how horrifying constant guerilla warfare was. It had been the norm where she grew up. "The Federation is grieved to hear that such a thing is happening to people we were hoping to welcome among us."

"Then surely the Federation will send help!" said Nalavia. "The people want peace, and a say in their government— but terrorists are murdering their elected officials. The legislature has been forced to suspend its meetings, just at the crucial time when the new constitution must be tested and amended."

They were interrupted by the information that dinner was ready—a sumptuous feast during which Nalavia played the gracious hostess, refusing to discuss the purpose of their visit until they were once more in her parlor, sipping Saurian brandy.

"What do these terrorists want?" Data asked.

"A return to the old ways, warlords ruling by force rather than the rule of the people through duly elected officials."

"Warlords?" Yar asked suspiciously.

"They have united under the rule of one man now," Nalavia explained. "Rikan. Many of the country folk have joined his army, either out of fear of change and a yearning for the old ways . . . or because they believe he will win and are in terror for their lives and those of their families should his wrath then fall upon them."

"But this is an internal matter," said Data. "What can Starfleet do?"

Nalavia sat forward eagerly. "We know the location of Rikan's fortress! Our ground forces have attempted several times to take it, but Rikan has an impregnable position. For *our* weaponry. But for yours—all you need do is send a single starship, to blast his fortress from the sky! He cannot shoot down a starship as he does our small aircraft. In minutes you can free us from this tyrant—and Treva will bless you and eagerly join the Federation."

"That is not how Starfleet operates," said Yar. "We believe in the prevention of war. To be forced to use a weapon is itself a form of defeat."

Nalavia stared at her in ill-concealed frustration. "You would have us lie down like dogs, let this tyrant rule?" Her bosom heaved with emotion. "But then, you have not seen what the warlord's troops do to innocent people." She stood and walked to a wallscreen, pressed some switches, and scenes began to appear. First, the bomb in the marketplace which they had seen on the news broadcast. "This happened only yesterday," said Nalavia.

"Your army does not seem very efficient," Data observed.

"What army is, against an enemy that attacks civilians?" Nalavia replied. "Our troops cannot be everywhere. If Rikan would meet us in fair battle, we might have a chance. But these are his methods."

Another scene played, this time of what appeared to be an omnibus full of local people on a busy city street, suddenly erupting with armed men shooting passers-by at random. More armed personnel assaulted a school, forcing children out at gunpoint, to be carried away in ground vehicles. A child tried to break from the line and was shot down. Others began screaming—and those who panicked and tried to run were shot in cold blood.

Yar pulled her mind from the scenes of slaughter just as Data was asking, "How is it that cameras—"

"How is it that the ranks of your army have not swelled with volunteers," Yar spoke over his voice, "when there is such a terrible enemy attacking your people?"

Data glanced at her, and nodded. He would not pursue his question now, and Yar could only hope that he would not try again later. They must not let Nalavia know they had noticed that these "atrocities" were at least staged, if not faked entirely.

But the woman was ahead of them. "Since the attacks began, we have placed surveillance cameras throughout the capital city, to mobilize our forces against attack as quickly as possible. As to volunteers, Treva's citizens have been truly free for less than a generation; tradition tells them to let their leaders take care of them. We are trying, my friends, we are trying desperately—but if we are not to succumb once again to the tyranny of the warlords and the rule of eternal war, then we must have your help." Nalavia sounded as if she was fighting back tears.

Yar looked at Data and mouthed "Now." He looked puzzled for a moment, then nodded.

"A most affecting argument," said the android, going to Nalavia and taking her hand as if to lend her strength. "Starfleet will be very much interested in what you have told us, and in what we find here. But we can do nothing tonight. You must put aside these images of tragedy. You called us friends, Nalavia. I hope we will soon prove good friends indeed."

Yar blinked. God, Data was good! Nalavia took his hand in both of hers, and looked up at him, bravely blinking back tears. Yar smothered a smirk. Treva's President was no slouch in the flirtation department either. By the time she had watched the two of them for half an hour, Yar felt smothered in whipped cream and was beginning to worry slightly. Surely Data could not really be taken in by the heaving bosom, the batting lashes, the helpless act—?

Nah. Data was a *machine*. He couldn't possibly let feelings overcome his judgment.

Still, he *acted* as if he had feelings.

Oh, come on, Tasha—he had to ask your opinion about whether Nalavia is beautiful, she reminded herself, and excused herself after the brandy, pleading a long day and her habit when planetside of getting up at dawn to exercise in the morning light.

Nalavia graciously wished her a good night, but her attention was only too obviously on Data. *I really must try out his flirtation program myself,* Yar thought as she walked the long corridors back toward her room. Her Security Officer's mind noted with amusement that the guard seated near her door was asleep on the job, but she resisted the temptation to wake him. Let his replacement or his senior officer find him that way.

She opened her door, flicked the light switch—and nothing happened.

Instantly she whirled back toward the corridor, not even taking the time to add one plus one odd event—

It was already too late.

Strong hands pulled her back inside her room.

Her fighting was instinctive. There were two attackers, for someone closed the door behind her as she kicked out against the one who had grabbed her, garnering a satisfying yelp as she connected with his knee.

The drapes, which she had left open, were now closed; for some moments Yar's attackers had the advantage while her eyes adjusted after the brightly-lighted corridor. But she had often practiced fighting blind.

And there were only two. No problem usually, but these moved like trained fighters, and they were both larger than she was.

But she took no time to think, spinning out of the first kick to jab the man by the door in the ribs.

"Bloody hell!" he gasped, and Yar grinned in the darkness.

Her next kick took the wind out of her other opponent, but as she was thus off-balance the first man kicked her standing leg out from under her.

She stumbled but managed not to fall.

Recovering, she felt hands grasp her arms—and before she could orient to break his hold a strong hand closed where her neck met her shoulder.

Only then did she think to scream—too late. She got out only a tiny squeak as she blacked out.

Yar came to in her worst nightmare. She was tied hand and foot and being carried roughly over someone's shoulder, her face smothered in a hood.

For a terrible moment she was on New Paris, in the clutches of the rape gang!

Then the present came back. She had been kidnapped from Nalavia's palace.

Damn—if only she had tried to wake the guard and found he was out cold! No. *If only's* wouldn't help.

How much time had passed? Were they still on the palace grounds?

Testing her bonds alerted the man carrying her. "She's comin' round."

"He said she's tough," said the other voice. "Damn it—I'm gonna limp for a week!"

"Yeah, well, me ribs'll be sportin' a nice bruise, but you don't hear me complainin'."

"He jests at scars that never felt a wound."

Yar's captor laughed, and shifted her. "She's heavy fer such a little thing."

"Want me t'take her?" The other man didn't sound very eager.

"Nah—we're here."

In a few more steps, Yar felt a sharp turn, and the sense of entering a room. "We got 'er!" her captor said brightly, and dumped her unceremoniously to the floor.

"Get that thing off her head!" a new voice exploded in fury.

Only it wasn't a new voice—

"Okay, okay—didn't want her t'see the way, did we?" protested the one who had carried her, pulling off the hood covering Yar's head.

In disbelieving *déjà vu* she found herself nose to toes with shining black boots, then managed to turn onto her back, her eyes following long legs up, farther up, past a torso clad in black and gray, to a cruel and angry face staring down at her. The expression was the same one seared into her memory from the last time she had seen . . .

. . . the face of Darryl Adin.

Chapter Five

ENSIGN TASHA YAR could not imagine anybody in the universe being happier than she was. She had graduated from Starfleet Academy with honors, and her first training cruise was such a success that the *Starbound* had been given a genuine, responsible assignment on its way back to Earth: carrying a consignment of dilithium crystals from the cracking station on Tarba to Starfleet's shipyard on Mars. But it was not just the success of her new career that had Yar wondering if the artificial gravity had ceased to function.

After the utter misery of the first fifteen years of her life, she had barely adjusted to the idea of a hopeful future when Federation Immigration threatened to send her back to the hell-hole she had escaped from. Historians discovered in records no one on the planet remembered that the turning point on New Paris had come when it seceded *in absentia* from the Federation it blamed for abandoning the colony. Not knowing about the wars and technological breakdowns going on back on Earth, the government of New Paris seceded in order not to be bound by the very laws whose abandonment led to Earth's worst war and the Post-Atomic Horrors. Ironically, New Paris took longer than its founding planet to sink into degradation . . . but the eventual result was similar, and unlike Earth, New Paris never recovered.

But Dare found Starfleet legal counsel to present Yar's case. In the end, though, it was neither the legal counsel's skills nor Dare's eloquent descriptions of the life he had rescued "the child" from that won her the right to stay on Earth: the most powerful druglord on New Paris, whom the Federation perforce had to recognize as spokesman for his planet, simply didn't want her! "What's another starving girl-child? You want her, you keep her—in fact, take any of the rest of the strays that want to go with you!"

Only after she was at last secure in her new life could Yar begin to mold herself into something civilized, to achieve her dream of attending Starfleet Academy. The struggle merely to survive was over. Whole new vistas opened to her.

At last, it seemed, fate had turned a kindly face toward the young woman it had previously scorned. When Darryl Adin returned to Starfleet Academy for a refresher course in the latest security techniques, just as her final training placed Yar in the same courses, they had rediscovered one another. The difference in their ages, so important when he was a Starfleet officer and she a terrified adolescent, was insignificant now that Yar was almost twenty-three. Inevitably, they had fallen in love.

Nor could they have chosen a better time for it. In the past, Starfleet marriages were risky endeavors, often doomed in the attempt to balance two careers, forcing choices between refused promotions or long separations. Either way, domestic pressures added to an already stressful lifestyle resulted in an unconscionably high rate of broken marriages.

But now, in recognition of the human need for family, Starfleet was building new Galaxy class starships, designed for long exploratory voyages upon which whole families would journey together. Darryl Adin and Tasha Yar had put in their application both for permission to marry, and for assignment together to such a ship. Their first request had already been granted: they would be married in the Academy Chapel upon their return to Earth. It was too early for announcements about the second, but Dare had been assured by friends in Starfleet Command that while the competition for other posts was the fiercest they had ever seen, there were few applicants for positions in Security. To people adventurous enough to choose a career in Starfleet Security, a ship safe enough to carry children held little appeal.

So Yar had high hopes that she and Dare would not only be able to serve together, but also raise a family in which their children would have both parents close at hand, all within the extended family of Starfleet . . . the only true family she had ever known.

As usual on a training voyage, the *Starbound* was crewed mostly by newly-graduated Starfleet Cadets with just a few seasoned officers to guide them. Their mission was real enough, carrying supplies to a number of planets along the well-traveled star lanes; it was simply neither dangerous nor crucial. They weathered ion storms, learned to keep to a schedule, and visited worlds where conditions were very different from those on the planets where they had grown up. They learned to man their posts, care for their ship, and work together on away teams, all from day-to-day experience. When the training voyage was over, they would go to their first assignments on ships or starbases, qualified to work side by side with seasoned Starfleet personnel.

Dare was one of the experienced officers on the *Starbound,* acting as Security Chief. Some of Yar's female friends had warned her that having her fiance as her superior would never work—but better to learn it now than after they were married. When the dire predictions did not come true, she put the comments down to jealousy. Now the six-month voyage was more than half over, they had secretly loaded the dilithium crystals at Starbase 36, and they headed back toward Earth with their precious cargo and heady sense of accomplishment.

One day Yar was on the firing range, trying to equal Dare's accuracy with a single-shot pistol. A phaser or other continuous-fire weapon was no true test of skill; the user moved it onto target while still firing. Practice only with such weapons led to sloppy shooting and the habit of wasting the weapon's charge—critical if one could not recharge it.

So Security personnel practiced with guns that shot brief bursts of light, at light-sensitive targets. Yar was the best in her class . . . but Dare's accuracy was legendary. He had been Starfleet champion for the past nine years, and no one yet came close to displacing him.

The light gun made a slight zapping sound, and the target beeped various notes, depending on where one hit it. Yar's shots made a monotonous repeated "boink" as she placed them consistently within the ten-centimeter-diameter center circle at a distance of thirty meters.

At that distance she could not see the target well enough to discern the pattern of white light made by her strikes, except that it seemed a little too large—again. She stepped back and looked up at the monitor over her head. Indeed, her shots were scattered over the center circle. Dare had been known to put fifteen shots dead center, one on top of the other, so that it appeared he had struck only once.

Yar took a deep breath, stretched her fingers, and tried again. Six shots pinged the same note, but the seventh rang a deeper tone. "Damn," Yar muttered. She was getting worse.

"Tension, love."

She closed her eyes, clenched her hands and jaw, and through gritted teeth said, "Go away, Dare. You know I hate it when you sneak up on me."

"Why was I able to?" he countered.

"Because this is not survival practice on the holodeck. This is target practice, and I'm trying to concentrate. There have to be some places where a person doesn't have to worry about being attacked."

"How about my quarters, after your next watch?"

"It's a date. Now go away and let me work."

"Is it work, Tasha?" He came up behind her, strong square hands on her shoulders, kneading her tension away. "Yes—you're working too hard. Relax. The gun is an extension of your hand. Point it like a finger. Target practice is just a game—"

"*Just* a game? That from the man who moped for three days because the ship's computer beat him at chess?"

"Someone on the last crew programmed it to cheat," he asserted staunchly. "Sestok had to reprogram it. And don't change the subject. You don't need this kind of accuracy to take out an enemy—you're just honing your skills here."

"Mm-hmm. You don't want me good enough to beat you." She said it lightly, but there were times Yar resented Dare's competitive nature, especially when it came head to head with her own. She could not make him understand the difference between them: Dare played to win. Yar worked to survive.

But her fiancé understood her desires, if not her motivations. His hands were still on her shoulders. Now he turned her to face him. "Tasha," he said, "I *want* you to be as good as I am."

"Not better?"

His smile was self-mocking. "Better than perfect?"

She chuckled. "Nobody's perfect."

"No, not at everything. But there are some things— Tasha, why do you think I push you so hard? I want you to be happy, and to you that means perfecting your skills as a Security officer."

"Not entirely. Having you. . . ." She let the sentence trail off.

His smile was sweet and open this time, and then he kissed her. She melted contentedly into his arms.

When they broke apart, he murmured, "Relaxed now? Feeling good?"

"Mmmm."

"Try the target again."

"Dare!" She stiffened in outrage.

"Go on," he urged. "That's an order, Ensign."

"Damn you," she muttered under her breath—not loud enough for her superior officer to hear, even though it was Dare—turned, and put fifteen rounds smack into the center of the target.

Dare was looking up at the monitor when she turned back to him. He grinned. "Personal best."

She looked up. Sure enough, every shot was clustered within a five-centimeter radius. When she looked at Dare, so smug and self-satisfied, fury at him and delight at her performance combined to prevent her from speaking.

"Now," said Dare, "tell me you didn't pretend it was me you were shooting at."

Yar gasped. "Of course I didn't!" Then she added, "Not that you wouldn't deserve it if I had."

"That's my clever girl," Dare approved. "Use your feelings—don't let them use you. See you after watch."

And he left her there, half indignant, half aroused, half delighted, half confused . . . and with never a thought to how many halves that added up to since she had enough emotions stirring for at least two people anyway.

Later, when they were both off duty and relaxing in Dare's quarters, she asked him, "Do you use the same technique you used on me today with all the trainees?"

He laughed. "I don't think it would work very well with Henderson, do you?"

Jack Henderson was a good head taller than Dare and built like an ore carrier. What he lacked in agility he made up for in sheer weight and muscle power. When he had a chance to set himself, not one of the security personnel aboard the *Starbound* could knock him over, including Darryl Adin.

"All your female trainees, then?"

"I've *been* nerve-pinched in the line of duty, Tasha; I don't care to casually invite it," he replied.

Oh, yes—T'Seya.

"Besides," Dare continued, "teaching security procedures is like being in the field: one uses what is available, and adapts it to the target."

"Oh—so now you're thinking of *me* as a target?"

He did not answer immediately, instead studying her for a moment. He was wearing a meditation robe, and sitting cross-legged on the bunk. The *Starbound* was a small ship, and while the Chief of Security did have a private cabin it was neither large nor luxurious. There were only two chairs, a comfortable armchair where Yar sat, and the straight-backed desk chair.

Yar was still in her uniform, as she had come here directly from her watch, which had been spent at the boring but necessary task of weapons inventory. Surprisingly, she had found seven phasers out of order, and sent them to Maintenance.

Dare watched her for a few moments, his eyes dark and unreadable in the soft cabin lighting. His golden brown hair had the soft and fluffy look of being freshly washed. Unparted, it spilled over his forehead like a young boy's, softening his harsh features. What Yar really wanted to do was sit beside him and run her fingers through it, then let him make her forget everything except the two of them. But something held her in her chair—perhaps his piercing stare.

Finally Dare said, "Are you angry with me, Tasha?"

"I don't know."

"That sounds like an honest answer. But you *are* angry."

"Don't play Ship's Counselor, Dare. You're no more qualified than I am."

His eyes widened, and his mouth quirked in an apologetic smile. He was beautiful to her in such moments, when his features softened. "So that's it. I'm sorry, Tasha. You thought I was playing games with your feelings this afternoon."

"Weren't you?"

"No. And yes."

"That *doesn't* sound like an honest answer."

"Yes, inasmuch as I wanted to break your nervous tension and call up your competitive spirit—as I should try to do for anyone in that situation. No, inasmuch as even though I used my right to touch you—" he smiled again "—my desire to touch you—it was individual without being personal."

"What?"

"I encouraged you to use disciplines you have already conquered. Tasha, it's little wonder you anger easily, considering your early life. But you have learned to turn that anger to positive use—and I had nothing to do with that. When I left you on Earth, you were a primed rocket, ready to go off in any direction, on any excuse. When I returned, I found a strong, beautiful young woman who can be relied on to act wisely."

"That's not what my instructors said," Yar pointed out.

"Style, Tasha, that's all. Your style is to act quickly. So is mine. We're both survivors, love. That's why we make such a good team."

"I thought opposites were supposed to attract."

"Well, now—I think we have enough differences to make life interesting," he replied in his sexiest voice.

Yar could not help laughing. Dare could always break through her defenses. No wonder she loved him! She left her chair for the warmth of his waiting arms.

Darryl Adin might be competitive in every other area of life, but he was most generous in their intimacy, giving Yar the tenderness and caring she so desperately needed. He was her first love and first lover, for although the years of counseling she had received through Starfleet had rid her of the fear and distrust of men she had carried from her life on New Paris, she had never gone beyond friendship with any man before Dare reappeared in her life.

It was incredible now to think that when he first rescued her she had cynically expected him to use her. She had been both drawn to him and terrified of him, her apprehension increasing as their journey progressed and she was cleansed, given proper nutrition, her teeth repaired. She feared that by the time she met his standards she would *owe* him whatever he wanted because she had accepted it all, including a great deal of his personal attention.

Finally, unable to stand the suspense any longer, when he dismissed her one evening after a lesson in arithmetic she had blurted out, "When're ya gonna do it, then? When do I start payin' fer the clothes, the medicine, the lessons? Ain't I good enough for ya yet, clean enough, smart enough?"

And he had looked at her with such bewilderment, his expressive eyes so openly puzzled that for the first time she knew, actually believed, that he expected no payment at all.

Even as she was assimilating that, he realized what she meant, what fears she had been hiding, and his mouth opened in horror and pity. "Oh, Tasha," he whispered. "Oh, child—no! Nobody's going to hurt you that way, ever again. I thought you understood. We're not like that." He had started to reach toward her, realized she could mistake the gesture, and turned away—but not before she saw the pain her undeserved accusation had caused him.

And she had been as bewildered as he, not least at her incomprehensible sense of rejection.

It was only years later, when they met again as adults, that she understood just how unfounded her accusations had been—and how they had echoed through the years even when they were reunited, preventing him from acknowledging his own feelings until she took the initiative. But then, if there was one quality Tasha Yar had in abundance, it was initiative.

Another was her sense of responsibility. That was why, on that particular evening on the *Starbound,* although she would have loved to spend the entire ship's night with Dare, she had left early because tomorrow there was a routine schedule change that placed her on the early watch. As she prepared to leave, she commented, "More inventory tomorrow. Everybody hates inventory, but at least today it was justified."

"Hmmm?" Dare asked, obviously much more interested in looking at her than in what she was saying.

She told him about the seven defective phasers—and suddenly had his undivided attention. *"Seven!* Tasha, that's far too many for coincidence. Somebody's misusing them."

"How? Most of them haven't been used at all."

"They're stored wrong, then."

"No they're not, Dare. They were stored properly in the charging units." She blinked. "Could the units be defective? I didn't think to jump ahead of schedule on the checklist. To be honest, it never occurred to me that there was anything out of line about finding seven defective phasers out of fifty. I mean—finding and repairing them is what the inventory's for, right?"

"Right—but you could only know from experience that one or two would be unusual enough, only four months out from Earth. That's why I'm here, Tasha. In two days the inventory report would have been completed and given to me, and I'd have spotted the discrepancy. As it is, I shall check the Weapons Room myself tomorrow."

The next morning Dare joined Yar and the other two Security trainees taking inventory. By the time they were finished, he was pale and tight-lipped. The barely-suppressed anger turned his face into such a threatening mask that the other two trainees were shaking. But Yar knew his anger was not at them—it was at the as-yet-unknown source of the devastation in the Weapons Room.

Not only were there five more damaged hand phasers, but nearly all of the booster handles they fitted into were completely discharged—useless. Dare ran the diagnostics himself, his voice becoming tighter and more nasal with each new discovery. The baffling thing was, everything operated perfectly now.

"Tasha," he instructed, "check the duty roster for everyone who has worked in here since the last inventory. Assemble them in the main briefing room at 0900 tomorrow morning. In the meantime, we must recharge as many units as possible. Get Bosinney from Engineering. I want to know what *caused* these burnouts and power drains! It will do no good to recharge the units if they simply discharge again."

"Uh, Commander—" Yar said hesitantly.

At her formal use of his title, Dare's head came up abruptly. "You mean after we report to the Captain?" she asked.

For one moment his anger was turned on her—but Dare had many years of experience at controlling his temper, and almost at once said, "Yes, it could be a breach of Security, Ensign. You take the report to Captain Jarvis. I'll call Engineering."

Yar was not surprised that Dare wanted the young trainee, Bosinney, rather than Chief Engineer Nichols; the training voyage assignment was a way of easing a man losing the sharp edge he had once had through the final months he needed to retire on full pension. Bosinney was a mechanical and electronic genius, and no one in Engineering was a part of the command structure, so there was no danger to the ship in this particular Starfleet kindness.

When Yar reported the debacle over weaponry to Captain Enid Jarvis, she insisted on accompanying the Ensign to the Weapons Room. By that time George Bosinney was there, disassembling one of the charging units and setting up diagnostics. Bosinney was one of those young men cursed not only with genius, but with an appearance younger than his true age. At barely twenty, he was the youngest graduate in their class, but anyone seeing him out of uniform would think him no more than sixteen at best. He was awkward and thin, his skin had not yet cleared nor his voice completely changed, but the hands working over the boards and connectors were sure and strong.

"What happened?" Captain Jarvis asked Dare.

"That's what we're trying to find out."

"Commander Adin!" Bosinney's voice was even higher pitched than usual in his excitement. "Look at this circuit breaker!"

Dare stared, puzzled. Neither could Yar see anything odd about the part the boy had pulled loose.

It was Jarvis who demanded, "Well—what's wrong with it?"

Bosinney gulped, but held his ground. "It's the wrong power level—too low for this connection."

"That would just mean it would blow out and have to be reset," said Jarvis.

"But on *this* voyage," said Dare, "the Weapons Room staff have changed almost daily."

"That's right!" said Yar. "I was scheduled to two watches here, then on to auxiliary power."

"How often would that breaker go out?" Jarvis asked.

"Each time there was an overload," Bosinney replied. "It'll be in the log—" He went to the computer terminal, calling up charts and graphs that flicked by too fast for Yar to make sense of what was not her field.

"On the average," said Bosinney, "the breaker was reset

every two point six days. Actually, it formed a random pattern ranging from zero point eight to five point four. And here," he indicated a low point following a spike on one of the graphs with one hand, and the Weapons Room Log entries with the other, "where it blew twice in one day, it was not while the same person was on duty."

"But how could a power loss every couple of days damage so many weapons?" Yar asked. "They're all on backup circuits."

"I think I know," said Bosinney, and began calling up more graphs. "Yes—that's it. Power fluctuations decreased the life of the storage batteries. They were partly drained until someone noticed and reset the breaker, but never fully drained and then recharged. Once or twice wouldn't hurt, but this pattern of a small drain followed by recharge occurred repeatedly. Finally it damaged the batteries, and they allowed the booster handles to discharge."

"Replace those damaged batteries," said Captain Jarvis. "Mr. Adin, how long will it take to recharge the booster handles?"

"Not more than—"

He was interrupted when warning lights began to flash.

The intercom clicked on. "Yellow alert. Unidentified vessel approaching—does not respond to hailing frequencies. Captain to the bridge, please. Yellow alert!" The voice was young and female, high-pitched with tension.

Darryl Adin and Enid Jarvis, experienced line officers, looked at one another for one moment. Dare's frown was ominous. "I do not believe in coincidence. Advise systems checks of all weaponry."

Jarvis went to the intercom. "Jarvis here. Go to red alert, shields up. Run check of all weapons systems. I'm on my way."

Before the Weapons Room door opened at the Captain's approach, the klaxon began sounding, and the flashing lights changed to red. The voice on the ship's intercom shook now, but sent out the message: "Red alert. All hands to battle stations. This is not a drill. Red alert."

Then Dare was at the intercom. "Security personnel to

Weapons Room." He turned to Yar. "Ensign—take the Security post on the bridge. I must decide who gets what weapons we have operational. Who's up there now?"

Yar glanced at the posted roster. "Henderson."

Dare handed her two phasers. "He's not our best shot, but he's tough and he doesn't panic. Keep him with you. You can always hide behind him, come to that."

"Dare—you can't think there's any danger of being boarded!" Yar exclaimed.

"We must prepare for any eventuality. You have your orders, Ensign."

What happened in the next hour would always have for Tasha Yar the quality of nightmare, far more so than the induced illusion of the Priam IV test. The *Starbound* was a small training vessel, not a battleship. Even though Dare's suspicions proved unfounded, and the external weapons worked perfectly, *Starbound*'s armament was intended as a deterrent only for such slight dangers as were occasionally met within Federation space. Despite a generation of peace and plenty, political or religious disputes still occasionally erupted into war or terrorism—although *Starbound*'s itinerary kept her well away from disputed territories.

Then there were the smugglers of contraband—forbid something on one planet, and someone would bring it in from another. "Free traders," of course, could be found anywhere, but as they used very small, very fast ships, they could not carry armament to attack a Starfleet vessel, even a small training ship.

So, there ought to be nothing in this area of space hostile to the *Starbound*. When they had loaded the dilithium a month ago, Starfleet Security had assured them that no one could even know about their precious cargo. But what, then, was a deep-space vessel doing on an intercept course with them at warp speed, refusing to answer their requests for identification?

When Jarvis and Yar reached the bridge, the young crew were already nervous. Jarvis took the central chair, to the obvious relief of the trainee holding the position. Yar went to the Security post. Jack Henderson stepped back gladly to give her room to study the board, saying, "D'you think we should call for Mr. Adin?"

"He's busy in the Weapons Room," Yar replied. "Here—I brought yours."

He stared at it. "He thinks we might need—?"

"Be prepared," Yar replied. The board before her showed the identification request broadcast to the oncoming vessel on all frequencies, translator circuits on so that it would be picked up in virtually any language. "No response on any frequency, Captain," she reported.

On another screen, sensor readings of the oncoming vessel were displayed in three dimensions, detail increasing as the distance between them decreased.

"Their communications may be out," Jarvis said calmly. "Helm, change course to zero zero seven, mark six."

"Course locked in."

"Oncoming vessel has changed course to compensate," Yar reported as the information came up on her screens. "Still on intercept course."

"Can you identify?" the Captain asked.

"No identity beacon," Yar replied. "Shape indicates a standard deep-space vehicle, approximately three times the size of *Starbound*. No visible characteristics identify origin. Ms. Sethan," she said to the tiny Hemanite Science Officer, "can you get life-form readings?"

"Numerous life forms," Sethan reported. "At this distance the instruments cannot yet distinguish—"

"They're firing at us!"

The shout came from the helmsman.

"Shields up," said Captain Jarvis. "Arm photon torpedoes. Send out a distress call to any Starfleet vessel within range: Training ship *Starbound* under attack from unidentified vessel."

Yar got out "Message sent," just before the first shot hit them.

The ship rocked with the blow, but the shields held—for three volleys.

Starbound fired back, but its torpedoes spent themselves futilely against the attacker's shields.

"Captain," Yar reported, "they're jamming subspace radio!"

"Just keep sending the message, Ensign," Jarvis said calmly.

Yar left the signal on automatic. "Front starboard shield thirty-five percent functional," she advised.

"Change course," ordered the Captain. "One zero three mark seventeen, warp three. Let's see if we can outrun them."

The maneuver placed the undamaged aft shields between the *Starbound* and her attacker. However, the enemy ship pursued, easily matching their speed through warp four . . . five . . . five point eight—

"Warp engine overload!" came the warning from Nichols at the Engineering console. "Bosinney, what the hell're you—?"

"Bosinney's in the Weapons Room, sir," Yar told him.

"Damn! Get him down to nurse those engines! If anyone can get warp six out of them, he can."

By the time Yar turned, the Captain was looking at her. "Do it."

The ship shook from another blast.

"Only three torpedoes left," the helmsman reported in a frightened voice even as Yar relayed the message to send Bosinney to Engineering.

"Go, boy!" she heard Dare tell Bosinney, then his voice just a bit clearer as he turned back to the intercom, "Security armed and deployed to transporter and shuttle bay, and at least one phaser issued to each department. I'm on my way to the bridge with arms for all of you."

The *Starbound* was too small to have a turbolift. By the time Dare reached the bridge, Jarvis had deployed the last of the torpedoes and only the shields stood between them and the enemy.

One of Yar's screens whited out with overload. When it came back, she reported, "Aft shield out, Captain."

"Captain," reported Sethan, who had kept at her controls all this time, "I have life-form identification on the hostile ship. Copper-based blood. From size, body temperature, ship's atmosphere, and attack pattern—" she swung around in her chair, a doll-like figure pronouncing their doom, "—they can only be Orions."

This isn't happening, thought Yar. *It's another test—it has to be! Orions never come this far into Federation space—*

But as the back of her mind tried to deny it, the foreground kept her to Starfleet efficiency. "Engineering reports damage to portside warp engine in that last blast, Captain. We're losing power."

"Losing speed," reported the helmsman. "Warp four point six. Warp four. Warp three point five . . . and holding."

"Hostile ship closing!" Yar reported.

"Surrender," said Captain Jarvis.

"Captain?" Yar spoke without thinking.

Jarvis spun her chair to face Yar. "Surrender, Ensign! We've no weapons left, our engines are damaged, and our distress signal is jammed on all channels. If Orions take us alive, Starfleet has a chance to ransom us."

Yar clamped her teeth over the automatic response, *If they can find us.*

"Better alive," said Dare, although his thunderous expression told how much he hated to admit defeat. "Always better alive."

He was right, of course. There was only one reason for Orions to take such an incredible risk: they had to know about the dilithium. Slaves were not worth an incursion so deep into Federation territory . . . which meant that the people were expendable. If they did not surrender, the Orions would simply blast the crippled *Starbound* to rubble, and from the remains sift out the impervious dilithium crystals.

Before she had even thought it through, Yar's reluctant hand had set the surrender signal broadcasting.

There was . . . "No response!" she reported in astonishment. "Captain—they don't acknowledge our surrender!"

"What the hell?!" demanded Dare, pushing Yar away from the Security console. He double-checked the signal. "It's broadcasting, and the visual light display is active if their jamming keeps them from picking up the radio signal. What can they want beyond surrender?"

What the Orions wanted, apparently, was to cripple the *Starbound* totally. They sent another barrage of torpedoes against the helpless training ship, then came alongside and boarded via a docking tube to the shuttle bay hatch. Since their surrender had not been accepted, Security and other armed personnel met them there. With only Phaser One operative they had little chance against the Orions' disruptors, phasers, and blasters.

"Dare," Yar objected as they watched the slaughter on the ship's monitor, "shouldn't we send the personnel from the transporter now that—"

"That's just what they hoped we'd do, Ensign!" he interrupted. "There they come!"

Sure enough, Orions were now transporting aboard—and the Security trainees Dare had placed in the transporter room blasted them before they were recovered enough to move. "Good work!" he told them over the intercom. "Stay there for a moment—"

"Dare!" Yar gasped, directing his attention to the viewscreen that showed the chaos in Engineering. Orions were beaming in there—obviously they had scanned the *Starbound* thoroughly now, since her shields were down, and did not have to aim for the transporter pad.

"Form a circle!" Dare instructed at once. Not even Captain Jarvis questioned the order, and they were all at the perimeter of the bridge when a knot of Orions appeared in the middle. With a cold smile, Dare was the first to fire, but the rest of the bridge crew were not far behind, and the boarding party fell as fast as it materialized.

For a few glorious moments, Yar thought that the crew of the *Starbound* might yet drive off the pirates.

But Orions were materializing everywhere now, and still coming steadily through the shuttle bay. And where they entered, they killed.

On the monitors, the bridge crew followed the progress of a contingent of Orions toward the bridge. As the enemy approached, the Starfleet members prepared. They had locked the doors to the corridor, of course, but it didn't take long for a barrage of phaser and disruptor fire to melt them away. Orions surged onto the bridge.

Sheltering behind the central consoles, the bridge crew gave a good accounting, but without full weaponry they had no chance. Henderson went down, then Captain Jarvis. Chief Engineer Nichols swore loudly as he drilled one of the Orions full center in his breastplate—but his voice cut off abruptly as another's shot took off the side of his head, blood and brains spattering Yar and Sethan.

Dare was shooting coolly, every shot counting—but for what?

Yar's phaser was discharged. She dropped it, scuttled behind the Captain's body to find the one she had dropped —and shouted "Dare—look out!" as one of the fallen Orions in the center of the bridge moved, aiming a disruptor at the Security Chief.

Dare turned, felled that Orion, but was exposed to one of those by the doors, who shot him in the back.

As her fiance fell, Yar felt something inside turn to ice. She rose to her knees, took aim at the one who had shot Dare, and drilled him through the forehead. And she kept shooting until *that* phaser was discharged, and she was the last of the bridge crew taken, backhanded by the Orion who finally captured her. She struck the wall, and blessed oblivion overcame her.

Tasha Yar came to in the *Starbound* sickbay with the worst headache of her life. She had a concussion, Dr. Trent informed her, and applied an instrument behind her ear which quickly dispensed with the headache.

But not her heartache. "Doctor—what happened?" she demanded.

"The Orions are gone," the doctor said grimly. "They took the dilithium crystals—turns out we were carrying some consignment Starfleet Command thought would be safe aboard because no one would expect it here—damn their little brass hearts!"

"But . . . they left us here?"

"Starfleet personnel don't make good slaves," the medic said bitterly. "Too strong-willed and determined."

"How many survived?" Yar asked, the scenes of slaughter returning to her reluctant memory.

"Most of the trainees, for all the good it does us."

"We're alive," Yar said, pushing out of her mind the fact that Dare was not. "We can still get back to Earth." She sat up. "Who's in command? The Captain—?"

"Dead. They killed every experienced officer except Adin and me, and since he's unconscious I guess that leaves me in command."

Yar heard only one thing in the doctor's statement. "Commander Adin's *alive?!* Where is he?"

"Hey—you shouldn't get up yet!" the doctor began. Then, "What the hell—we'll all be dead in a few days anyway. Adin's over—"

Yar found Dare in one of the sickbay life-support beds, waxen pale and barely breathing. One of the nurses told her, "The setting the Orions use kills instantly if the target is the brain. But if they hit somewhere else, the person can be revived with life support—if he's worth bothering with." She looked sadly from Dare to the other patients in the same condition. "Slavers' mentality, I suppose. After twenty or thirty minutes the victim is brain-dead." A tear slipped her control. "We lost at least ten people because we didn't have support beds or personnel to save them!"

But the immediate losses were not the worst of it. Once assured that Dare would not regain consciousness for hours yet, although he would survive unimpaired, Yar set out to discover the condition of the ship. The few people moving about had been conscious to the end—and their reports were grim indeed.

The Orions had left most of the medical personnel unharmed, but it was a brutal kindness. They had removed not only the dilithium crystals from the cargo, but those from the *Starbound*'s own warp engines—and then methodically wrecked the impulse engines, the single shuttlecraft, and the life capsules. They had also removed irreplaceable components from the subspace radio, so the ship could not call for help. Finally, they had gone through the severely stunned victims of their attack and shot all the officers in the head—except for the chief medical officer and two experienced nurses.

When the pirates had gone, the medics worked their hearts out to save as many lives as they possibly could . . . only to learn that they had doomed them to a lingering death. With neither the warp engines nor the impulse engines operational, battery-operated life support would fail in six days—and by the time Starfleet began to wonder why *Starbound* was late for her next planetfall, everyone on board would be many days dead.

Yar roamed the corridors, anguishedly searching for someone—anyone—with an idea to save them. But the trainees were too stunned to think, and there were no experienced officers left to guide them.

Except Dare.

How had he survived? All Yar could remember was his being struck in the back. He had fallen forward over some others of the bridge crew. Perhaps the Orions had not turned him over to see his face or insignia. However it had happened, Yar breathed a prayer of thanks to any god who might have had a hand in saving him. Even if only so that she and he could die together.

But Darryl Adin was not a man to accept death without a fight. Over and over Dare had drilled into the trainees, "Learn to be survivors. Your job is to protect other people—how much protection is a dead security guard?"

Yar was sitting by his bed when he finally came to—and despite the warnings of Dr. Trent that he needed rest he soon had out of them the condition in which the Orions had left the *Starbound*.

"Who's in command?" he demanded at once.

"I suppose you are," Dr. Trent told him.

"But who has the con?"

"Nobody, really," said Yar. "Karin Orlov and Brian Hayakawa are on the bridge trying to rig some sort of radio transmitter, but without subspace the chance of a signal reaching another ship before——"

"Any chance is better than none!" Dare said. "Who else is taking action?"

"Uh . . . what else is there——?"

Dare sat up and swung his legs over the side of the couch.

"You're in no condition to get up!" protested Dr. Trent as Dare winced sharply.

Dare opened his eyes and pinned the medic with his dark gaze. "If I don't, who will? You're needed here, and the trainees don't have the experience. Who survived from Engineering?"

"T'Irnya, Zkun, Donal, and Bosinney, but——"

"Where's Bosinney?"

"Mr. Adin," said Dr. Trent, "Ensign Bosinney is injured. He won't be able to work on the engines, if that's what you have in mind."

"Why not? Is he unconscious?"

"No, but I had to tranquilize him. When the Orions broke into Engineering and the crew ran out of phaser power, they used their tools as weapons. Bosinney had a welder, one of the Orions tried to shoot it out of his hand—and destroyed Bosinney's right hand."

"Oh, God," Dare said, looking down at his own hands in his lap for a moment. But then he lifted his head. "If he can't do the work—he can still direct it. There's nothing wrong with his brain, I take it?"

"He is in severe shock," Trent said angrily.

"Well the best thing to bring him out of it," said Dare, "is getting back to work. Can he move about?"

"*Mr.* Adin!" the doctor objected.

Dare stood, wobbly but determined. "If there is a chance in hell of restoring impulse power, George Bosinney is the only one who can do it. I'm sorry if I insult your sensibilities, Doctor, but if we cannot restore power we'll all be dead anyway. Now let me talk to Bosinney."

The young Engineer lay listlessly on one of the treatment couches, two round tranquilizer pads attached to his forehead. Like Dare, he was dressed in a blue sickbay coverall.

Bosinney's right arm disappeared from the elbow down into a healing unit. His eyes were open, but they stared blankly at nothing.

Without waiting for the doctor's permission, Dare pulled one of the tranquilizer pads off. Bosinney blinked, and attempted to focus on him. "Mr. Adin," he said, somewhat thickly. "I'm glad . . . you survived, sir."

"And we're all glad you did, son." It was the first time Yar had ever heard him address a trainee so familiarly—except herself, of course, and that only in private. "We need your help, George. If we can't get the impulse engines running, we're all going to die."

"Wish I . . . could help, sir. But . . . my hand—"

"George," said Dare, "you can't think straight, tranquilized that way. If I remove the other pad, you'll have to face what has happened to you. Can you cope . . . for the good of your shipmates?"

The unfocused stare told them nothing. But apparently it simply took Bosinney longer than usual to assemble his thoughts under the effects of the tranquilizer, for just as Yar had decided he had tuned them out he said, "For . . . shipmates. I'll . . . try, sir."

"Good job," said Dare, and removed the other pad.

Bosinney's eyes focused at once, and he blinked. He looked toward his right arm, and said, "I can feel my hand. It itches."

"That's from the healing in your arm," said Dr. Trent. "If you want—" He gestured toward the pads Dare had laid on the bedside table.

"No!" Bosinney's eyes turned to Dare again. "You said we're all going to die."

"Not if you can get the impulse engines running."

"How can I?" Bosinney demanded, his voice squeaking in anguish. Tears leaked from the corners of his eyes.

"It's your mind that's your strong point, Bosinney, not your hands!" Dare told him. "I'm sure Dr. Trent has reminded you of the many members of Starfleet with prosthetic limbs. You'll have a new hand that works just as well as the original—but only if we get the *Starbound* to

Starbase 18. It's thirty-five days from here on impulse power—and we'll have life support once the engines are working."

"But how?"

"You're going to sit back and give the orders, son. As Acting Captain of the U.S.S. *Starbound,* I'm appointing you Acting Chief Engineer. You know the other trainees. Which ones are the most skilled at this kind of work?"

"I won't know till I assess the damage," Bosinney answered.

"Very well." Dare turned to Trent. "How soon can he start work, Doctor?"

"Another few hours—"

"Can I do any harm that will prevent getting a prosthetic hand if I get up now?" Bosinney asked.

"You'll still have pain, itching—and the possibility of shock—"

"That wasn't what I asked," said the boy, suddenly sounding very much a man.

The doctor gave Dare an annoyed look and replied, "No, you can't do any more damage now, unless you fall on it."

"Then please remove the healing unit, Doctor."

In the next few hours, Yar watched the man she loved bring the terrified and hopeless trainees back to Starfleet levels of discipline. A new duty roster was posted and all departments were manned, if with fewer personnel than usual.

All Dare really did was to proceed according to Starfleet protocols, but ordering, threatening, cajoling, and manipulating the trainees and the reluctant medical staff into following those procedures took tremendous effort. On the first day, Orlov and Hayakawa got their distress signal working, but it could only be sent by pre-warp methods of transmission. It would be months before the signal reached Starbase 18. The only hope it offered was the chance of a ship passing near enough to receive it, before the *Starbound* ran out of power.

Nonetheless, the news that the signal was broadcasting was the first ray of hope.

Dare followed it with the mass funeral for the crew who fell in the Orion massacre.

That was also Starfleet regs, but Yar was horrified nonetheless when Dare assembled all off-duty personnel for the standard Starfleet service, and broadcast it throughout the ship for those who could not attend. When he put his mind to it, Dare could read aloud beautifully and effectively, and as for the first time the young crew heard the words of hope and consolation read over the bodies of friends fallen in the line of duty, they wept shamelessly.

The bodies were then committed to the vastness of space, whose exploration was the purpose to which their lives had been dedicated. There were no Orion bodies to dispose of; the pirates had carried their own dead away with them, a surprising act among a people renowned for having no honor or loyalty.

As surprising as their leaving anyone alive aboard the *Starbound.*

It was only when the funeral service was over, and Yar found herself wiping away tears and proceeding to her watch on the bridge with a new sense of dedication, that she realized Dare was right. Starfleet regs were right. Instead of increasing their depression, the funeral service provided a catharsis.

For the next three days, Yar doubted Dare slept at all. He visited every part of the ship, inspecting repairs, encouraging hope, ordering people to meals and to rest as often as to duty. And when he was not prowling the corridors, he was in Engineering, supporting George Bosinney, who seethed with frustration at not being able to do the work with his own hands. Then he got the idea of strapping an instrument to the stump of his right wrist, to perform some delicate maneuver that not even T'Irnya was able to complete to his satisfaction.

What he did, he explained, was to build one functioning impulse engine out of the ruins of three. It wouldn't give them much power beyond barest life support and motion— but if it got them to Starbase 18 it would save their lives.

And the day they finally tested it, and began to move, the corridors of the U.S.S. *Starbound* rang with cheers.

Once they were underway, and it became apparent that the engine would hold, the trip to Starbase 18 became routine. Two days out from base, their radio signal suddenly brought an answer. A starship was sent to tow the crippled training ship in, while the joyful crew were taken aboard, wined, dined—and debriefed. There was talk of medals and commendations, and Yar glowed with pride in her young shipmates, and particularly the man she loved.

A few hours later they were able to transport to the Starbase. Yar, who had been acting more or less as second in command, stood at Dare's right, George Bosinney on his left, in the last group to transport over. As they materialized on the platform, Yar was surprised to see none of their shipmates lingering, and no admiral or even commodore waiting to greet the heroes.

Instead, a contingent of Starfleet Security marched forward, their leader facing Dare. "Darryl Adin," he announced, "I arrest you in the name of Starfleet Command. You are hereby relieved of duty, stripped of rank, and consigned to a Security holding area until a board of inquiry determines whether there are grounds for court-martial on charges of conspiracy, treason, and murder."

Tasha Yar and the other survivors of the *Starbound* were kept away from Darryl Adin for several days, until the Starfleet board of inquiry had done its work. To their horror, the board found enough evidence to court-martial the man who had given them the strength, courage, and guidance to survive after the Orions left them to die.

Once that was determined, though, Yar refused to answer the defense attorney's questions until the man arranged for her to see Dare.

By that time she knew what he was accused of: conspiring with the Orions to steal the dilithium crystals, in return for a fortune in numbered bank accounts on Oriana. Starfleet Command had discovered that the leak to the Orions had taken place on Starbase 36, where they had loaded the crystals. Adin's complicity would account for his being left alive when the Orions killed the other officers.

Yar wanted George Bosinney to talk to Dare as well, but he refused. At first Bosinney had been as staunch as she in defending Dare—until he was reminded of the discharged phaser boosters discovered just before the attack. The young engineer told the investigating board about the wrong circuit breaker in the charging unit. Of course Dare had put the right one in after they restored power, and logged doing so. What the investigators found, though, was that according to the ship's log, the correct breaker had been installed at the beginning of the journey, and there was no record of anyone's changing it.

The Chief of Security had access to the Weapons Room at any time. And . . . he made up the Security staff duty roster. "He put routine inventory of the Weapons Room off as long as regs allow after our stop at Starbase 36," Bosinney reminded Yar. "And, I'm not Security staff, but it gets around who the smartest and most conscientious people are in each department. He put you last on the list to take inventory, Tasha—because you were most likely to discover the sabotage. My guess is, the Orions were late. If they'd shown up even twelve hours earlier, no one but Adin would have known about that circuit breaker, and in the chaos after the battle he could have replaced it with no one the wiser."

"How dare you!" gasped Yar. "After he saved all our lives, you actually think Dare capable of treason?"

Bosinney held up the stump where his right hand used to be. "If he did what they say, he's responsible for this. I'll manage, but a prosthesis won't be the same, no matter what the doctors say. And I'm one of the lucky ones, Tasha. Fourteen of our classmates and seven good Starfleet officers are dead. If Darryl Adin betrayed us, he deserves to die! A rehabilitation colony's too good for a man who would betray his own shipmates."

"He didn't!" Yar insisted. "George—help me prove he didn't do it! At least talk to him."

110

"What good would that do?" he asked. "If he's guilty, he'd only lie. Think like a Starfleet officer instead of a lovesick teenager, Tasha. I hope, for your sake, that Adin proves innocent, but so far I haven't seen much chance of that. Once all the facts are uncovered, the truth will come out."

Oddly enough, when she did get to see Dare, he told her the same thing—except that he was quietly confident that he would be exonerated. He looked pale and thin, with dark circles around his eyes. Wearing a shapeless tan coverall, he seemed smaller than she remembered—she wanted to take him in her arms, protect him from whoever was doing this terrible thing to him, but they were separated by a force field.

"What should I do?" she asked. "Dare, I was witness to all the events. I was there when George found the circuit breaker. And they keep questioning me about our private conversations. What am I going to do, Dare?"

"Tell the truth!" he urged. "Tasha, I *didn't do it*. The truth can only prove me innocent. Don't be afraid, love. Trust the Starfleet investigators—they're the best there are. You may have noticed some important clue that I didn't. Tell them everything you know. That's the only way to set me free."

But at the court-martial, the truth only condemned her love. There were suspicious messages on record within Starbase 36, from public comcons in the hotel where the *Starbound* crew had stayed for a few days of shore leave. Although they were paid for with tokens, Dare's credit code had been used to purchase such tokens.

This was early in the proceedings, and Dare was still supremely confident. When the prosecution asked him about the tokens, he replied, "I did not purchase them. If I were committing treason, would I be so stupid as to use my credit code? I would have deposited coins."

"The tokens were purchased on the other side of the base, far from your hotel," the prosecutor told him.

"And of course no Starfleet officer knows how easily computer records are traced," Dare replied sarcastically. "Someone else used my code to purchase comcon tokens.

No identification would be required for an amount that small. What you are proving, sir, is that someone systematically set me up to take the blame for the attack on *Starbound*."

"Yes, Mr. Adin," said the prosecutor, "we shall prove that is exactly what happened."

Slowly but implacably, the prosecution built a case that the Orions had targeted Darryl Adin after he led the Starfleet Security team that defeated them at Conquiidor. Rather than kill him, they decided to discredit him. According to this hypothesis, they had approached him at some unspecified time, offering him money. He was known to be a gambler; possibly he owed money to underground associates of the Orions.

Although Dare's attorney objected loudly, the prosecution continued to suggest that the Orions had found Dare's weakness and used it against him. But they could not have done it without his cooperation. Presumably he provided them with the information about the dilithium and the plan for taking the *Starbound,* believing the Orions would leave the crew unharmed and that he was safe because an informer inside Starfleet would be of continuing value to them.

But, according to the prosecution's theory, the Orions' real purpose was to destroy Darryl Adin, and at the same time make Starfleet question the reliability of all its Security personnel. And the theme of the prosecution's case was that for the Orions to achieve their goal, Dare had had to cooperate.

Dare's response was a sarcastic laugh, and "Anyone who would do a deal with the Orions would have to be mad!"

Unfortunately, the evidence suggested he was right.

The comcon messages were to guests at another hotel on Starbase 36, to set up meetings. But when Starfleet checked the identities of those guests, it turned out that they did not exist. Their identity documents were forged. Their credit accounts were real enough, but had been opened just before and closed out immediately after they paid off the expenses of that trip to Starbase 36. Furthermore, all financial arrangements had been made from a rather backward planet through keyboard-access computers, so there were no images or voiceprints on record.

Nor could Dare account for all of his time on Starbase 36. The supposed meetings had taken place during times when he was asleep—alone—or on his own somewhere on the base. Yar blushed to think they had been watched so closely that whoever set him up knew which nights they had spent together, and the two nights they had been apart, during a seminar for the trainees aboard a Starfleet cruiser docked at the base. The seminar was hardly classified knowledge, but it did not help Dare's case that he freely admitted spending both evenings gambling, a pursuit in which Yar never joined him.

Then there was the afternoon when she wanted to explore the famous sensory museum with the other trainees, and Dare had told her to go ahead, he had been there many times and wanted to do some shopping.

Dare had had several presents for her when they met again that evening . . . but as the evidence unfolded, Yar could not help thinking that there had been plenty of time, as well, for him to meet someone for a brief strategy session.

Her own testimony came very late in the court martial. By that time Dare was sitting as expressionlessly as a Vulcan, listening to the damning evidence against him. Still, he managed an encouraging smile for Yar—he obviously counted on her testimony to exonerate him of the charges that he had sabotaged the *Starbound*.

But . . . what could she say? She had to tell the truth. She clung fast to his insistence that she do so—surely his certainty that the truth would set him free was the best proof she could have of his innocence!

Yes, she answered the prosecutor, she had taken top honors in Security in her graduating class. Yes, Darryl Adin had made out the Security duty rosters aboard *Starbound*. Yes, the weapons inventory had been delayed for almost the maximum thirty days after leaving Starbase 36.

"You began to discover defective weapons as soon as you started the phaser inventory?"

"Yes."

"What did you do about it?"

"I told Dare—Commander Adin—that same evening."

"Is that standard procedure?"

"No. I could have logged the defective phasers out to Maintenance and thought no more about it," she said triumphantly. "Mr. Adin would not have known there was anything unusual until the end of the following day, when I turned in the completed inventory report. But we had a . . . an appointment that evening. So, scheduling me for inventory duty meant that he was informed and had to repair them sooner, rather than later."

"And did he?" the prosecutor asked.

"Repair them? Of course. That's what we were doing when the Orions attacked."

"No, Ensign—did Mr. Adin begin repairs on the defective weapons *sooner?* Your preliminary statement indicates that even though you reported them that evening, he did nothing until the following day."

"That is correct," she admitted, feeling Dare's eyes on her but unable to look his way. "First thing next morning he was in the Weapons Room. The phasers were only unusual; we didn't know there was anything seriously wrong until we found the boosters discharged. You cannot blame Mr. Adin for not resolving an emergency when he did not know it existed."

The questioning continued, and Yar was forced to relive those hours in the Weapons Room, pointing out that Dare had acted according to Starfleet procedure in each step, including calling for the best person aboard to trace the fault and effect repairs.

"I have here the Weapons Room log," said the prosecutor. "Let me play the section in which you discovered the problem with the boosters."

An overview of the *Starbound* Weapons Room appeared on screen.

Yar and Adin discovered that the phaser booster handles were discharged. Adin ran the diagnostics, his voice becoming tighter and more nasal with each new discovery.

"Tasha," he instructed, "check the duty roster for everyone

*who has worked in here since the last inventory. Assemble
them in the main briefing room at 0900 tomorrow morning.
In the meantime, we must recharge as many units as
possible. Get Bosinney from Engineering. I want to know
what caused these burnouts and power drains! It will do us no
good to recharge the units if they simply discharge again."*

"Uh, Commander—" Yar said hesitantly.

*Dare's head came up abruptly. The camera picked up a
front view of his face, showing his lips pull back from his teeth
almost in a snarl.*

*Yar was behind him, and could not see the grimace. "You
mean after we report to the Captain?" she asked.*

*Adin swung on her, the anger plain on his face for just one
moment before he controlled it. Then, "Yes," he said calmly,
"it could be a breach of Security, Ensign. You take the report
to Captain Jarvis. I'll call Engineering."*

The screen blanked.

The prosecutor rounded on Yar. "Is it Starfleet procedure
to inform the ship's commanding officer of a breach of
Security?"

"Of course," she replied. "However, we did not know that
it was a breach of Security. In fact, we still do not know that
the weapons failure was not a terrible coincidence."

"Oh, come now, Ensign Yar!" said the prosecutor. "We
know the *cause:* an improper circuit breaker, whose installa-
tion was *unlogged.* Expert witnesses have testified that the
power losses and surges caused by repeated failure and
resetting of that breaker for nearly thirty days damaged the
booster units, and once they failed the hand phasers started
to deteriorate. It would take approximately twenty-five days
to guarantee that no boosters would be in working order.
Mr. Adin did not schedule inventory of the Weapons Room
until twenty-seven days out from Starbase 36. You discovered some defective hand phasers on the twenty-eighth day,
and the rest of the damage on the twenty-ninth."

"And immediately started repairs!" Yar insisted.

"Which were interrupted by the arrival of the Orions.
Now, Ensign, several of your shipmates have testified that
after the battle the Orions collected the bodies of their dead

companions and removed them from the *Starbound*. Is that correct?"

"I was unconscious," she replied. "All I know is that there were no Orion bodies aboard when I recovered."

"Do you know why?"

Yar had no idea where that question was leading, so all she could answer was, "No, sir."

"How many people aboard *Starbound* knew about the consignment of dilithium crystals?"

"The Captain, First Officer, and Security staff."

"Why were *you* told, Ensign? You were only a trainee."

"Except for Commander Adin, the Security staff were all trainees. In order to do our job, we had to know about the dilithium crystals."

"Mm-hmm. Mr. Adin exercised his judgment to waive your security clearance in that instance, proper procedure under the circumstances. Interestingly, though, he did not share with you another piece of information which he had learned at Starbase 36. Ensign Yar, if you expect to encounter hostile Orions, with what weapon would you arm your away team?"

"At least Phaser Two, sir."

"Why not simply hand phasers?"

"Orion males are very difficult to kill with a hand phaser. You must hit a vital organ, or the Orion will only be injured. While we are taught to avoid battle if at all possible, it is sometimes necessary to threaten—and in the case of Orions, Phaser Two can be a deterrent. If they start a fight, they're risking their lives from any direct hit at the higher settings."

"So—reducing your weaponry to hand phasers gave the Orions a great advantage. But was everyone aboard the *Starbound* such a poor shot that not a single Orion was hit in a vital organ?"

Yar remembered drilling a few very precisely herself. "No, sir, I don't think so."

The prosecutor smiled smugly at her. "And you are right not to think so, Ensign. The information Mr. Adin did not share with you is that the Orions have developed a new personal armor. It's lightweight, flexible as heavy cloth—and it absorbs and diffuses enough of the energy from a phaser bolt that a hand phaser kill-setting shot to the heart may stun for a few moments, at most. Any other body shot won't even drop your target. It's even some protection against Phaser Two—but these Orion pirates made certain none of the *Starbound* crew had Phaser Two or higher available. In other words, there were no Orion bodies after the battle because none of the Orions were killed."

Yar stared from the prosecutor to Dare, and back. "And . . . you claim Commander Adin knew this?" she asked.

"He learned of it in a Security briefing at Starbase 36. Can you think of any reason he did not share the information with the *Starbound* Security staff?"

Dare looked as if he had been hit by a stun bolt. His defense attorney was staring at him, surprise, disgust, and anger mingled in his expression.

Yar had no answer for the prosecutor, but she did have a question. "You mean it was hopeless? There was no way we could have stopped them?"

"Oh, you *did* stop a few—in fact, an amazing number. The logs show quite remarkable sharpshooting from Security trainees in their first test under fire. But the Orions were only stunned. In that armor, with the protective helmets they always wear, an Orion can be killed only by a direct shot through the eye. Not much of a target."

"Oh," Yar said weakly.

Dare had known: they couldn't kill the Orions, but the Orions could kill them.

"We should have surrendered!" she blurted out. She stared at Dare, who stared back wild-eyed and pale. "Oh, Dare—why? Why did you let us fight? The Orions would have had no reason to kill if we had just let them board, made no effort to stop them! Maybe . . . maybe they still would have slaughtered the officers, but there'd have been no cause for them to shoot trainees."

Dare shook his head, slowly. "No," he said. His defense attorney put his hand on his arm, but Dare shook him off.

"No!" he insisted. "There was no such Security briefing on Starbase 36—or if there was, I was not notified. Check the records! If it happened, I wasn't there. I didn't *know*!"

He played right into the prosecutor's hands. The records were produced. It was a secured meeting, in which some highly classified information was discussed; therefore no computer log of the meeting could be presented in open court. But the agenda could—parts of it blanked out on the screen for security reasons. The matter of Orion armor, though, was unclassified and high on the list of announcements.

There was also a roster of attendees. Near the top, among the A's, was the name Darryl Adin. "This was a high-security meeting," said the prosecutor. "All attendees were computer-checked by voiceprint, fingerprints, and retinal scan. As you can see, Darryl Adin *was* in attendance."

He turned to the admirals who made up the jury. "So, ladies and gentlemen, if he were not charged with conspiracy, treason, and murder, Darryl Adin would still be guilty of gross neglect of duty, first for not informing the officers and Security staff of the *Starbound* of this vital information, and second for allowing his shipmates to attempt to fight off the Orions with only hand phasers, resulting in unnecessary injury and loss of life."

From that point on, Yar hardly heard the proceedings. It was a foregone conclusion that Dare would be found guilty . . . for he was. The only reason he could possibly have allowed them to fight was to set up his own shooting— on stun, of course. And she had thought him a hero!

She had trusted him, with her life . . . with her heart.

A few times Yar felt Dare's eyes on her—and when he drew her gaze she found his cold, hard, accusing. He whispered something to his attorney, who shook his head, but asked for a recess. When they returned, Dare's face was shuttered, and his attorney's was tight-lipped and grim.

The defense tried, but the evidence against Dare was indisputable.

The verdict came quickly, and Dare was consigned to a rehabilitation colony, where the doctors and counselors would try to find out what had turned a loyal Starfleet officer into a traitor. If they could, they would cure him and return him to society. If they could not, he would be confined there for the rest of his life.

Dare took the verdict and sentence quietly enough, although cold fury turned his ever-changing features as ugly as Yar had ever seen them.

To her surprise, his defense attorney called her that evening. Dare had asked to see her. "You don't have to," he told her. "In fact, I advise you to refuse."

"No," said Yar. "I want to see him. I need to ask him why."

But it was Dare who demanded the moment they were face to face, "Why, Tasha? Why did you betray me?"

"What?" she asked, confused.

He was back in the tan prison coverall, but he did not look small or vulnerable now. His anger sustained him. "It had to be you," he said. "Where was I when the message came about the Security briefing? In the shower? Gone for a bottle of wine? It was a Starfleet Security play/erase; the hotel records show only that there was one, not what it said."

"Dare—I couldn't have accessed your message!"

"Why not? You had examples of my voice on tricorder, and you know my ID number. Was it curiosity? Mischief? Did you not tell me about the meeting because we were enjoying ourselves, and you didn't want our shore leave broken up a second time?"

"Dare—" she protested helplessly. Although she wanted desperately to prove the records wrong, she simply could not remember whether they had been together at the time of the Security meeting—which meant she could not dispute the evidence that he had been there. "Dare, the truth verifier—"

"You know how to fool a bloody truth verifier!" he rasped. His voice, although pitched low so as to keep the guards from interrupting, was harsh with the intensity of his emotions. "I taught you myself, damn you. I actually believed that you loved me. I never thought you would use what I've taught you, what Starfleet has taught you, to betray me! We were together at the time the meeting took place. Why didn't you tell them? It's my *life* against a reprimand to you for making me miss a meeting."

"Dare—did you expect me to lie for you?" she gasped.

His eyes were almost black with fury. "What did they pay you, Tasha? What could the Orions possibly give you that would outweigh what you've found in Starfleet?"

Stunned at the accusation, she struck back. "That's what I came here to ask *you*!"

His jaw set, and then his lips pulled back to reveal his teeth in a smile that was much more a snarl. "You bloody cold bitch. You never let up on your act—but then, we're being recorded, aren't we? You have to play the innocent for the cameras." But she could see in his eyes that while he might think her capable of the gross stupidity of making him miss a meeting, he didn't truly think her capable of conspiracy.

Did that mean he was innocent? Or only that he could not let go his pretense of innocence—that the best way to persuade her he was falsely convicted was to accuse *her*?

Dare glanced around, although the cameras that were certainly there were well-hidden. Then he laughed, a hollow, empty sound. "I'll tell you anyway, because stupid as Starfleet just proved, they're not so stupid as to expect me to go like the lamb to the slaughter. Starfleet know I'm a survivor—they taught me how to survive."

The wolfish smile flashed again, and he continued, "There's a lesson you haven't learned yet, from the side of the captor, although when we first met you knew it from the side of the victim. Desperation, Tasha. I'm the freest man in this galaxy right now. Do you know why?"

"No," she whispered, mesmerized by his stare.

"Because it's all gone, everything I believed in. Starfleet. You. I'm bound by no rules but my own. The only thing left is myself—and that I'll never let them take. They'll never get me to a rehabilitation colony. Rehabilitation! Brainwashing—that's what they do in those hell pits, no matter how they try to disguise it. The patients might seem happy—but they're drugged or hypnotized into submission until their wills are broken."

"Dare, you *know* there's nothing like that in the Federation! They're going to help you," Yar pleaded, hating the anger in his face, knowing the pain it hid. Her love for him hadn't died in the courtroom. She hated the deed he had done . . . but she loved the man. "Let them heal you, Dare, so you can come back to me."

"Come back!" he growled. Then he tilted his head to one side. "Oh, yes—I'll come back, Tasha. Wait for the day, love. I'll escape—and then, you beautiful lying bitch, I'll find you again. Watch your back, Tasha—for one day we will meet again."

Chapter Six

Lieutenant Tasha Yar was frozen in *déjà vu* as she stared up at the angry face of her captor.

Darryl Adin had made good his promise to escape before he could be confined in a rehabilitation colony—and then had disappeared from the face of the galaxy. He was still in Starfleet Security criminal records, though: there was no statute of limitations on either treason or murder.

Now he had made good his promise to find her again. What did he intend to do with her?

Floods of memory overwhelmed her, less of when she had seen him last than of when she had seen him first, on New Paris, lying helpless at his feet, not knowing what he wanted with her, not trusting—

And, just like the first time, he stooped down to her, examining her for injury. Then he helped her to her feet.

Yar allowed him to give her a hand up, biding her time while they assessed one another.

Dare looked different, although his distinctive features made it impossible not to know him at once. He was thinner than she remembered, yet somehow taller and more imposing. The added height, she saw, came from thick-soled boots, while his costume was an archaic design of black tailored jacket worn open over a gray shirt and black trousers. She remembered learning somewhere that the basic concept of that male costume had been invented in the nineteenth century, variations on it worn by men of power for more than two centuries. Now Dare had adopted it, to good effect.

But his manner of dress was the least of the changes in his appearance. His hair was longer, parted and combed to the side, revealing his broad forehead. Its severity, in contrast to the shake-into-place style he had worn in Starfleet, accented new vertical lines in his face. His eyes seemed to be deeper, more shadowed and mysterious, and yet, against the thinner contours of his face, larger and more luminous.

His mouth was as curved, lips as full as she remembered, but gone was the old sense that they would quirk into a smile or open in a laugh at any moment. The Darryl Adin Yar had loved had been a man of quicksilver emotions; this man seemed to have halved the range, retaining only the negative ones.

"So, Tasha," Dare said at last, "you are still in Starfleet."

"And you are still alive," was the only response she could manage.

"I'm a survivor. What are you doing here?" he asked as he led her to a table that would seat a dozen people, although at the moment there were only four in the room.

"Don't you get the news broadcasts?"

"For what they're worth. Has Starfleet sent you and your pet robot to blow us to pieces?" Dare sat opposite her, studying her face.

"*You* are the warlord Nalavia wants us to dispose of?"

His laugh was without mirth. "No. I'm here to help the people of Treva throw off Nalavia's oppression."

"Oh," she said with heavy sarcasm, "you're a freedom fighter."

He raised his eyebrows and a sardonic smile twitched at his lips. "You might say so. If I'm paid well enough."

"Paid?"

"I'm a hired gun, Tasha—the best in the galaxy. Adrian Dareau is the name I go by these days."

"The Silver Paladin? You?"

She had heard of him, but never connected his growing legend on the planets of the outer rim with the man she had once loved and lost. "I should have made the connection, but no one's ever seen Dareau. So—now you're wanted not only by the Federation but by the Ferengi, the Zertanians, and rumor has it by the Romulans as well."

"Indeed? Sdan, have we done anything to stir up the Romulans?"

For the first time, Yar looked at the other two men, the ones who had so unceremoniously captured her. Dare's best men, she assumed; they had to be good to take her so easily.

The one Dare addressed as Sdan looked vaguely Vulcan, as the name and the cramp in her neck suggested, but his black hair fell in untamed waves almost to shoulder length, and he quirked a grin as he replied, "That little episode with the Omani, prob'ly. The Roms weren't too happy when they decided t'go Fed."

"Nothin' t'worry about," said the third man, a rather nondescript human of medium height and build, with thinning medium-brown hair. He wore browns and tans that blended into the background. His only distinctive feature was that he wore glasses—actual frames that held lenses in front of his eyes. Yar had never seen an adult wear them; some children did until they were old enough to have the chemical treatment that gave everyone perfect vision.

"The Romulans rarely act; they prefer to react," the man continued, taking the chair next to Yar. She looked through his lenses to see that he had another distinctive feature: lively brown eyes actually darker than Dare's, sparkling with a keen intelligence that belied the first impression of his appearance. "A nice bit o' tension, maybe a detente or even a cold war between the Feds and the Roms, and we'll have so much business we won't know where to turn next. Make a fortune—money's the sinews of war."

"Aren't you rich enough yet, Poet?" asked Dare. "You could buy your own planet."

"Gold which he cannot spend will make no man rich," Poet replied with a twinkle. "However, pretty lady," he added to Yar, "if you've a yen to be a rich man's plaything—or have a rich man for a plaything—I'd be happy to oblige."

Something in that knowing glance suggested he knew as many "multiple techniques of pleasuring" as Data—and was just as unthreatening. But Yar was in no mood for flirtation. "I hardly think that's why you've brought me here," she said harshly.

"No," said Dare, "we brought you here to show you what's *really* happening on Treva."

"Why?" she asked suspiciously.

"Because Nalavia's certainly not going to let you see it!" Dare replied angrily. "You've seen the news broadcasts?"

"Yes—and I agree, attacks by the 'enemies of the people' happen too conveniently in front of cameras. Nalavia claims that's because she has installed surveillance cameras to locate terrorist activity and get her army there fast."

"Haven't succeeded very well, have they?" This from Sdan, who had taken up a position behind Dare, guarding his back. Yar looked at him again, trying to guess his origins. He had the slanted eyebrows and pointed ears of Vulcanoid races, and the pale skin that spoke of green blood running beneath it. But unlike most Vulcans he was solid and muscular, almost stocky. His eyes were blue, rare but not unseen among Vulcans.

But it was Sdan's dress and demeanor that proclaimed him not Vulcan—or at least not Vulcan raised. He stood behind Dare in the universal military "at ease" position, relaxed but alert, his face reacting openly to everything being said. He smiled easily, but if more frequent and less threatening than Dare's, Sdan's smile was also that of a dangerous man.

His clothes matched the casualness of his shaggy hair, loose shirt of blue silky material open half-way down his chest, black trousers, and high boots with fronts that came up over the kneecap. Yar wondered whether he chose them as protection from a kick to that vulnerable spot, or because of their swashbuckling appearance. As Dare had done when Yar had known him back at Starfleet Academy, Sdan casually exuded sex appeal.

Dare, however, was emotionally contained and shielded now, as if he had raised barriers against what he and Yar had once shared. Realizing how she was sitting, straight-backed, both feet flat on the floor, she realized that she was unconsciously doing the same thing. Both were determined not to let their former relationship cloud their thinking.

Yar said, "Tell me your side of the story."

"It's not *ours*," said Poet. "It's the side of the Trevans. They're rebelling against Nalavia's tyranny."

"Tyranny?" Yar asked. "She is the duly-elected President."

"So were Adolf Hitler," Dare replied, "Baravis the Incomparable, and Immea of Kaveran. Nalavia used the new democratic system to get elected—and now she is systematically destroying it. There should have been a general election this year, but she suspended it for the 'planetary emergency.' Those who can see what she's doing are trying to put a stop to it, but Nalavia controls the army."

"Besides," said Poet, "most people are happy with Nalavia. Life's better than the older folks can ever remember, and the younguns have their bread and circuses. For that they're willing to forgo a bit o' freedom."

"A familiar story," Yar said with a nod. "But what does it have to do with you?"

"We're not Starfleet," Dare replied. "We don't worry about the Prime Directive. Some Trevans tried to rebel against Nalavia, but they were defeated—and those who were captured were executed publicly, without trial."

Yar felt her jaw clench, but gave back Starfleet dogma: "This world is still developing. By our standards its customs may seem primitive, even savage, but they are the customs of the people of Treva. We can hope that they will eventually become more civilized, but in the meantime we may not interfere with Trevan law."

"It's Nalavia interfering with Trevan law," said Poet. "The new constitution calls for a trial before anyone can be convicted or punished, and the system has been in operation for years. Nalavia suspended it, and acted as judge, jury, and executioner."

"None of this was in the reports sent to Starfleet," Yar pointed out.

"I assume," Dare replied, "that that is why you are here. *We* were invited, as well," again the wolfish smile, "by the opposing faction. Isn't it intriguing that Nalavia feels threatened enough to call in the might of Starfleet?"

"If what you're saying is true," said Yar, "she won't get it. Dare, private citizens may not be bound by the Prime Directive, but Federation policy is that non-Federation worlds be left to handle their own internal affairs."

"And then," said Sdan, "Nalavia will make a big thing outta Starfleet refusing to help her poor beleaguered people. She sets everything up so she can't lose."

"If Nalavia is as tyrannical as you claim," said Yar, "eventually she will go too far, and her own people will rebel."

"Not very likely," said Poet. "Nalavia's too clever to make the majority unhappy till she's got all their necks firmly in the noose."

"Tomorrow morning," said Dare, "you will meet Rikan, the last of the Trevan warlords. Perhaps you will believe him more easily than you do us. In the meantime, a room has been prepared for you." He reached across the table. "I'll take the combadge."

Oh, I am an idiot! Yar thought—but it was probably better that she had not attempted to contact Data earlier. He might still have been with Nalavia.

As she raised her hand to tap the badge, Yar realized two things simultaneously: the badge was no longer pinned to her uniform, and Dare was reaching not to her but to Poet. His henchman dropped her combadge into Dare's hand.

The other man might be a skilled pickpocket, but Dare wasn't. By reflex, Yar snatched the badge from him and tapped it firmly.

It chirped, but there was no response—and faster than she could try again, her wrist was gripped in an iron hand. Not Dare's; Poet's.

The ineffectual-looking man had a grip like a tractor

beam. "Naughty, naughty," he said, retrieving the badge with his other hand and tossing it to Dare.

Dare caught it with a frown, obviously considered giving it a tap himself, but instead passed it to Sdan. "The channel didn't open when she touched it. Test it out, Sdan—but make sure you don't trigger it. The robot may be able to trace her from even a single signal."

"Mr. Data is an android, not a robot," said Yar. "He is also a Starfleet officer, my shipmate, and my friend."

"You used to have better taste in friends."

"At least I don't have to worry about where Data's loyalties lie!" she spat in return, sorry the moment she said it. Frustration was her greatest enemy; when she felt helpless, outmaneuvered, she acted without thinking. Why hadn't she pretended to be partly won over? Now they'd be guarded against her, lessening her chances of escape.

Dare said coldly, "I see. You still believe in my guilt. And your duty as a Starfleet officer is to apprehend a fugitive from justice should you happen upon one in the course of an assignment." His face had the same hauteur with which he had listened to the verdict at his court-martial. Even his eyes were ice. "Poet," he said, "put her in the blue room, and bar the door." And with that he stood up and walked out.

In the Presidential Palace, Lieutenant Commander Data used every piece of programming in his flirtation files to disengage himself from Nalavia's clutches.

He was having an unfamiliar reaction: it was not merely that he and Tasha had decided that restricting his actions to flirtation was the best way to "soften up" the President. No . . . Data discovered that he did not want to be intimate with Nalavia. He had never experienced such antipathy before, and as he finally walked through the corridors toward his room, much later than he had intended, he analyzed his response.

Why, when it was obvious that Nalavia would test and perhaps expand his limits, did he find himself hoping that it would not become necessary?

It was curious: he felt as if he had changed more in the

months he had been aboard the *Enterprise* than in all the years he had been conscious before that. He had served on other starships, visited numerous worlds, gathered gigabytes of data . . . and still, on those other assignments, he remained more a piece of convenient equipment than a fellow crew member to the people he worked among. And the more he sensed that he was shut out of their camaraderie, the more he yearned to be human . . . until by the time he was assigned to the *Enterprise* he had actually dared to articulate the desire.

And was not laughed at.

Even Will Riker, who was occasionally insensitive to his aspirations to such human attributes as creativity, had laughed with, not at, him the day they met—or had intended to, not yet knowing that Data laughed even less competently than he whistled. "Nice to meet you . . . Pinocchio."

He had had to search the ship's data banks for the reference, but when he found and accessed it seconds later, even though Riker passed it off as a joke, he was stunned at being compared to the subject of a story about the magical power of love.

Love was something Data had never had the temerity to analyze . . . and yet he sometimes wondered if that was the underlying reason for his sudden growth in his new assignment. He was given more freedom by Picard than by any other Captain he had served with, and when he used it to pursue his own interests there was never a reprimand, except when he occasionally allowed his voracious curiosity to interfere with his duty. He was ashamed of how frequently that happened—yet how could he resist revelling in an opportunity he had never had before?

Along with freedom had come responsibility. Data had been amazed when he learned that his assignment to the *Enterprise* was not in the science department, or even as Science Officer, the highest post he had ever aspired to. When he accessed his new orders and saw that he was third in command he had at first believed it to be human error. Someone had input the wrong serial number, surely.

But it was true—and not only was he suddenly a member of the command structure heretofore reserved strictly for organic beings, but Captain Picard casually turned the ship over to him from time to time, as easily as he did to Riker.

And nobody protested!

In such an atmosphere of acceptance, Data made friends, real friends who shared their problems and their successes rather than simply using him for his physical strength or his rapid data access. Friends like Geordi LaForge, who would tell him jokes and encourage him to try any human activity that aroused his curiosity.

And friends like Tasha Yar.

When she had seduced him, so early in the voyage, he had been pleased that she had chosen him, even if it was while she was under the influence of the intoxicating virus. Her later denial, "It never happened," had hurt and the incident had limited the progress of their friendship for a time, although it had not interfered with their working relationship. Recently, though, Data had come to recognize the emotion of embarrassment, and with that understanding and the passage of time they had grown closer once again.

Their last assignment together had been on Minos, the planet where the people had been destroyed by the weapons they built—where Tasha and Data had come as close as he cared to consider to dying together. That experience had crushed the final barriers.

Tasha was the last woman with whom Data had exercised his sexual function. Now he realized that he was comparing Nalavia to Tasha—and that was why he would prefer not to function with the President of Treva if he could avoid it. Tasha might have been under the influence of an intoxicant, but she had shared mutual pleasure. Nalavia's primary motivation was clearly novelty. To her he was not a person but a toy, a bit of exotic spice for her jaded palate.

That was an intriguing thought: a year ago he would not have known that Nalavia was jaded, nor cared. And a year ago he would not have had the suspicion that she would treat an organic male exactly as she treated an android.

As Data approached his room, he noticed that there was

no light under Tasha's door. She would be asleep by this time. It was a pity that humans had to sleep in order to function properly; he would have liked to discuss his latest self-discovery with Tasha.

However, it was an ideal time to attempt to access Nalavia's computer system; he had no responsibilities until the appointment with Nalavia in the morning, when she was to join her two guests on a tour of the capital city.

As Data approached, the guard posted near their rooms looked up groggily, frowned, and stretched, giving a grunt of surprise and then rubbing his right shoulder with his left hand. The man must have fallen asleep sitting up and gotten a cramp. If he fell asleep on duty once he would probably do so again, making it easy for Data to sneak out to locate a computer terminal. So as he went by, he said, "Good night," and opened the door to his room.

The guard stared at him. "You sleep?" he asked.

"No," Data replied with automatic honesty—and then "could have kicked himself," as the saying went. He knew perfectly well how to lie when the situation called for it; he simply had more trouble than humans recognizing such a situation. "But I . . . must recharge." Let the man think he would be out of commission for a time.

"Hey—you won't blow out the power system?"

Oh what a tangled web we weave—

"No," Data assured him, recalling Tasha's briefings to the officers who most frequently formed away teams: if you must lie, keep it simple. "I brought what I need with me."

"Oh. Well, good night, then."

Data breathed a sigh of relief as he closed the door behind him.

To give the guard time to relax, he exchanged his dress uniform for a standard one, then turned out the light. He could still see—not on as many frequencies as Geordi, but simple infrared made his environment as bright as day, while his internal processor interpreted the color shifts.

After a time, he carefully cracked the door open—only to have the guard look up and ask, "Is there something you need, sir?"

"No, thank you," Data replied. The guard did not appear at all sleepy now. "Please do not allow anyone to disturb me for the next four point six hours," he improvised.

"Yes, sir," the guard replied. "I'll tell my relief."

Data pulled back into his room and looked for another exit. His tricorder had already told him sensors of an alarm system surrounded the windows. The suite consisted of an anteroom, a bedroom, and a bath. The only extra door opened on a closet, with no concealed exits. There were no trapdoors beneath the carpets.

Weren't palaces supposed to come equipped with secret passageways? Apparently only in fiction.

The bathroom was equipped with water plumbing, not sonics. Its small window was frosted, but sealed shut and also equipped with alarm sensors. Data wondered if they had been installed for Tasha and himself, or if Nalavia frequently entertained "guests" who might seek to sneak or break out. If challenged, she would undoubtedly claim it was protection against anyone trying to break *in*.

Data examined the fixtures, accessing all his knowledge of water plumbing. Assuming the culture had proper pipes that neither broke nor leached poisons into the drinking water, its primary weakness was a tendency for drains to stop up. Chemical cleansers could be used to prevent or correct the problem . . . but there were times when the pipes themselves had to be replaced. There should be access panels, then—

As it turned out, the entire floor of the bath lifted out, to expose all the pipes coming in and out of the small room. Data lowered himself into the crawlspace, and began worming his way toward the area of the palace where Nalavia had first greeted them. The communications and information center would presumably be in that area.

He listened carefully for sounds above, to tell him what kinds of rooms he crawled beneath, knowing he was past the sleeping apartments when the pattern of plumbing leading to a bath every few meters ceased.

Ultimately, he pushed up the floor in a tiny lavatory and

found it connected to a suite of three small offices. There were no computer terminals to be seen. Although the door to the corridor was locked, it had no alarm sensors; whatever went on in here was obviously not security sensitive.

He didn't have to pick the lock, as it opened with a knob from the inside. There was no one outside, so he slipped a stylus from one of the desks between door and frame to keep it from locking behind him, and crept down the deserted corridor, every sense alert.

Two live guards stood outside the computer room, and the door sported an array of sensors that his infrared could perceive from twenty meters away. But he had no intention of going in through the door.

Now that he knew where the main computer was, Data moved swiftly but silently back to the suite of offices, climbed back down into the crawlspace, and carefully pulled the lavatory floor back into place above him. Then, unerringly, he crawled through mostly empty space until he was directly under the computer—he could see the warmth of its motor above him. He then followed the pipes to the nearest lavatory, hoping it was attached to the computer room.

It was. But there was someone at the computer.

He knew several dozen ways to render her unconscious but unharmed . . . but he dared not risk crossing the space to do so. If she turned and saw him, even if he stopped her before she sounded an alarm she would never be persuaded that she had simply fallen asleep at her work—and Nalavia would guess that Data had accessed the computer.

Data ducked back into the lavatory, where he waited for almost an hour before the woman logged off, turned out the lights, and left. Almost instantly, he was in the seat she had vacated, sorting through the routines of the archaic instrument until he got through its security codes, then erasing all evidence that he had done so.

Since he did not know what other insomniac computer user might appear at any moment, Data did not linger in the computer room. He determined the communications frequencies the computer was capable of, chose one not presently in use, adapted the modem in his tricorder to that frequency, and deleted all evidence of his tampering.

Then he returned to his suite of rooms as he had come. When he had replaced the floor, he almost left the bath at once . . . until it occurred to him to check his appearance. He switched on the light, adjusted his vision to humanoid spectrum—and found that he was filthy!

He had a spare uniform, of course—but he could neither put this one in the closet nor ask the palace staff to clean it without risking questions as to how it had gotten into this condition. Fortunately, Starfleet's latest uniforms were nearly indestructible and could be cleaned by almost every method known, including soap and water.

Data stripped, stepped into the shower, and washed both himself and his uniform. The uniform he left hanging in the bath, where it would dry in an hour or two.

Then he gave his full concentration to his tricorder, ever alert for safeguards or for other computer access. Nalavia's was an old computer design with limited memory; Data could not draw information from it at normal speed, but had to wait for it to feed at its own baud rate. At one point someone else accessed the system for a check of palace security, and Data shut down his search lest it perceptibly slow the other user's access.

The slow data feed gave him time to analyze some of the information as it flashed by—at least enough to recognize a pattern. Orders to Nalavia's army indicated that the "terrorists" in those raids they had been shown were neither rebels nor the henchmen of a warlord: Nalavia's own troopers had committed those atrocities.

When he had finally stored everything from the tricorder, Data needed time to analyze it. He expected that a servant would come to "wake" him in the morning. Therefore he slid beneath the bed covers, so as to appear as normal as possible to someone unaccustomed to androids, and add credence to the lie that he was "recharging" should he be disturbed before he had finished his analysis.

By morning Data had reached one significant conclusion:

Nalavia was lying on almost every count. Far from the duly-elected and benevolent President she claimed to be, Nalavia was a cruel and power-mad tyrant. He could not understand why the people had not risen against her *en masse*.

Just as he was beginning to sort the data into a form that would be comprehensible to Tasha, the door to Data's room opened and a servant entered with a tray. "President Nalavia will meet you in half an hour, sir, in the reception hall."

"Thank you," Data responded automatically.

The man set the tray on a table, uncovered several dishes, and then left. Data got up, ignored the food he did not need after indulging his curiosity to taste a large variety of dishes last evening, dressed, and went to knock at Tasha's door.

The guard in the hall said, "The young lady's gone already, sir."

Data felt himself frown. It was not late; if Tasha had been up early, why hadn't she contacted him? He tapped his combadge. It chirped but the channel did not open. Still, Tasha could have knocked at his door.

"I wonder if she remembered—" he said casually, entering Tasha's room.

Everything was as neat as Tasha herself, the bed made, her toilet items precisely laid out on the dresser.

Suspicious nevertheless, Data opened the closet. In it hung Tasha's dressing gown and two everyday uniforms.

Her dress uniform was not there.

Why was she wearing her dress uniform again this morning?

Or was it "still" rather than "again"? Had Tasha ever returned to her room last night? After spending the night awash in impersonal records of Nalavia's treachery, Data did not put anything past Treva's President.

Data scanned the entire room, the closet, the bath, the dresser drawers. He could not analyze the information now; for the moment, he had to concentrate on keeping Nalavia's suspicions away from himself.

He left the room, saying to the guard, "Good, she took it with her," and headed for the reception area.

Nalavia was waiting . . . but there was no sign of Tasha.

The President was in another parody of uniform, this one in blue. She smiled seductively at Data, and said, "Good morning. I trust you rested well. Just how much sleep do you need, sweet android? Less than us fully organic creatures, I should think."

"Considerably less," he evaded.

"Ah—that should make some things very interesting."

But Data refused to access his flirtation files this morning. "Where is Lieutenant Yar?" he asked bluntly.

"Up with the dawn, to tour some agricultural sites. She expressed an interest in our dairy products, you remember."

Accepting a second helping of a foamy dessert made from the milk of some local animal hardly constituted a request to tour dairy farms, but Data pretended to accept Nalavia's story at face value. "Yes, I remember. But then, I remember everything that occurs in my presence."

Nalavia's smile froze just the slightest bit. Then she cooed, "I shall have to watch what I say to you, won't I? I certainly wouldn't want to make promises I don't intend to keep."

She was testing him. Should he ask to be taken to Tasha? She might be in custody—and Nalavia knew Data's strength well enough from those Starfleet information tapes; if she imprisoned him, she would make certain he could not break out. If Tasha had simply been diverted for some reason, Data would reveal his suspicions by asking for her.

Until he was certain Tasha was in trouble, he would do her the best service by remaining free and learning as much as possible about Treva.

"You promised to show us the city," he reminded her. "Even if Lieutenant Yar has chosen a different itinerary, I would like to see it." *And perhaps pick up some clues to what is happening here.* He put on his blandest, most innocent air, the one guaranteed to drive sophisticated people to shouting at him if he kept it up long enough. There had been a time when it was his only mode of interaction with humanoids.

Nalavia did not shout. As they looked out at the world from her transparent groundcar, she put up with childlike curiosity about her city and her people for almost an hour. Finally, though, she had enough of "Inquiry—"

"Let's stop the games, Mr. Data. Last night you were an entirely different person. Stop playing the walking machine —you have far more interesting modes of interaction."

Perhaps the most startling thing about his reaction was the pleasant warmth at her casual assertion that he was "playing" a machine. It meant she thought of him as a person. But then he reminded himself of who—and especially what—she was. He had not told her of his wish to be human, but could she have learned it from Tasha?

"It is not completely inaccurate," he pointed out in the most reasonable tone, "to refer to me as a 'walking machine.' However, as I am only partly mechanical, and have a considerable organic component—"

"Stuff it," she said in imperious tones.

He blinked. "Stuff . . . it?"

"I don't want your imitation Vulcan act, either. You were a most interesting companion last night. I want to know why that has changed."

Why me? Why is it not Will Riker here? He is the one you send to handle beautiful, clever, and powerful women!

But Commander Riker was many light-years away, and Data had to do something here and now. *What would Riker do?* he asked himself. The problem was, he didn't know what had happened behind the doors of Beata's chamber on Angel One, and on several other occasions.

No—wait. He did know one thing: Riker always gave the woman a present, something rare and beautiful.

So he said, "I feel . . . awkward. You are such a gracious hostess, have provided us with luxurious accommodations, excellent food—and I have nothing to give you in return."

She smiled lasciviously. "Oh, you will give me something in return, Mr. Data—this evening, I think, after we have met with the members of my cabinet."

In desperation, he accessed his flirtation files. "Ah, but that will be as much for me as for you, Madame President. I wish to give you something special, something as beautiful as you are . . . something for you alone."

"Why, what a lovely thought," she said. "But I have all I could ever ask of material goods. I shall take the thought as the gift." And then, to Data's relief, after a pensive pause Nalavia deliberately changed the subject.

With a sad little sigh, she looked away from him, to the swarming city outside the groundcar and said, "There is one gift you can give me, you know: persuade Starfleet to help my people."

And, when she put it that way, Data was able to say with perfect sincerity, "Oh, yes, President Nalavia, I shall certainly try to do that."

Data was watched every moment. Although he was quite capable of doing two things at once, only one of those things could occupy his immediate consciousness. Thus while fencing with Nalavia he could merely set his data processor to indexing the material he had input during the night, so that later he could access the rest of it in an organized fashion, and ponder its meaning.

They returned to the palace for luncheon with representatives of the victims of the "terrorist raids." Data pitied those who had had friends and families killed or maimed, even though Nalavia had staged the attacks. It was obvious her people did not know that.

It was Data's first chance to meet Trevans other than the palace staff, for they had never left Nalavia's groundcar during the tour of the city. There were two spokespersons for the terrorist victims, and eight people who had either been injured or had a loved one killed. Data was puzzled by the lack of anger or anguish in the victims. They were wistfully sad, and spoke lovingly of those they had lost, but they seemed to have no interest in placing blame or exacting retribution. Data wished Dr. Crusher or Counselor Troi were here, for he could not tell if their reactions were unnatural, or normal for Trevans.

After the meal, Data spoke individually with some of their guests, but even when they told of their grief, it was with a kind of distanced sadness. As if somehow they could not find the emotional strength to really care. The spokespersons were little better; they seemed pleased that Nalavia was giving monetary compensation to their clients, and trusted that the government would prevent further tragedies.

Data had come prepared for a difficult session of trying to explain why the Prime Directive would not allow Starfleet to come in and kill off those who had so hurt these people. But the tough questions never came, and afterward he asked Nalavia, "Are these people in shock?"

"Oh, no—no, Mr. Data. They're just members of the old peasant class. Even though we are educating them and making their lives far better than they used to be, it will take generations to raise their sensibilities. In the meantime, we must protect them as the childlike creatures they are."

He pretended to accept her explanation, and also to be interested in the visit to a nearby school scheduled for the afternoon, even though he would have preferred to stay at the palace. He was concerned about Tasha's continued absence—had his colleague really been sent on a time-wasting tour, or had something more sinister happened to her?

At least Nalavia would be meeting with her counselors that afternoon; Data was free to act on automatic programming while his mind concentrated on the information he had only begun to sort through in the night.

Children were fascinated by Data, and quickly got over being frightened or shy. He had a well-rehearsed routine, which he was conscious of only enough to recognize that the children responded in an apparently normal fashion. Possibly Nalavia was right—perhaps class attitudes were so strongly embedded in Trevan society that only the young people could be educated out of them.

On the other hand, while the children did shout and giggle, there were no outbursts of anger or crying, even among the youngest. Coincidence? Insufficient information.

So he put most of his attention on the megabytes of information he had gleaned from Nalavia's computer. Much of it he could discard as inapplicable: public transport schedules, weather data, crop reports, manufacturing quotas. But wait—an inordinate amount of intoxicating substance seemed to be produced on Treva, and the records indicated that little was exported. He remembered the video broadcasts he and Tasha had monitored, full of advertising for intoxicants as beverage, inhalant, even topical application cream.

Intoxicants might be the reason for the Trevans' dulled sensibilities. The children seemed more normal because they did not use those substances. He focused his concentration for a moment on the teacher of the class he was visiting, to lead the conversation around so he could ask, "Are you educating the children against the use of intoxicants?"

The teacher seemed completely puzzled. "Why should we do that? Intoxicants put joy in life—a well-earned pleasure after a job well done." She was parrotting one of the advertisements, apparently quite unaware of the source.

Data's guide hastily thanked the teacher, and moved them on to another class. Data went back to playing friendly android, while internally he concentrated on the revenue figures for intoxicants and advertising of same. They were huge . . . but when he looked into the production figures he found something peculiar: chemical substances were a giant industry, but the substance with the highest production rate was something called "Riatine," which had no advertising budget whatsoever. However, Data was able to trace the largest stockholders in the companies manufacturing it: Nalavia, and several members of her cabinet.

Perhaps the substance was called something else in the form in which it was sold to the public. But no—it was not sold, and it was not exported. In the files indexed under manufacturing, the substance was produced . . . and there the information ended.

Data's internal programming, however, was a thousand times more efficient than that of Nalavia's computer. He searched for any reference to Riatine in any file—and found it in open government records: Riatine was a purifier distributed to all city water systems.

No great mystery, then. And yet . . . he searched the files

for the chemical formula for Riatine. Not in the open government files. Not in the manufacturing records. Treva did not have anything like a patent office, it seemed—but continuation of the global search for the term "Riatine" located it in a top security eyes-only file coded to Nalavia and only two other people.

Data read the formula, and then began a search of his own data banks for the effect of such a chemical on humanoids of Treva's genetic makeup. "Creates susceptibility to hypnotic command while suppressing negative emotions," the file told him. "Nonaddictive. As adjunct to psychotherapy, used to control excessive anger or grief. Commonly used as an aid in sleep-learning. No negative short-term side effects. Not recommended for long-term use."

The long-term effects included "emotional deprivation, suppression of assertiveness. Deprived of emotional outlet, subject loses self-reliance and turns to external sources for mental and emotional stimuli. If not carefully supervised, subject may seek chemical stimuli to induce emotion. Side effects disappear once Riatine is discontinued."

So there it was: Nalavia's people were undemanding and unaggressive because they were drugged and hypnotized. They turned to video entertainment and intoxicants to put feelings into their emotionally deadened lives, while in turn the video programs told them what to believe, even if today's assertions contradicted yesterday's.

He had to find Tasha! Nalavia could have *her* drugged by now. Why hadn't he insisted on being taken to join her on her supposed "agricultural tour"?

No. As long as Nalavia thought he did not suspect anything, Data remained free. But if the President did not produce Tasha by dinnertime, Data could no longer pretend to be fooled. Before then, he must find out where Tasha was being held, and rescue her.

So he prattled to his guide about school systems in the Federation until they were back at the Presidential Palace. Then he excused himself, "to dress for dinner," and hurried to his room, first assuring himself that Tasha was not in hers.

Finally he had time to take apart his combadge. There

was nothing wrong with it—except that it wouldn't work! His tricorder confirmed external interference to the signal.

In an hour, when it was time to go to dinner, the masquerade would end, for Data could not pretend to accept whatever lame excuse Nalavia gave for Tasha's continued absence. Desperate now, he accessed Nalavia's computer again, even though it was in use. He hoped that simply spying through the tricorder would not be detected, and might provide him a clue to Tasha's whereabouts.

There were business dealings going on at one terminal, military orders being issued at another. The main communications terminal was not in use when he began listening . . . but after a time someone accessed it to call "Droo." When Droo answered, the caller said, "She's fuming, Droo. You better have found that Yar woman!"

"I tell ya, she's nowhere on the grounds!" Droo replied. "She musta got clean away—no tellin' where she'll be by now."

"Damn you—it'll be my—"

"It *is* your head, Jokane," Nalavia suddenly interrupted on her private line. "Report to foot patrol duty. And Droo, you have my authority to conscript half the army if need be. I can't stall the android much longer—get that woman back here by sunset, or you'll be guarding an ice mine on an asteroid. If I'm going to deal with Starfleet, I cannot have one of my hostages at large!"

Chapter Seven

TASHA YAR WAS Starfleet Security trained. Once she was certain that no one was going to attack her in the night, and that the door was indeed barred, not locked in some way that could be picked or jimmied, she prowled the bare but adequate room that Darryl Adin had her locked into, only long enough to ascertain that there was no escape.

The building was stone, with hand-laid parquet floors of the kind made only in times when manual labor is cheap. Without a tricorder, she could not be sure there were no hidden sensors, but she could not imagine where they would be installed unless parts of the wall were false. The stone felt real, and gave back a solid thump when she struck it. The wooden door frames had the patina of genuine age, and she could detect no tampering with them.

There were no windows, and the only doors were the one to the hall and one leading into a primitive but functional bath. The only mirror, small but clear, was in there, hung above the basin, but it was not positioned to take in the bedroom, making it an unlikely candidate for spy device.

The bed consisted of a thick pad on a wooden frame, covered with soft blue linens. Yar took it all apart, felt every bit of the mattress, and then remade the bed. There was nothing, and no devices on its underside.

What would they expect to find out by spying on her anyway? Dare had her combadge. She couldn't communicate with Data. Dare would expect her to do exactly what she was doing, and then, when it became obvious that she could not get out, rest so that she could face whatever happened in the morning.

There was no closet, only a peg rail. A soft blue robe hung on it, with a pair of soft slippers on the floor beneath. Yar decided to accept the invitation; her dress uniform had been through enough this evening without being slept in.

The bath had no cabinet; a wooden shelf held comb, hairbrush, toothbrush, dentifrice, soap, towels, and a tube of shampoo. She recognized the last item: Dare's personal preference, made with herbs from Rigel Seven. It was part of his individual scent even now, she recognized as she sniffed it, a wave of nostalgia washing over her.

But she could not allow herself to be overwhelmed by yesterday. Darryl Adin was a traitor and a murderer, and now, by his own admission, a mercenary. He was no more to be trusted than President Nalavia—and Yar feared that she and Data had been thrust into one of those gray situations in which neither side was in the right.

Since there was nothing to do until morning, though, she put all that out of her mind, and slept.

Starfleet officers—star travelers in general—did not allow their bodies to settle into a fixed circadian rhythm, as each planet they visited had different days and nights, and they might beam down to noon or midnight, winter or summer. Yar slept for five hours, got up and exercised, showered and dressed, and waited for someone to come for her.

It wasn't long before Poet appeared, all playful gallantry, to escort her to breakfast. He was not in camouflage this morning, but boasted a soft yellow tunic over black trousers, a wide black belt defining his waist. He did not appear to be armed—now that she thought of it, she had seen no evidence of weapons on any of the men last night. She *had* seen lots of loose clothing, though. Starfleet uniforms made concealing weapons virtually impossible; the loose tunics, shirts, and jackets she saw here might conceal any variety of phasers, blasters, knives, slings—Starfleet Security training had rendered Dare, like herself, expert in virtually every weapon known, and she had little doubt his chosen henchmen were equally versatile.

Should she make a break for freedom? She already knew Poet was stronger and more skilled than he looked, and she did not know her way around this . . . place. What was it—a castle? She decided to ask Poet.

"That's right," he told her. "Rikan's castle, the center of the resistance movement against Nalavia. Someone will show you around later." He paused, making her automatically stop as well, and turn toward him. Light glinted off the lenses of his glasses, making his eyes unreadable. She wondered if that was why he wore them. "You're the one, aren't you?" he asked suspiciously.

"The . . . one?"

"The woman in the case. The reason he chats up little fine-boned blondes, an' then either leaves 'em frustrated or comes back the next day frustrated as hell himself. A Starfleet Officer! Always did say Dare was a glutton fer punishment."

At her look of astonishment, he added, "Oh, yeah, we all know Dare was Starfleet—and how they screwed him. How you—" His eyes raked over her in obvious distaste. "Womankind more joy discovers/Making fools, than keeping lovers."

So Dare still blames me.

They walked the rest of the way in silence.

Breakfast was served in one of the most beautiful rooms Yar had ever seen. It was one of several that ran along the outside of the building, windows on the outer wall overlooking a deep chasm filled with bright-colored trees, solid walls with fireplaces and hangings on the inner wall. The dining room table would seat at least twenty people, completely set, although just three were currently eating. Yar knew only one of them: Sdan.

Tapestries, damask furnishings, old and beautifully pol-

ished wood for the table, porcelain and gold place settings—
the splendor took Yar's breath away, vying for her attention
with the magnificent view through the windows. Imagine
living here, amid the beauty of nature blended so perfectly
with the finest work of artists and artisans. For a moment
she could do nothing but let the effect sweep over her. Then
she deliberately pulled the cloak of Starfleet efficiency about
her, and approached the table.

The two strangers were a man and a woman. The woman
appeared human, with olive skin and thick straight black
hair cut as short as Yar's and tied with a kerchief about her
forehead. She was neither pretty nor beautiful, but exuded
power even seated, eating and talking with her companions.
She wore a sleeveless shirt that displayed arms more muscular than most men's—clearly another of Dare's mercenary
band.

If the woman was intriguing, the man was impelling. He
was human or Trevan and quite old, with thick white hair,
leathery skin, and clear hazel eyes. Yar did not know the
aging patterns of Trevans, but for a human he would have to
be well over eighty. Yet he sat straight, his eyes were alert,
and the moment she approached he stood, all old-fashioned
gallantry, as natural as Poet's was contrived.

"You must be Natasha Yar," he said. "I am Rikan.
Welcome to Warrior's Rest, Miss Yar."

Her translator chose the term "Miss," obsolete even in
Starfleet now although it had survived there until last
century, to represent whatever Trevan term he had used to
address her. An extremely useful item, the universal translator even suggested the flavor of his language, apparently
archaic even among Trevans.

"I am glad to meet you, sir," Yar replied, stopping short of
the table and standing at attention, "but you greet me as if I
were a guest. In actuality, I am your prisoner."

"Nonsense," the warlord replied. "You are my guest.
Please sit down. The servants will bring you breakfast."

Yar remained exactly where she was. "Where I come
from, Lord Rikan, guests are not locked into their rooms."

He smiled charmingly, revealing worn but well cared for teeth. "Then you will wish to eat so as to replenish your strength, in case you should decide to attempt escape."

Yar looked into the wise old eyes and saw that he knew exactly what was going on in her mind. She gave up, and allowed Poet to seat her. The food smelled wonderful and tasted better—if she stayed on this planet long, Trevan cuisine just might spoil the line of her form-fitting uniform.

Rikan introduced the other woman at the table as Barbara. "That's Barb," she corrected. "Don't nobody call me Barbara, and especially don't nobody call me Babs!" This last with a glare at Poet.

"What's in a name?" he replied. "A rose by any other name would smell as sweet."

Barb bared her teeth at him. *"This* rose has thorns!"

"Natasha—" Rikan began.

As long as they were getting names straight, "It's Tasha," Yar corrected. "It probably comes from Natasha, and that was put down in my early records, but all either my mother or the woman who raised me called me was Tasha."

Barb said, "Ain't no use tellin' him, Tasha. Dunno why *I* bother, when it don't do no good."

Rikan ignored the interruption and continued, "My young friend Adrian—" There was a snort from Poet, who must know Dare disliked being called anything but his chosen nickname. Well, if Dare couldn't pierce Rikan's habit of formality no one could. "—did not believe you would visit me voluntarily, even if it had been possible for an invitation to reach you through Nalavia's security."

"He was wrong," Yar said firmly. "If the alleged terrorist warlord had invited us, Data and I would certainly have made every effort to meet with you."

"Data—the android?"

So Rikan understood what Data really was. Yar was sure Dare did, too; he was simply scornful of everything connected with Starfleet these days. "Yes, Data is an android, but that doesn't make him any less a person."

"Indeed? I should like to meet him."

"If you keep me here long, you will certainly have the opportunity," Yar replied confidently.

Another voice interrupted from behind Yar. "I'm sure your walking computer can work out where you are, but it will never get within ten kilometers of this place."

Yar turned, and watched Dare enter and take his place opposite her as she said, *"He* will if he decides that is the best course to take." She did not continue because her attention turned elsewhere. Dare had not come in alone; a woman walked beside him as if she belonged there, and Dare seated her beside him as if he agreed.

"Aurora," he addressed the woman, "may I present Lieutenant Tasha Yar. Tasha, my tactical advisor, Aurora."

Aurora was a stunning woman who appeared to be only slightly older than Yar but made the Security officer feel awkward and childish in comparison with the other woman's easy confidence. On second glance, she was not beautiful, hardly even pretty, but she had the regal attitude of born nobility.

Her hair was dark brown, with red highlights brought out by the same exposure to sun that had sprinkled freckles across her fair complexion. Her eyes were a warm brown, almost Vulcan in their depth. Otherwise, taken piece by piece she was quite ordinary: cheeks a little too round, jaw a little too square, figure not at all fat but neither slender enough to be called willowy nor buxom enough to be called voluptuous. Yet exquisitely dressed in a cherry-red jacket over a white satin blouse and black full trousers, she made Yar feel . . . she could imagine Data finding the word "tacky" in his memory banks . . . even in her dress uniform. *Especially* in her dress uniform, which was totally inappropriate at breakfast.

Aurora gave Yar an appraising look, saying, "I'm pleased to meet you, Tasha. Dare tells me you are highly skilled at combat. I hope you will be persuaded to help us."

That was the last comment Yar was expecting. She frowned, looked at Dare, then Rikan. "Help *you?*"

Rikan said, "I know what Nalavia has told you. We have seen those terrible pictures, too, of innocent people attacked, little children murdered. All this she blames on me and those who fight against her tyranny."

"Data and I already know those raids were faked," said Yar. "Or at least staged or edited, just as she edited and slanted the information about Data and me, and Starfleet itself. I trust Dare has told you it's not a war fleet?"

She glanced back at her former love, who lounged in his chair with the sneer that met any mention of Starfleet. This morning he was dressed in an outfit similar to the one last night, but today's shirt was a silky black material with a pattern of silver running through it. On the breast pocket of a more square-cut jacket was a symbol etched in silver. It was a stylized helmet, Yar realized, such as had been worn by medieval knights on Earth. The Silver Paladin.

Rikan answered Yar's question, "He has told me Starfleet will not do as I feared: take up Nalavia's invitation to come here and destroy our resistance, and then turn on her as well so as to take control of our planet for the Federation."

"Oh, no—surely you must know that is against both the rules of Starfleet and the laws of the Federation!"

The old man nodded. "So I thought, from the research we did many years ago. I was a member of the Council when Treva sought to join the Federation. But since Nalavia came to power she has contradicted what we learned. Her evidence suggests that the Federation gobbles up planets by making them protectorates, lulling them into a sense of security, then annexing them and taxing their products and natural resources. Then, when they can no longer produce enough to satisfy the Federation's greed, stripped and gutted of their resources, they are left to die, their people to starve."

Tasha was horrified. "Dare—"

"I've told him that's not true," he replied. "The Federation certainly have their faults, but if anything they lie in the opposite direction: there is so much of everything to go around that people grow weak with indulgence. No one has to struggle to survive anymore—and without struggle there is no strength."

"Dare," said Tasha, "your own strength gives the lie to that statement."

Rikan said, "This corresponds more closely with what I saw when I visited the Federation years ago—but as I saw only four planets, I could have been fooled, you see."

Sdan spoke up for the first time, "She's tellin' the truth. The Federation's not evil; it just has its problems with people that don't fit into convenient niches."

"What do you mean?" Yar asked. "There are so many different worlds, so many different cultures—how could anyone be so different as not to find a home somewhere?"

Barb gave a derisive snort.

Sdan grinned sardonically. "Try bein' a mix of Vulcan, human, Romulan, Orion, an' maybe a touch of Aldebaran shell-mouth fer the stubborn streak!" he replied. "Then throw in bein' the black sheep of the family besides, an' you may just have a bit o' trouble fittin' in."

Well, now she knew why he didn't act like the Vulcan he appeared to be. "Did you break Federation law, Sdan?"

"Only me family's. Hate t'study, y'see—can't stand bein' cooped up indoors all the time, seein' life through a computer screen. Come from a line of mathematicians, scientists, doctors, researchers—but I'm a throwback to me great-grandad, it seems. He was a free trader, human, married an Orion woman an' started this whole parcel of hybrid vigor." He chuckled. "Lotsa vigor, it seems. Got me three brothers and five sisters, and the Great Bird knows how many cousins runnin' around. Ever' last one of 'em a scholar's scholar. Not me! I need adventure, or I'll shrivel up an' die."

"Quiet to quick bosoms is a hell," Poet put in.

"Did you consider Starfleet?" Yar asked Sdan.

"Too many rules," he replied. "Rules was made to be broken—but Starfleet don't think that way."

"So you have joined Dare in making a career of breaking the most important rule of all." But she was looking at her former lover as she spoke.

Dare was making a great show of concentration on peeling a piece of fruit, but at that he set it down on his plate and looked directly across the table at Yar. "For what it's worth, I have never broken the Prime Directive. All our jobs have been strictly by invitation, and none have been on primitive planets where our presence could disrupt the evolution of native culture."

"You mean no primitive culture has the wherewithal to pay your price," Yar said scornfully.

Something had happened to Dare's quick temper. It seemed to smolder rather than flame now, but its containment might actually produce greater heat.

Instead of flaring at Yar, he smiled—but it didn't reach his eyes. "That is true. I am paid very, very well . . . and I'm worth every credit. But there are certain things I will not do, no matter how high the price." The smile became a smug grin. "Think about it, Tasha: who on Treva could offer me a higher price, Rikan or Nalavia?"

"Which one actually made you an offer?" she countered.

He emitted a bark of laughter, but now there was something about his humor as artificial as Data's. "Rikan," he admitted.

Aurora spoke up. "We could have approached Nalavia for a counter-offer. Or, we could have refused Rikan's as we have dozens of others since I have been with Dare. However, it became clear once we investigated the situation here that Nalavia is a ruthless tyrant who must be stopped while there is still time."

Rikan shook his head sadly. "The time may be past. I do not know what has happened to the independent spirit of Treva's people. The country folk still have it—but those who have succumbed to the lure of soft living in the cities seem to care about nothing except good food, soft beds, strong ale, and entertainment." He frowned. "Nalavia makes intoxicants available cheap, and people spend the time when they're not working in a stupor. No one plays sports except professional athletes. People don't even go to the games—they watch everything on video. Natasha, this change has taken place within only three years, after Nalavia had entrenched her powers. As she suspended civil rights,

151

then free elections, I thought the people would rise up—but only those outside the cities seem to *care*. So . . . I sent for help."

"Why didn't *you* ask the Federation?" Yar asked.

"I no longer represent the Trevan government. In the last election I was turned out of office, along with every other legislator who opposed Nalavia's schemes. My personal efforts to contact Federation officials met with bureaucratic stalling, and ultimate refusals. When I returned home I found myself charged with interfering with the actions of the duly-elected government, and my passport revoked."

There was a pause. Then Barb said, "What he ain't gonna tell you is that he spent two months in one of Nalavia's prisons. Woulda died there if some of his people hadn't broke him out. I been in places like that—rats live better. We freed a bunch of political prisoners that day, an' all of 'em are workin' with us now."

"Us?" Yar asked. "You are Trevan? I thought you were one of Dare's . . . people."

"Oh, Barb is one of my . . . gang," Dare supplied the word Yar had diplomatically avoided. "She took the prison break as a private job while we were between assignments. Of all of us, Barb is the least tolerant of inactivity. I don't care what outside jobs she takes, so long as they're brief and she neither gets herself killed nor brings reprisals down on the rest of us. She came back with Rikan's invitation, and a report of what she had seen on Treva. So here we are."

Yar no longer trusted her instincts about Darryl Adin, but Rikan seemed sincere, and she had seen the video broadcasts and the advertisements for intoxicants. Her instincts certainly told her to distrust Nalavia.

"I am beginning to believe you," she said. "Let me go back to Nalavia's palace—it's considerably west of here, isn't it? Give me my combadge to contact Data, and possibly I can figure out how to get back in. Ah! The sleeping guard—"

"He wasn't asleep," said Sdan. "He was nerve-pinched."

"Doesn't matter. I'll claim whoever was on guard this morning was asleep when I went out to run. If one of you can lend me clothing that could pass as exercise gear, I can get through the perimeter defenses while Data creates a diversion. But we must hurry, or it will be too late to claim I have been out running. Data and I will tap into Nalavia's computer if he hasn't done so already, and find out what's really going on. If you'll give me a frequency on which to contact you—" she said, pushing her chair back from the table.

"Sit down, Tasha," Dare said flatly.

"But there's no time—"

"Sit *down*. You are not going anywhere, and you are not contacting the android."

"Couldn't anyway," Sdan added. "Nothin' wrong with yer combadge; there's jamming on all Starfleet frequencies."

"*If* that is true," said Yar, "Data will verify it. That makes it even more important that I go back—"

"You are not going back," said Dare. "I have a job to do here, which I will not abandon because you or your android reports my whereabouts to Starfleet. You are not going anywhere, Tasha, until either you believe what I say and help me to help Rikan . . . or I have done the job without your help and got clear of Treva and Starfleet's jurisdiction."

Lieutenant Commander Data adjusted the frequency on his combadge one more time. Static. Although he was virtually certain Nalavia was jamming Starfleet frequencies, it *could* be a most inconvenient ion storm in the vicinity of Treva.

Whatever the reason, he could not contact Tasha and he could not patch into the shuttle's more powerful radio to send a message to the *Enterprise*.

So Nalavia considered Data and Tasha hostages . . . and had lost track of Tasha. That was the last thing Data had expected; he had thought Nalavia had Tasha imprisoned. While he worked on the combadge, Data kept his tricorder's circuits open to Nalavia's communications center, hoping to pick up a clue to what had happened to Tasha. There was much concern, and fear of Nalavia's retribution, but no hint of the Starfleet Lieutenant's whereabouts.

But where would Tasha go? And why had she not left some message for Data? Or . . . had she?

He crossed the hallway to knock at Tasha's door, for the benefit of the guard. "Not back yet," the man spoke up.

"That is strange," said Data. "We are having dinner with the cabinet members in an hour."

"Groundcar mighta broke down," the guard suggested.

Different shift, different guard. Data hoped this one found nothing suspicious in his saying, "I must borrow something; Lieutenant Yar will not mind," and entering her room.

Tasha's tricorder was gone. Of course; Nalavia's people had obviously searched the room while the President kept Data occupied. If she had left him a message in that obvious place, it was coded so that no one else could read it—but neither could he without the instrument.

But it had been here this morning. So he had been in here before the search, although after someone else had discovered Tasha missing. Whatever evidence had been here then was now scuffed about, turned over, muddled by the searchers even though they had carefully put everything back except the tricorder.

Data, however, had a perfect record in his memory banks of how the room had looked this morning. Remembering that he had told the guard he had come in to borrow something, he picked up Tasha's shoe polisher and returned to his own room, making sure the guard looked up and saw him enter . . . for he did not expect to stay there long.

Quickly, he ran through the morning's images of Tasha's room. Nothing at ordinary focus. Wait . . . the chair by the door was at an odd angle. He focused in on the carpet, and could see the impressions its legs had left where it usually sat—where it sat once again this evening—along with a scuff mark where it had been shoved out of place.

A human would have had to squat down and examine the carpeting with special equipment. Data was able to magnify and home in on every square centimeter he had looked at, even with peripheral vision. There were the prints of three different sets of shoes—Tasha's Starfleet issue boots, one set belonging to an average-sized humanoid male or rather large female who had wandered all over the room, and one set belonging to someone very heavy for the size of his feet, who had stood near the door, back against the wall, for some time.

Immediately in front of the door, Data's own small but deep footprints walked straight through the signs of a fight—many footprints at various angles, other marks caused by other parts of bodies hitting the floor.

The carpeting held impressions best, but now that he knew what he was looking for Data found the scuffs on the door and walls. Tasha had fought two opponents who had been hiding in her room, waiting for her. Why hadn't the guard heard?

Because he was part of the scheme? No, Nalavia didn't have Tasha.

Because he was paid off? Unlikely—Nalavia's displeasure did not seem worth the risk.

Because he was either away from his post or unconscious, then.

Data replayed his own return last night. The guard seemed to have been just waking up, rubbing his neck—

If he had been drugged he would probably have stayed unconscious. If he had been hit on the head he would have had pain. But a cramp in the neck where it joined the shoulder—

He had been put out with a Vulcan nerve pinch, then, which accounted for the heavier-than-human person in Tasha's room. But . . . a Vulcan? On Treva without the Federation's knowledge? Oh, no . . . not a Romulan, please!

This was no time for fruitless speculation. A Vulcanoid person and probably a human had kidnapped Tasha. They were not Nalavia's people, which meant she was not on the palace grounds. Either she was hidden in the city, or she had been taken elsewhere. That depended on who had taken her.

There was only one likely prospect: Nalavia's enemy, the warlord Rikan. He had a stronghold somewhere to the east of here. Data accessed the information on Rikan he had gleaned from Nalavia's computers. Too far for her captors to have taken her on foot. Groundcar or flyer, then.

Data had no groundcar, but he did have a shuttlecraft . . . hangared at the city's landing field.

Even if he was wrong about who had taken Tasha, he needed the shuttle's radio to inform the *Enterprise* of today's events. It would not be a wasted journey even if once there, where he could also access the aircraft control records, he found nothing that indicated a journey in the right direction.

All of this took less than five minutes. In forty-seven minutes, Data was expected at dinner. Soon thereafter, Nalavia would send someone for him—but by that time he planned to be far away from her Presidential Palace, "hot on the trail" of Tasha Yar.

Taking both phaser and tricorder, Data went out through the floor of the bath again, carefully fitting it back above him to leave his method of escape a mystery. He worked his way to the back of the palace, beneath the kitchen, where as he expected he found an opening to the grounds. It was twilight, an excellent time to fool humanoid eyes. Full day or full dark, while Data's uniform was not bad camouflage amid the browns and greens typical of class-M planets' vegetation, his pale face and hands would stand out far more than human coloring, even though he deliberately smeared dirt on them.

Switching to infrared vision again, he set out across the grounds, dodging from one ornamental planting to another and avoiding open lawns. The perimeter defenses were primitive by Starfleet standards; Data observed the visual scanners until both in range of him were turned away, then sprinted between them. The touch-sensitive fence he merely leaped over. Then he set out for the landing field at a run.

Data could not run much faster than the fastest human; the shape of his body determined that. His advantage lay in his inorganic substructure, which would not fatigue and force him to slow or rest. He maintained the speed of a sprinter all the way to the landing field, actually moving faster afoot than they had in the groundcar on their arrival. He took alternative roads to avoid populated areas, but the map of the city he had accessed from Nalavia's computer showed him a route shorter than the one on which the visitors from Starfleet had been displayed. The only breaks in his journey came when he hid to allow cars to pass.

He had to slow at the landing field, for there were people about. Unfortunately, a dirty android was as conspicuous in a crowd as a clean one.

So he crept through the shadows, every sense alert for alarms. It seemed he had not yet been missed, for surely the shuttlecraft was the first place they would look for him. He found the hangar unguarded. It was locked, but there was no need to risk attracting attention by using his phaser; the simple external lock broke easily under android strength.

The shuttlecraft was gone.

There were many times that Data wished he were human, but none more so than when he needed an outlet for frustration. As false as his laughter was, his rare attempts to use expletives were even more so.

He should have *known!*

Wherever Nalavia had had the shuttle moved, he was quite sure it was not here at the landing field.

Which was more important, finding the shuttle and sending a message that the *Enterprise* would not receive for days, or locating Tasha? His friend and fellow crew member was certainly in danger. His first duty was to rescue her.

Except that he had only a . . . was this what humans called a "hunch"?

No, it was a logical deduction. Nalavia and Rikan were enemies. If Nalavia did not have Tasha—then the laws of probability said she was most likely in Rikan's clutches.

Data surveyed the flyers tethered nearby, chose a small, fast, versatile one, broke the external lock, picked the lock on the power source with a set of tools he found inside— although the owner probably had no idea they could be used for that purpose—and accessed its onboard computer. In seconds he knew who he was supposed to be—and in minutes had filed a flight plan this craft had flown many times before, was cleared with field control, and was wished a speedy flight as he took off into gathering darkness. He flew on the flight plan until he was out of sensor range, then sped east.

The flyer's scanning system did not notify him of the sensors at the outer perimeter of Rikan's territory, but they showed on his tricorder, which he had set to monitor all bands. A sophisticated system, much newer than anything at Nalavia's palace, but all such systems had their blind spots around the projectors. Few human pilots could have maneuvered a strange craft through the tiny null zone, but Data skimmed easily through it and continued toward his goal.

Rikan's stronghold sat on a cliff overlooking a steep chasm. Data sought access to computerized control of the small landing site . . . but there was none! His infrared vision told him *people* were there instead, ready to fight off any aircraft that got through the perimeter defense, or perhaps guide an expected flyer down with lights.

How could they operate that way? Not all nights were as clear as this one; that tiny landing site would be inaccessible to most pilots much of the time without a guidance system. Might there be sensors here neither the flyer's nor his own equipment could detect? The people stood or walked casually about, seemingly unaware of him. They were too far away for even Vulcans to hear the soft swish of the flyer's antigravs, and he had turned off the running lights as soon as he passed through the perimeter defenses.

He kept his distance, studying the layout of the buildings and grounds . . . and the Starfleet shuttlecraft inside a wooden shed, hidden from normal vision but not infrared. So Nalavia had not moved the shuttle; Tasha's captors had.

Giving the impression that Tasha had left on her own.

Or . . . was it only an impression?

No—Data had seen the signs of her struggle, and she was far too good an officer to leave without reporting to him. The presence of the shuttlecraft confirmed that Data was not on a "wild goose chase."

Still, there were personnel watching the skies, and some

rather wicked-looking anti-aircraft weapons in one of the outbuildings. Data dared not circle Rikan's castle closely; he would have to leave the flyer and go in on foot.

Go *up* on foot.

Data found a clearing in the forest and set the flyer down, pulling the light craft in as close under the trees as he could, then piling branches over the parts still in the clear. If he and Tasha could not recapture their shuttle, they would have secondary transport.

But he had to find Tasha first.

It was a steep climb up to Rikan's castle, difficult for humans but not for an android. Data watched for surveillance devices, but no infrared glows indicated cameras, light beams, or other sensors. Rikan probably anticipated attack by air; this approach was hardly suitable for an infantry assault.

Data finally reached the top of the plateau, and saw the castle through the trees. He crept forward, drawing his phaser as he approached the clearing—

And was suddenly grasped from all sides at once, enmeshed and entangled and lifted into the air, to the accompaniment of raucous clanging!

Netted!

It took only microseconds for Data to realize that a net of natural fibers, the same temperature as the ground cover, had been hidden under leaves and twigs. It triggered when he stepped onto it. Bells attached to the ropes made the awful clangor when he moved.

Data's weight held the springy trees bent over, but he was nonetheless helpless as their motion dragged him to and fro.

Hopelessly tangled, Data flopped onto his back and struggled to bring his hands to grasp a section of rope and tear it apart. It was amazingly resilient, but could not hold against his android strength.

When it parted, though, it made only one tiny hole in the net—it would take too long to tear through the strands necessary to make a slit large enough to crawl through. He would have to phaser it.

His phaser was lying on his chest, the springy net hindering his attempt to grasp it. The bells clashed and clanged with every movement. Even as he tried to escape, people converged on him, weapons pointed.

He was surrounded by six people, male and female, armed with phasers, disruptors, and similar hand weapons. One of them of a Vulcanoid race, presumably the same man who had helped capture Tasha, moved in front of him. "I'll take that phaser now—and don't get no fancy ideas, Robot. You might get me, but trussed up like that you ain't takin' out nobody else before my friends get *you*. Don't know what yer made outta, but I'd bet it can't take a blast from *five* weapons."

"It cannot," Data admitted, allowing the man to take his phaser. He was intensely annoyed at his ineptitude in eluding their trap . . . and yet he did not see how he could have possibly detected the net. In daylight, perhaps, if he knew what he was looking for—

Four of his captors kept their weapons trained on him, while two released Data from the net. Then they stayed to reset the trap, while the others escorted him to the castle. No one seemed concerned that he might have a companion; apparently they had been expecting him, and him alone.

His deduction was confirmed when they entered the castle, and one of the women stopped before a large blank screen. She flicked a switch; sensors and detectors came to life. They had been expecting him, all right—and known he could elude normal surveillance. On his last mission he had almost been destroyed by the most sophisticated, self-improving weapon ever devised. *That* he had eluded and helped to destroy . . . only to prove vulnerable tonight to a simple net!

Irony. There was a human feeling Data understood only too well at this moment.

He was taken into the castle, through a number of large halls and corridors, to a series of rooms overlooking the cliff. In one of these, a fire crackled in the fireplace. Three people were ranged before it, apparently visiting casually, comfortably.

One of those people was Tasha Yar.

She did not appear to be held prisoner. Rather, she was seated on a settee facing the fire, her feet drawn up under her, staring into the flames as she sipped pensively at a drink in a small, elegant goblet. She was wearing a long, loose dress of a softer gold color than her uniform . . . the first time Data seen her in a skirt since—

Tasha turned as the group entered, and her eyes widened with surprise. "Data! Are you all right?!"

"Yes, I am all right," he replied, realizing her concern was due to his dirty and disheveled state. "Merely chagrined. I came here to rescue you."

"Yes, well, there is some question as to whether or not I require rescue," she told him. "Lord Rikan," she said to an old man seated on the other side of the fire, "this is my colleague, Lt. Commander Data."

The man rose, tall and imposing despite his advanced years. "I am most interested to meet you, Mr. Data. I hope we may have the opportunity for discussion. I have never met an android before."

"How do you do, sir," Data replied politely, taking his cue from Tasha.

"And this," said Tasha, turning to the man standing behind her near the fire, leaning on the mantelpiece, his face in the shadows, "is Adrian Dareau, better known as—"

But when Data focused on the man's face, his pupils automatically opened to allow him to see clearly even in the dim light. He knew that face from Starfleet Security files— an open file, besmirching Starfleet's otherwise perfect record of policing her own.

Ignoring the four weapons still covering him, Data stepped forward, interrupting Tasha, shifting instantly into command mode.

"—better known as former Starfleet Commander Darryl Adin," he supplied, "the most wanted criminal in the Federation."

And that gave Data a duty to perform, no matter how hopeless its full implementation might be: "As an authorized representative of Starfleet, I arrest you, sir, on the charge of unlawful flight from custody after being found guilty in a properly-convened and conducted court-martial, on twenty-one counts of murder, two counts of conspiracy, and three counts of treason against the United Federation of Planets."

"Data!" Tasha gasped.

But Data took no notice of her, his attention fixed on the very dangerous man before him.

Darryl Adin simply stared at him, dumbfounded, for a moment . . . and then his mouth quirked. His eyes crinkled as he looked Data up and down, choked bursts of humor escaped his control—and finally he simply threw back his head, and laughed out loud.

Chapter Eight

TASHA YAR had had no idea what Data was doing during her day of captivity, but she knew that Nalavia could not keep him ignorant that she was missing. She decided to assess her situation before determining her next move.

After that most uncomfortable breakfast, Rikan had offered to show Yar his home, explaining as he took her from one magnificent room to another how things had changed on Treva since he had been born in this very castle. "Once we made contact with other planets, if we wanted the medical advances, the technology, the creature comforts they offered, we had to trade something in return. We didn't know that it would change our entire way of life."

He described a pattern Yar had learned about in her required studies in history and sociology, one repeated time after time across the galaxy. Some governments were wise enough, as Treva's council of warlords had been, to recognize that trading away natural resources was planetary suicide. The only other choice was industrialization.

But as the level of technology on a planet climbed, the education of its workers had to follow or there would be no one capable of designing the equipment or doing the work. With education quickly came discontent—and insistence on sharing in the wealth they created.

Once the people acquired economic power, political power quickly followed. Governments changed from tyrannies, monarchies, oligarchies, to the many variants of rule by the people. On Treva, Rikan said, bemused, "We ruling families found to our astonishment that our lives were no worse than before. At least for those of us who bowed to the inevitable. My father no longer ruled by right of birth, but he was elected to the new Legislative Council, and when he died I replaced him. It was the same for all the great families. The power of the sword was replaced by the power of the vote—but it was still power."

His face grew sad as he continued, "Some there were who would not give up the old ways. They actually did what Nalavia accuses me of: built armies and attempted to win by might over those who welcomed the new ways." He sighed. "My father said, 'You cannot fight the future.' He was forced to take arms against some of his oldest friends. They called him a coward and a weakling, but they were wrong."

By this time they were standing on a balcony overlooking the chasm that formed a natural defense for the castle. "They were wrong," Rikan repeated . . . but Yar heard something in his voice. . . .

"Do you doubt that?" she asked.

"They said the common people could not be trusted, that they were weak and lazy and stupid. The warlords died fighting, like men—and cursing those like my father who, they said, turned against their own kind." His mouth thinned. "We were four, four who looked to the future and trusted in our people. Now all the others are gone."

Yar suddenly remembered, "Three members of the Legislative Council were murdered. Not—?"

Rikan nodded. "Yes—the other warlords. And suspicion cast on me, although of course there was no proof. I am the last, and I am childless. When I die, there will be no more warlords on Treva . . . and I have survived to see the prophecy come true: the people elected Nalavia, and now as she takes their power to herself they don't seem to *care!* As long as they have life's necessities plus entertainment and intoxicants, they don't think of the future. Weak and lazy and stupid."

"Then why do you fight?" Yar asked.

"There are days when I ask myself that," Rikan replied, "and cannot find an answer. But then I go among my own people, here in the countryside. They work eagerly, play hard, live well—and I say no, Nalavia will not turn these people into her slaves! Not so long as I have breath and strength, or the wherewithal to get help for their struggle."

"So you hired Dare."

"His reputation has it that he can organize a small number of people to be as efficient as an army."

Oh, yes—Starfleet Security training had certainly taught him that.

"And has he done so?"

"Yes. His people trained and drilled us—and then these so-called terrorist attacks began, and the blame was placed on me. It cost me a large number of supporters." He turned the open, young hazel eyes, so incongruous in the old, wrinkled face, on Yar. "Natasha—those attacks are not Adrian's doing, nor mine. We believe they may be perpetrated by Nalavia herself, to rouse her people's hatred against us, but we have no proof."

"If that's so," Yar said, "Data will find out."

"Data? The android has such powers?"

She told him about her friend and colleague. It was easy to talk to Rikan . . . but Dare as he was now made her extremely uncomfortable. He stayed out of her way all morning, and Yar began to plot escape once she knew the general layout of the castle.

Poet joined her with Rikan for a time, then Barb . . . and Yar realized that once she knew her way around she was no longer to be left alone with the old man. Dammit—Dare knew she had to try to escape, and while Rikan was certainly hale and hearty for his age, with her skills she could overpower him easily. What her captor could not know was that until Dare's people began to protect him it had never crossed her mind to attack the aging warlord . . . although she now realized she had thus missed her best chance to get away.

She must not miss another ... even if it did mean attacking Rikan. Her Security training included methods to render someone unconscious without causing serious harm.

Unlike standard uniform, Yar's dress uniform included pockets in the trousers, covered by the long-skirted jacket—a place to carry a comb or a credit chit on a formal occasion. She knew better than to try to palm anything while Poet was around, but neither Barb nor Rikan noticed when she slipped a small but heavy stone sculpture first into her hand, then into her pocket. Its weight was reassuring: there were no sharp edges to do serious damage, but with scientific positioning of the blow it would make a very effective cosh.

If she was to get out of the castle, though, she had to wait until she was alone with one person.

Just before noon Rikan and Barb turned her over to Dare. He took her to the room where they had first met last night. The table stood as it had then, bare and polished. Now, though, Yar took note of the cupboards lining the walls, and two shiny surfaces that could be viewscreens, although such technology seemed out of place in the ancient castle.

"This is our strategy room," Dare said. "I wish I could trust you enough to show you everything, Tasha—but how can I?"

"You wish *you* could trust *me?*" she asked sarcastically.

"Look at you!" he replied, a burst of anger escaping for a moment before he controlled it to quiet bitterness. "Security Chief on a Galaxy-class starship, at your age. I'm surprised you're not a lieutenant commander."

"I don't have the minimum time in rank yet," she replied automatically, eliciting from him a snort of acid laughter.

"So you are a success," he said. "I always knew you would be."

"You encouraged me," she recalled.

"Oh, yes, I did encourage you, didn't I? Look where it got me: when the crunch came, you chose your career over me."

"Dare!" she gasped.

"You can stop being indignant," he said. "At least you're consistent—I can trust that, can't I? Tasha Yar will always do what's best for her career. Even betray someone she purports to love."

She turned away. "You still think I betrayed you."

"And you still think I won't shoot or stab you in the back," he replied. "If I betrayed everything I believed in, how can you trust me"—he came up behind her and put his hands about her throat—"not to simply snap your neck?"

She knew half a dozen ways to break his hold, but she used none of them, her ingrained defenses overpowered by the memory of what his touch used to mean to her, the scent of him in her nostrils as he leaned forward over her shoulder to watch her expression.

"I believe you know I told the truth and nothing more on the witness stand," she replied calmly.

The hands dropped, and he walked away from her. "Unfortunately, I do believe that," he said. "The more fool I."

"It's the truth," she said, turning to see that he now stood more than two meters from her, his back to her in his turn.

It was her chance to escape . . . but too obviously so. He'd have her before she reached the door.

Instead she moved closer, willing him to remain turned away from her as she took the stone sculpture from her pocket, closed it within her hand so that the blunt surface was exposed, saying, "I loved you, but I had a higher duty, one that you yourself taught me. Not to my own success, but to Starfleet."

When he turned, she was so close that he looked into her face, not down at the hand she kept carefully out of his line of sight.

"There was a time," she continued, holding his eyes with hers, "when, to me, Starfleet meant Darryl Adin. When you betrayed Starfleet, what did you expect me to do—run away and become an outlaw? Or just pine away and die of love like the heroine of some opera?"

On the last words of her speech she swung. He wasn't expecting it—not as the tag to her series of questions. Even

Dare's reflexes were not fast enough to block such an unexpected blow.

Years of experience told her how to knock him unconscious without serious injury.

Before his body hit the floor, she was gone.

Yar darted down the corridor the way they had come, but instead of taking the stairs back up to the gallery suite she scurried down a hallway toward the back of the castle. There was no escape via the chasm in front—not without mountain climbing equipment.

She heard no alarms, nor were there footsteps behind her.

She didn't question her luck, but sped past the kitchens, from which delicious aromas drifted, then up a ramp that wound several times at a shallow angle—apparently the means by which heavy provision carts were taken down to the kitchens. That augured well for coming out into the courtyard.

By the time she reached the top of the ramp, Yar was panting. The thick double doors were barred from the inside; she wished for Data's strength as she shoved at the heavy wooden bar, bruising her shoulder using leverage against the doorframe before she finally slid it out of place.

Peering out into brilliant sunshine, she looked all around the courtyard . . . and saw nobody.

Still no alarm. Dammit, she *knew* her job! Dare should have been unconscious for no more than thirty seconds, groggy for perhaps a minute after that. By this time there ought to be people searching for her.

She was tempted to go back, to see if she had hurt him more than she intended. Or if he had injured himself on impact with the stone floor—

But her duty was to escape; Starfleet had not sent her to Treva to be captured by outlaws! Data must be suspicious about her absence by now, and possibly a good portion of Nalavia's army was out looking for her.

Keeping to the shadows, she crept farther out into the courtyard. No one, absolutely no one, was there.

Shivers ran up her spine. This was wrong.

There was nothing to do but keep going until she encountered the trap surely set for her, and hope she could escape once she tripped it.

She scuttled from the shadow of one outbuilding to another until she came to one with the tracks of wheels before it. Groundcars—maybe flyers. Surely she would set off an alarm if she tried to steal a vehicle, perhaps just if she opened the door. The answer was speed.

The door lock was a simple one any Starfleet Security trainee could open. Yar sprang it, darted inside—

There were three vehicles: a groundcar, a flyer . . . and the Starfleet shuttle she and Data had flown to Treva!

Dare had always been a class act. His people had not only kidnapped her, but carried her away in her own shuttle.

She took no time to consider the implications. The door opened to her ID code, she climbed in, and the lights came on.

"What took you so long, Tasha?"

In the pilot's position sat Darryl Adin.

Too bitterly furious at herself to answer, she sat down in the co-pilot's seat, turning the chair toward him as she tried to collect herself.

He gave her that sardonic twist of his lips that had replaced his once-sweet smile. "You don't have the edge over me anymore, little kitten."

"What?"

"You've forgotten what it's like to have no one to rely on but yourself, whilst danger lurks at every turn. To trust no one."

"Dare—"

"Don't apologize."

"I wasn't going to. It's my duty to escape, Dare."

"I know. That's why I had to show you it's impossible."

"You set me up!"

He inclined his head, as if acknowledging a compliment. "For what it's worth, you did catch me off guard—I was preparing to set you up a few moments later. No one saw you take the sculpture, but you did me no permanent injury." The humorless smile again. "Perhaps if you had it to do over you would reconsider the latter."

"There was a time," she said, "when you would have put me on report for such a foolish stunt as attempting to recapture an escaped prisoner alone, without backup."

As if on cue there was a soft chime, and Dare tapped the paladin insignia on his jacket. Yar realized it was a combadge. Poet's voice was clear but tinny through its tiny speaker. "Dare? You all right? D'ja find 'er?"

"Right where I expected, Poet. Everything's under control. You can call off the search."

Yar gritted her teeth. "Now that you've made me feel like a total fool, what are you going to do with me?"

"Try to persuade you to wait, learn the truth, and report that to Starfleet. Which you cannot do with the shuttle's subspace radio, by the way—Sdan has been trying to pierce the jamming all morning. If he can't do it, it can't be done."

"All I have to do," said Yar, "is take the shuttle into orbit, beyond Nalavia's jamming."

"And from there just keep going," he replied, "forcing me to abandon my work here before a Starfleet Security squad arrive. No, Tasha, I cannot allow you to take the shuttle."

"I can't abandon Data," she protested.

"An expensive piece of equipment, but replaceable."

"As I told you before," she said, exasperated, "a friend and colleague, no more expendable than any other member of an away team. And definitely *not* replaceable. If we ever do recover the technology to create androids like Data, each will have a unique personality, born of individual life experience. Just like a human being, Dare. Data is more human than a good many flesh-and-blood people I've met."

She saw that controlled anger in his eyes as he said, "There are some things flesh and blood can do that no machine will ever learn." He leaned forward, took her by the upper arms to pull her toward him, and kissed her.

It was not a pleasant kiss, more a demonstration of power than a gesture of affection. Yar did not fight, but she did not respond, either. When Dare let her go, she deliberately wiped her mouth and said fiercely, "Don't bet on it!"

His lips parted in astonishment—an expression only

Dare and Data, of all the men she knew, shared in common. Then his mouth curled into a sneer such as Data would never attempt, and he said scornfully, "I might have known. I don't suppose any *man* will ever be good enough for you."

"At least Data would never do what you just did. There was a time, Dare, when you protected me against unwanted attention."

He went dead pale . . . and then said, "I'm sorry." For one moment he was the man she had known, anguished to discover an unwelcome side of the man he had become. But Adrian Dareau could not expose any form of vulnerability. The mask closed down once more. "I still cannot let you take the shuttle."

"You could come with me, to make certain I return."

"No. Nalavia's defenses will be primed for this vehicle, Tasha. It would be dangerous enough just to use it as a flyer—but if you try to orbit, she'll shoot it down."

"You may be right," she conceded. "Why didn't you say that in the first place?"

"It might be possible to escape on a straight liftoff. In orbit you're a sitting target."

"Then . . . how can I send a message? If Data and I *don't* report, in a few days Starfleet will start an investigation. They may send another shuttle, or possibly a ship. But if Captain Picard is satisfied that we can handle things here he won't send in the cavalry."

"We're playing for time then," said Dare. "One way or another, Starfleet *will* send more personnel to Treva. The best I can hope for is to do what I came for and be gone before they arrive. Very well, Tasha. If you can calculate the location of the *Enterprise* when the signal reaches it, we will send your message by non-Starfleet frequencies. Nalavia's own communications channels are clear."

"Data can calculate it," Yar said. "I can't."

"You could ask Sdan."

"Give him classified information about the route of a Starfleet vessel? Really, Dare."

He grinned. "I'm good, but I'm not *that* good! Not even

the Silver Paladin could take a Galaxy-class starship using only nine people and four ships, the best of which can manage warp 3.7 on a good day. Besides, the *Enterprise* is far too conspicuous a vessel for my purposes."

Not if you took the battle bridge and abandoned the saucer, Yar couldn't help her warrior's instincts from reminding her—but after staying so carefully out of Starfleet's way all these years she doubted Dare would risk setting the dogs on himself with such a rash move. Besides, if what he had just said was true— "Nine people? There are only *nine* of you?" She had assumed he had an army of several hundred from everything he had supposedly accomplished.

"If the local people aren't willing to do their own fighting, I don't take the job," he replied. "What I provide is leadership, planning, technology, and technique."

"Has anyone else in your gang had Starfleet training?"

"Barb—but she left the Academy after two years because she's a fighter, not a student. She's the one who got me started in this business. She happened to be in a bar on Nornius Beta when some thugs decided I looked an easy mark. When I left them draped over the chandeliers, she invited me to join her in rescuing a kidnap victim. I had nothing better to do . . . and the rest is history."

"Dare . . . everything I've ever heard about the Silver Paladin's work has been positive. If I'd known it was you, I'd have been following more closely—"

"To apprehend me?"

"I'm a Starfleet officer, not a bounty hunter. I have no call to go in search of wanted criminals." She looked into his eyes. "*Would* you allow me to send a message to the *Enterprise*, if your man can figure out where to send it?"

"Yes—provided I monitor what you transmit."

"You don't trust me not to tell them you're here."

"It would be your duty to do so if you saw the opportunity."

He knew her only too well . . . perhaps better now than before. "Then I will give you the flight plan. You were in Starfleet long enough to know that it's a rare thing for a starship to stay on its filed plan for more than a few days. We may just beam a message into limbo."

"But you have to try," he said. "I understand. I will allow you to do it—on two conditions."

"I won't mention you," she said. "What is the other?"

"I want your word that you will not try to escape again."

"Dare—"

"Nalavia can't stall your android much longer. Once it knows you're gone, it'll come looking for you. If it finds this place—"

"He will."

"—we'll let it . . . him in."

"And have two hostages. But you won't take Data as easily as you did me. He has some built-in electronic sensors; you can't take it all away from him with his tricorder."

"Useful information," said Dare. "Thank you. Now, your word. Tasha, I promise, if what you see here does not persuade you that Rikan and not Nalavia represents what is best for Treva, we'll let you go."

"It is not Starfleet's business to decide who is right and who is wrong on Treva. The Prime Directive—"

"—ceased to apply when Nalavia called for help. Starfleet can refuse to provide it, though."

"Leaving the field clear for you to aid Rikan."

"Yes," he said, the cynicism gone from his voice. "Rikan represents what is best for Treva. You may say I have no right to judge, but that is what Nalavia is asking *you* to do. Please promise to stay long enough to compare Rikan's people to Nalavia's."

He seemed so open and honest at that moment that she almost forgot the crimes he was convicted of. As his prisoner, she could hardly arrest him. If she had escaped, she would also have escaped that duty. The longer she remained with Dare, the greater the possibility that the time would come when she would be forced to apprehend him.

She didn't want to. Each time she got a glimpse through his armor of the man she had once known and loved, her dread of that duty grew stronger.

If she gave him her word, she would have to keep it. If she didn't, he would have no choice but to lock her up again. If she gave her word, she would be allowed to send a message to the *Enterprise*. Her duty—

"I give you my word," she said, stifling the pain in her heart.

He smiled—a very small, quiet smile, but it brought back for the first time the handsomeness lurking beneath the stern lines of his face. Then he pulled her combadge from his pocket. "It still won't transmit on Starfleet channels, but if you decide to work with us we'll adjust it to the frequencies we use. Now let's find Sdan, and see if he can calculate the position of the *Enterprise*."

In the strategy room, Sdan had opened one of the cupboards to reveal a computer terminal far more modern than anything Yar had seen in Nalavia's castle. Like the ones aboard ship, it had no buttons or switches, but responded to either voice or touch control.

Sdan might claim to be no scholar, but he certainly knew the mathematics of space-time, calculating the probabilities of the ship's location along the continuum, and comparing them with the beam of the subspace radio traveling at a constant speed. The *Enterprise* would routinely monitor all messages on Starfleet frequencies, but the computer would ignore other frequencies unless there was something unusual about a message—such as its being beamed directly at the ship.

Dare left Sdan to his calculations, and showed Yar around the strategy room. It was all computerized, including a complete schematic of the castle with the position of every person in it. Yar felt her mouth thin as she realized, "You could trace my every move without leaving this room."

"Actually," said Dare, "Sdan watched the screens, Barb followed you, Poet was on the cliff side, and I made my way to the shuttle by the shortest route—which we had been careful not to show you earlier." He pointed out on the map that if she had gone back upstairs there was a corridor directly to the courtyard. As it was, she had dipped down to kitchen level, then climbed the winding ramp, reaching the courtyard well behind Dare even though he had started more than a minute after her.

Suddenly she realized, "I forgot to ask how badly I hurt you!"

"You did exactly what you intended. I blacked out—but Sdan was here to revive me, so I was on my way to the shuttle faster than you counted on."

"You took a stimulant? After a blow to the head? Dare—"

"No—just a painkiller. It's nothing, Tasha—all in a day's work in our profession."

She managed to bite back the automatic response that they were no longer in the same profession.

They joined Rikan again for a light luncheon, after which Aurora took Yar back to the strategy room. There she showed her what they knew of Nalavia's activities, the positions of her standing army, her armament and deployment systems.

Sdan was back at his console, calling up probabilities and swearing softly when they did not say what he wanted them to.

The two women worked at one of the large viewscreens, Yar becoming fascinated, appreciating Aurora's skills and forgetting for the moment that this woman had apparently taken her place with Dare. *No longer my place,* she reminded herself when it did occur to her. *I retired from the field years ago.* Caught up in strategy as if it were a game, Yar suggested positions for the troops Rikan could muster, if they wanted to take Nalavia's palace.

"Take the queen," said Aurora, "and the game is ours."

"It appears so," Yar agreed. "Nalavia does seem to be a one-person operation. Both the most dangerous kind of tyrant, and the most vulnerable."

"You are right," said Aurora. "She has not created in her people any vested interest in keeping *her* in power, only in the things which they associate with her. The council, though, is another matter."

"The people with the real power," said Yar. "It's an

ancient strategy, but it always works. They vote for what Nalavia wants, and she provides them with wealth and power."

"Such people have no real loyalty," said Aurora. "We've considered infiltrating the council somehow, persuading a councilor or two that he really ought to be President or at least not trust the present one."

"Good idea, but how do you implement it?" Yar asked.

"It's not easy in such a closed society. I tried setting up as a wealthy free trader and applying a bit of discreet flirtation. Unfortunately, since that is Nalavia's own stock in trade, she immediately created restrictions that made it impossible for me to trade profitably on Treva. I was forced to retreat to preserve my cover."

Yar frowned. "Dare let you—?"

"Oh, it wasn't particularly dangerous. But he refuses to do what *would* work."

"And what is that?" Yar asked.

"Go in himself. He can be incredibly sexy when he—" She broke off. Then, "Of course, you know that," she said softly. "But he won't use that power, cynical as he may be about everything else."

"Aurora," said Yar, "are you telling me that you suggested Dare—?"

"That he go in undercover, as it were, use his charms on Nalavia and the two most powerful women on the council . . . and then let the three of them find out about one another—after Dare was safely off-planet, of course. Considering the kind of person Nalavia is, the catfight would have been heard all the way to Earth! Divide and conquer among Nalavia's allies, and make Madame President look more than a little ridiculous. But you know Dare."

Do I? Do I know him at all anymore? Yar stared at Aurora. "I don't understand. How could you suggest such a thing when you and Dare . . . ?"

"Dare and I?" Aurora laughed. "Oh, no, Tasha—I can't take the moody, brooding type! I love Dare as a friend and colleague, but his idea of romantic love is far too solemn and serious for me. I'll take Poet any day—he knows how to make me laugh."

"Oh," Yar said, trying to hide her surprise. Her memories of loving Darryl Adin were all spun 'round with joy and laughter.

Finally Sdan reported, "If the *Enterprise* remained on the course you gave us, it should be approaching its destination just as a message sent thirty-seven minutes from now would intercept its path. How long will they orbit Brentis VI?"

"Probably at least a day."

"Then I suggest that we record your message now and transmit it every two hours for the next day."

"Nalavia will monitor the transmission," Aurora reminded them.

"Without my tricorder," said Yar, "I can't scramble it."

"Wouldn't matter," said Sdan. "Scrambled or plain, a message beamed subspace from here means that's where you have to be."

"Even so, if I could code it somehow, Nalavia wouldn't know exactly what I sent." She thought a moment, and suddenly recalled something that she could use. "Sdan—can you have the computer translate the message into binary code?"

"Well . . . sure, but that's easy enough to read with any computer."

"If you know what it is. Captain Picard and Commander Riker will recognize it at once—they recently had reason to learn quite memorably how it sounds."

"Ah," said Sdan, "we'll send it at top speed. Chances are Nalavia's never heard anything like it. We can hope her cipher experts take a while to deduce what it is."

So Yar composed her message: "Arrived Treva. Nalavia's reports unreliable. Standard subspace frequencies jammed. Assessing situation. Further reports will follow. Yar."

"Aren't you going to ask for help?" Aurora asked.

"You don't divert a starship unless you are certain it's needed," Yar replied. "Possibly Data and I can settle matters here and rendezvous with the *Enterprise* as originally planned."

"For an experienced Security officer," said Aurora, "you are unexpectedly optimistic." But Yar saw understanding in the woman's eyes, and realized shamefully that in her heart she sheltered the hope that they could, indeed, resolve things here and still allow Dare to escape.

Before dinner, Aurora took Yar to her quarters, and lent her some clothes. Like the men, Aurora wore her garments loose; as she was also taller than Yar, everything was too big. However, a bit of tucking and belting, and Yar began to look less like a child in her mother's clothes, and more like a disturbingly glamorous woman.

But when she wore the gold dress to dinner, and saw appreciation in Dare's eyes, she felt a dangerous warmth inside. *I must not let my feelings affect my judgment,* she reminded herself. *I am still Dare's prisoner, even if I did agree not to run.*

Nevertheless dinner was excellent, the conversation was fascinating, and afterward Dare and Yar joined Rikan in one of the salons.

Only to have alarms sound almost at once.

Dare tapped his combadge. "What's happening?"

"Flyer approaching, no recognition signal," came Barb's voice. "Cleared the outer defenses without triggerin' 'em."

"Data," said Yar. "It has to be."

Dare grinned wolfishly at her, then said into his combadge, "It's the android. Shut off electronic surveillance and follow the procedures we discussed this afternoon."

"Right!"

"What are you doing?" Yar asked as Dare turned to stare into the fire as if he hadn't a care in the world.

"Your android relies on electronic gadgetry. So we will take it with methods that do not involve electronics."

And Yar could do nothing but wait, knowing Data would not expect physical traps, hoping his strength and quickness would let him elude them.

But Dare's people were too good; in less than half an hour they herded the android into the salon. And when Yar tried to lessen the tension by making introductions, her sometimes impossibly naive colleague stepped forward and attempted to arrest his captor!

Yar stared from the dappled form of Lieutenant Commander Data to the dark shadow of Darryl Adin. The room lights were dimmed, so the flickering firelight could be appreciated. Despite the dirt smeared on it, Data's pale face was still clear enough that she could see his puzzled frown.

She had to turn to see Dare, although she first heard his choking attempt to keep from laughing. By the time she could see his silhouette, he had lost the battle and was laughing freely—the first genuine humor she had seen in him since her arrival. It took him several moments to regain control. Then he walked over to Data, and around him, still grinning as he looked the android over.

At the same time, Rikan did something to the arm of his chair, and the lights slowly came up.

Yar wanted to leap to Data's defense, but the situation was tense enough already. The android was, unfortunately, accustomed to being treated on first acquaintance as a fascinating piece of equipment; he remained still, allowing himself to be examined. Behind him, Sdan, Barb, and two of Rikan's men kept guns trained on him. He ignored them.

Dare completed his circuit, peering into Data's face. Data looked mildly back at him, taking his cue from Yar to wait. She was surprised at her own calm. Perhaps after the wild emotional swings of the day her nervous system simply could not attain red alert again.

Dare finally spoke, but it was to Yar instead of to Data. "Was that courage, or merely programming?"

"It was foolhardiness," she replied. "That's supposed to be my department, Data. How often do I have to remind you that you are not indestructible?"

"Nor invincible," he replied with genuine chagrin. "I came to rescue you, Lieutenant, but as you see . . ." He gave the tilt of his head that was his equivalent of a shrug, and smiled his small self-deprecating smile.

Dare stared at Data. "You *are* more than a machine," he said.

179

"Yes, sir. A portion of my structure is organic."

"No, not the physical. Tasha, you told me your colleague had a personality—but I wasn't expecting a sense of humor."

Yar saw Data's eyes widen. Dare couldn't know what that assessment from a stranger would mean to the android.

Dare turned back to Data. "Give me your word as a Starfleet officer that you won't try to escape—or to arrest me again—and I will dismiss these people. They have better things to do than guard you all night."

"Tasha?" Data asked.

"Dare has my word—until I have all the information he and Rikan can provide. They know the other side of what's happening here, Data. I think we should listen to them, compare their evidence with what Nalavia has told us and what we've found out for ourselves, and then decide what to do."

"Conditionally, then," Data agreed. "You have my word that I will make no attempt to escape while we are still investigating." He said nothing about arresting Dare, and Yar knew the omission did not go unnoted. She would have to tell Data later that she had not made that promise either.

At least she knew better than to come out with it as Data had, held helplessly at gunpoint. So why had he—?

Rikan, of course. The warlord now knew who it was he had hired—but out here beyond Federation space the reputation Dare had gained as the Silver Paladin far outweighed whatever had made him leave the Federation. Data would probably not understand that to a world attempting to overthrow a ruthless tyrant, a ruthless criminal—provided he had the reputation "Adrian Dareau" did for reliability—might seem precisely the hired gun they needed.

Still, Data's thinking that Rikan ought to know suggested that the android had discovered something after Yar was carried off . . . something that made him trust the warlord. Interesting.

"Very well," Dare was saying, "I accept your word . . . conditionally. Would you join us then? Or perhaps you would prefer to get cleaned up first?"

In the stronger light, Data appeared even more of a disaster area, several different kinds of mud and dust on his skin and uniform, leaves and twigs in his hair. Obviously he had had an interesting time getting here. Data glanced down at his filthy uniform, then at the silk-upholstered furnishings. "I think I ought to clean up first. There is a great deal to tell."

Rikan spoke. "Trell, give this man a room, and find him something to wear." Then to Data. "Please come back as quickly as you can. We are pooling our information in an attempt to demonstrate that Nalavia has not told you the truth."

"We knew that already," said Data. "Tasha, there is even more. I will hurry, for it is very important."

Yar remained huddled on the settee, suddenly feeling very much out of uniform. Data had steadfastly continued with his duties, while she—

Why should she feel guilty? Actually, she had continued with her duties as well, putting herself in a position to learn all about Rikan's plans. She had sent a report to the *Enterprise*. Not a bad day's work, really.

Data rejoined them, clean and dressed in trousers that bagged a bit, tucked into his own boots, with one of the loose shirts Dare's men affected belted around his slender waist. He looked as if he were off on one of his play-acting kicks again, Yar thought—all he needed was a bandanna, an eyepatch, and a gold earring!

Fortunately, telepathy was not a part of Data's programming. He sat, and accepted a glass of wine from Rikan, who seemed not in the least fazed to be host to an android. Yar recognized that she was watching true *noblesse oblige* in action, a tradition rarely seen in the galaxy today.

As Rikan was always Rikan, so Data was utterly himself, sniffing, then tasting the wine and commenting, "Excellent vintage—aged in wood, decanted—"

"Data!" Yar interrupted. "You have important information for us."

"Yes," he replied, setting the glass down and turning to business.

"One moment," said Rikan. "I do not know your requirements, Mr. Data. Do you need food or other sustenance?"

"No, thank you, sir. I have had adequate nourishment today. And Lieutenant Yar is correct that I have information to impart." He frowned. "Tasha, can we speak freely here?"

"These people are working to overthrow Nalavia, but claim they are not responsible for the terrorist attacks on her people."

"They are not," said Data. "I have copied all the data from Nalavia's computer, including military files. All the attacks were performed by her own army, to discredit Rikan."

Dare looked stunned, then delighted. "Mr. Data, despite our infortuitous introduction, I think I shall quickly grow to like you! What else did you find out?"

"A great deal. Of particular significance to our present situation is the fact that Nalavia's term for her visitors from Starfleet is . . . hostages. She was considerably agitated when Tasha was discovered to be missing, and by now I assume she knows that I am also no longer in her palace."

"Hostages," mused Yar. "So that was her plan: If she couldn't manipulate us into getting Starfleet to do what she wanted, she was going to try to force them by threatening us."

"It would not work," said Data.

"She doesn't know that," said Dare. "From out here, the Federation look very soft and unthreatening."

With his characteristic half-questioning intonation, Data said, "Indeed. Do you perceive Nalavia as unthreatening?"

"No, I do not," Dare replied.

"She has proved extremely successful," Rikan put in.

"Her efforts, however, have gone toward entrenching her own power rather than benefitting the people of Treva."

"Are you aware of how she has accomplished that?" Data asked the warlord.

"She encourages them to grow soft," he replied. "I do not understand it—there should be *some* who recognize what she is doing. Yet only outside the cities has there been rebellion against her."

"I assume that in the countryside the major sources of drinking water are untreated?"

"Wells and streams, for the most part. Mr. Data, are you suggesting that Nalavia drugs the water supply in the cities?" Rikan deduced at once.

"It is not a suggestion. It is a fact."

Dare frowned. "The people don't act drugged," he said. "They use intoxicants in their leisure time, but we've seen no signs of slowed production, increased industrial accident rate—anything to indicate that workers are chemically dependent."

"It is not that kind of drug," said Data. "Nalavia is using a chemical which opens people's minds to hypnotic suggestion. Then she uses the video broadcasts to . . . program them. The drug also suppresses strong negative emotions. It does not impair judgment or coordination; in fact, it makes people more efficient at their work because they are not distracted by anger or fear or grief."

"Or love," Yar murmured. Data glanced at her with the faintly puzzled frown that told her he was storing a response he did not comprehend for later analysis.

Data continued, "Intoxicants are sold freely, but under strict government control. They appear to be used to supply a substitute for the suppressed emotions."

"Yes," said Yar. "It's very easy to turn to chemical happiness when there is no other kind in your life."

Rikan was sitting up very straight now. "But how do we fight this?" he asked. "How do we stop it? Mr. Data, you have revealed Nalavia's secret, for which I thank you heartily. Now how can we stop Nalavia?"

Dare smiled his wolfish smile. "All we have to do," he said, "is substitute something innocuous for Nalavia's suppressant! Once it clears everyone's system—"

Data stared at nothing, nodding slowly and smiling faintly as he accessed the necessary information. "—they will have a sudden release of emotions. All that they should have felt during the time their emotions were suppressed will come on them at once."

"And that," said Rikan firmly, "is when we attack!"

Chapter Nine

LIEUTENANT COMMANDER DATA was intrigued with the warlord Rikan and his castle. The structure was genuinely old, yet outfitted with the latest technology, both for comfort and for defense. The computerized surveillance system was new, part of the service supplied by Darryl Adin, aka Adrian Dareau, aka the Silver Paladin.

Data found it confusing—hardly a new feeling in his life among humans—to be a prisoner, yet to be treated as a colleague, even a friend. Having accessed all the *Enterprise* Security files except the ones classified as "eyes only" to Tasha and her Security staff, he knew all about Darryl Adin. Knew facts, that is. The man did not seem to match the facts.

Someone capable of selling out the Federation, of arranging an attack that would endanger Starfleet trainees and personnel—and which in fact had resulted in the deaths of a number of them—ought to appear more of a hardened criminal. Not that Data's experience with hardened criminals was all that extensive; Cyrus Redblock and Felix Leech had been created by the holodeck program, after all, and based on characters from fiction.

Nevertheless, Data had passed the required psychology courses at the Academy. The activities of the Silver Paladin did not correspond with the profile of a criminal. If anything, except for the fact that he charged for his services, they seemed closer to the exploits of the legendary Robin Hood. A man falsely convicted, so the stories claimed, of the same crime of treason.

There was, however, another possibility: if, in a moment of weakness, an otherwise honest Adin had succumbed to the lure of riches; if, as some evidence at his trial suggested, he had been led to believe that the *Starbound* could be taken without loss of life; then his current pattern of activity could be a combination of remorse and the same greed that had led him to deal with the Orions.

And the evidence at Adin's trial had been conclusive.

Data's speculations could have no bearing on his actions: Adin was a fugitive from both Starfleet and the Federation, and Data's duty was to arrest him—next time, preferably, when he had some chance to take him in.

He was annoyed that he hadn't fooled Tasha into thinking his action naivete, especially as it had not accomplished his intention of making Rikan reconsider the man he had hired. Either the warlord already knew Adin's background, or else did not care, considering the reputation of "Adrian Dareau."

Data was concerned about Tasha Yar. She was the consummate Starfleet officer, her first priority the safety of the *Enterprise* and its crew, her first duty to Starfleet. If she was sometimes overeager, that was preferable to slackness. Yet now she had given her word not to escape.

But so have I, Data reminded himself. Adin's men had, after all, gone inside Nalavia's palace to capture Tasha, and then carried her off in her own shuttle. They were ruthlessly efficient, and Data had no doubt that they would either find an escape-proof cell to lock him in, or else disable him. The Vulcanoid, Sdan, had expressed a desire to "examine" Data, in terms which left no doubt that he meant to take him apart to see how he functioned. Limited freedom was certainly better than being locked away or incapacitated.

Furthermore, these people opposed Nalavia. Data had no doubt now that Rikan and Adin were the lesser evil; it was simply disturbing that Tasha had apparently decided that before the crucial evidence was in.

For the time being, Data joined in the plans to remove Nalavia's drug from the water supply. Sdan, once he accepted that Data was not a toy to be dismantled, worked with the android through the night, transferring the manufacturing and distribution information from Data's memory banks to the very fine computer system in the strategy room.

"I do not know why Nalavia has such an out-of-date system," Data commented.

"Serves 'er purposes," Sdan replied, "an' it's Trevan-built—come with the palace. Besides, she can't get one of these babies legally. This is the latest Federation technology, traded only to Federation planets, not even to allies."

"Then where did you get it?" Data asked. "Or should I not ask?"

"Built it!" Sdan replied. "Me an' Poet got no record in the Federation. Barb or Pris, neither, come to that, but if you can't use it to bust somebody's head, they're not interested. So Poet an' me, we hit the tech expos, then come back and build our own versions of the latest the Federation has to offer."

"Inside the Federation, that would be illegal," Data pointed out.

"Ain't inside the Federation, are we?"

"You could make a great deal of money by selling this technology to the Ferengi, the Orions, the—"

"Look, Computer Brain, if all we wanted was money we'd just steal it! Hell of a lot easier and safer. Ain't you twigged yet we're not some gang of common criminals?"

"And if you did sell the technology," Data pointed out, "it would not be exclusively yours, to provide to your . . . clients."

Sdan grinned. "True. Y'know, Data, you might have the makings of a devious mind there. Stick around long enough, and we may invite you to join us!"

"I think you are hoping that if I stay long enough, you will come upon an excuse to take me apart."

Sdan looked him up and down with a solemn nod. "Yeah. There's always that."

Tasha Yar spent a second night in the "blue room," but this time her door was not barred. In the morning, dressed in comfortable trousers and tunic, she found the same informality as yesterday at the breakfast table, people arriving when they pleased, leaving when they had finished eating, only Rikan there for the entire time.

The warlord appeared in the strategy room sometime after Yar joined the growing group before the viewscreens. She already knew Data, Dare, Sdan, Poet, Barb, and Aurora. Now she met Tuuk and Gerva, a mated pair of Tellarites; Jevsithian Drominiger, a Grokarian seer; and Pris Shenkley, a human woman who built expert weapons systems. The rest of Dare's "gang."

Jevsithian was archetypal: just about Yar's height, he was so old and wrinkled that a first glance could not identify his species. His hooded gray robe hid so much of him that only his eight-fingered hands, looking like nothing so much as spiders at the ends of his sleeves, provided the clue to what he was.

Yar had heard of Grokarians, but never met one before. Some of them were said to have the gift of prophecy, although she recalled that the Starfleet manual on species with so-called psi powers explained it as "a wild talent, the ability to calculate probabilities within the space/time continuum."

Jevsithian turned to her, eyes almost hidden in wrinkled folds, and announced, "You are the one with whom it changed."

"Hmmm?" Yar found the impression of staring into black holes unnerving.

"Your presence draws all possible futures into one. The Silver Paladin will win all, and yet lose. The bright knight of darkness transcends to legend."

"Hey—none o' that doomsayin'!" Sdan protested.

"Doom is but fate," Jevsithian replied, "and the fates of

all living beings are linked." He withdrew to a chair in one corner, apparently unconcerned with the plans the others were making. *Or,* thought Yar, *maybe he already knows everything we're going to do.*

"Tasha." Data's voice drew her away from her contemplation of the Grokarian. "We must talk."

"Hmm? What about?" she asked, following him away from the cluster of people around the computer.

"About how much aid we should give these people . . . if any."

Of course she should have known Data would not take that final step without careful consideration. Yar felt a sudden sinking feeling. "Priam IV," she said.

"Exactly."

She stared at him. "*You* took that test? How could they fool you, when you can see the walls of the holodeck no matter how it's programmed?"

"Do you mind if I do not explain how an android can be misled by computer experts? The point is that we face a similar paradox here. We know that Nalavia is so determined to maintain her tyranny that she has resorted to drugging her people. But this is not a Federation planet; we are not duty-bound to help the people of Treva regain their freedom."

"Are we duty-bound *not* to?" Yar asked. "Suppose we do nothing. Nalavia continues her rule—unless Rikan and Dare can put an end to it without our help."

"*My* help," said Data. "I have the information from Nalavia's computer which will allow them to remove the drug from the water supply."

"Allowing the people to decide for themselves whether to overthrow Nalavia," said Yar. "Isn't that closer to the spirit of the Prime Directive than leaving them unable to think for themselves?"

"It is not the spirit but the letter of the law that we are sworn to obey," Data pointed out. "If we interfere, we do not know the effect on Trevan culture."

"No, we only know what will happen if we *don't* interfere.

189

Things will get worse. You told us the long-term effects of Riatine. Data, last night you were ready to help Rikan and Dare. What happened?"

"I was reminded of the short-term effect of removing the drug: war."

Yar remembered Rikan's "That's when we attack!"

"War or drugged docility," she said. "It's Priam IV, all right. But Data . . . if I were a Trevan, I know which I would choose. You cannot imagine what it is to live drugged, to have no happiness except a false joy created by chemicals—"

"Your mother?" he murmured.

"And myself."

"What?!" he asked sharply.

"I don't remember anything but the pain," she admitted. "I . . . I was born addicted to joy dust, Data, because my mother was. She fed it to me to keep me quiet when I was a baby, but after a while she couldn't afford enough for both of us. She stopped giving it to me. My earliest memories are of the pain of withdrawal."

"Tasha, I had no idea—"

"Please don't tell anyone. Not even Dare knows that. The woman who cared for me after my mother finally abandoned me altogether kept me free of the stuff until I was old enough to understand that a free mind was worth the pain of life, even on New Paris. Data, you said Riatine doesn't have physical withdrawal symptoms. I say, free the minds of the people of Treva. Let them think for themselves, decide for themselves what to do about Nalavia!"

Data stared into her eyes for some seconds. Then he nodded. "I will provide the information Rikan and Adin require. Rikan is Trevan; he has the right to decide what to do with it."

Data provided the records of the manufacture and delivery of Riatine. "It would be simplest to exchange it where it is warehoused before use," he explained. "There are no guards—why would anyone want to steal water purifier? If we had a transporter, it would be child's play to substitute a placebo for the Riatine; an hour's work for the capital and all three other major cities."

"But we don't have a transporter," Dare said, putting a casual hand on Data's shoulder as he leaned forward to study the screen. Yar saw Data glance at the hand—on the *Enterprise,* only Geordi touched Data that way, as if he were just another person. She felt her lips quirk at the change in Dare's attitude once he actually met the android; obviously he had already forgotten that Data was a machine.

"Suppose," Dare was saying, "we ambush the lorries carrying the drug to the purification plants."

"Right!" said Barb.

"Fine if we just wanted to steal it," said Aurora, "but we want to substitute something for it. The regular deliverymen are probably known, and they would certainly be missed before the placebo was used."

"Mmm," Dare ruminated, "I was thinking of going in *fast,* hitting deliveries to all three cities in one night."

"We can do it," urged Barb. "If we just take the Riatine, they can't put it in the water."

Poet responded, "Who ever asks whether the enemy were defeated by strategy or valor?"

"I do!" Barb told him with a glare. "We're all gettin' fat an' lazy sittin' around here."

"The better part of valor is discretion," Poet reminded her.

"Dammit, Poet," the warrior woman said, "you talk like a coward. If I hadn't a seen you fight, I'd think you was some snivelin' worm."

Data interrupted the bickering. "The moment the Riatine is missed, Nalavia will know you have stolen it. If you replace it, the placebo may not be used immediately. If the drug wears off in only one city, Nalavia will test both the water and the chemical in the warehouse."

"You're right," said Dare. "The scheme will only work if it wears off for everyone before Nalavia realizes what has happened."

"And we must be ready to take advantage of it," Aurora

added. "A few riots won't do any good. Nalavia will send her army to quell them, and replace the drugs. Once the people have their free will back, they must be informed of Nalavia's treachery."

"If we can take over the radio and video broadcasts," said Sdan, "the word will spread very fast."

"And be believed," said Aurora, "because people will feel the difference in themselves."

"Why not simply destroy the plants manufacturing Riatine?" Yar asked. "Nalavia would know at once, but surely she could not manufacture enough to poison all the cities' water again before everyone woke up."

"That's the ticket!" Barb agreed.

Rikan said, "Many Trevan people work in those manufacturing centers. I am sure most of them think they are making water purifier. Is there a way to destroy the plants without killing and injuring innocent people?"

"I doubt it," Dare replied.

"Even if we could, consider Nalavia's reaction," said Aurora. "She wouldn't wait for the rioting to start; she'd institute martial law the moment she saw a danger of losing control."

"We must surprise her," Rikan agreed. "The plan to substitute something harmless for the Riatine seems best, if we can implement it."

"That's what you're paying us for," Dare replied. "Data, have you any records beyond the routes from the manufacturing plants to the water purification plants?"

Yar saw Data's head lift in the half-nod that said he did indeed. "I have the time schedules, including places where the drivers are exchanged, and where they stop for meals and fuel along the way. However . . ." he stared at nothing as he cross-referenced, ". . . possibly unbeknownst to the drivers, they are tracked by Nalavia's army units."

Unbeknownst? Yar was amused to hear Data doing his chameleon act, picking up the flavor of Dare's speech patterns.

"Tracked?" Dare asked. "How?"

"There are tracing devices in the trucks, by which a small

armed escort makes certain the vehicles follow the route and schedule. Where there are no parallel roads, the escort follows at a discreet distance, or else flyers are used. The patterns vary—" The android frowned in momentary puzzlement. "Ah, I see why. They travel through the open countryside, where undrugged citizens might wonder at a military escort for what is purported to be water purifier. Therefore the method of escort changes frequently, parallel, following, preceding, troop carriers, single-person vehicles, flyers—apparently Nalavia hopes no pattern will be noticed."

"It works," said Aurora. "We've heard no suspicions. But now that we know—"

"I have the schedules for the next four days," said Data. "There was nothing beyond that in Nalavia's computer."

Dare grinned at him, no sarcasm this time. "That's enough—give us those schedules, and we'll figure out how to manage a substitution. Mr. Data, how would you fancy leaving Starfleet for a life of danger and excitement on the outer edge of the galaxy?"

Yar knew it was said jokingly, but Data replied solemnly, "I am afraid I would not . . . fancy it at all."

One of the advantages of being an android was the ability to keep several ideas in one's consciousness at once, and many others within ready access. Data found in the next few hours that it was also a disadvantage.

Tasha seemed caught up in the hope of freeing Treva's city dwellers from the hypnotic chemical, forgetting that, even though they had a sort of trustee status, she and Data were prisoners here. Data could not forget who Darryl Adin really was, and that produced another, unanticipated, problem: he liked the man.

Adin was the glue that bound his small coterie together, just as Jean-Luc Picard was for the crew of the *Enterprise*. Adin's role was more difficult than Picard's. Although his followers were few, they were even more diverse than the motley bridge crew Data served among, for they had no common loyalty to an ideal, such as Starfleet, to hold them together. In the course of that first day, Data heard them squabble interminably, but *saw* them work toward a common goal.

And through it all, nothing Adin did suggested that Data was less than a person. Only Geordi LaForge, of all the people Data knew, had accepted him so unquestioningly upon first acquaintance.

No, he suddenly realized, the warlord had done exactly the same thing. But Data had little contact with Rikan that day, while he and Adin worked side by side for hours.

Before time for dinner, they had a plan. Sdan and Poet left with some of Rikan's people to borrow vehicles from heavy transport companies in Rikan's territory. Barb and the Tellarites went off with a "shopping list" for containers, paint, and stencils. Jevsithian had long since left them, while others had drifted in and out all day. Now Aurora joined Data at the computer, along with Pris Shenkley, the weapons designer, to go over the plan step by step for possible hazards.

Data could not help being aware when Adin and Tasha stopped participating, and then quietly left the strategy room together.

But he saw them again at dinner, his first meal since yesterday's luncheon with Nalavia. By this time his organic components were ready for a nutritional boost, and his curiosity led him to sample everything on the table. Rikan's board was as lavish as Nalavia's; if he had not had other things on his mind, Data could have spent his time contentedly analyzing the ingredients which contributed to the wide variety of flavors.

However, his consciousness was occupied with the dinnertime conversation, expansion of their plan to sabotage Nalavia, and watching Tasha and Adin.

Tasha was wearing the long gold dress again. Aurora was resplendent in crimson, Pris in pale blue. Rikan wore a richly-embroidered tunic and coat over a shirt with an elegant fall of white lace. Adin was in his usual black, with a white shirt and his silver emblem, while Data, when everyone had gone to "dress for dinner," had considered changing back into his uniform, which he found clean and neatly hung up in the room he had been assigned.

However, remembering the clothes he had seen last night, he put on what seemed most formal of the garments Trell had given him: jacket and trousers of deep gray-green, with a gold shirt almost exactly the color of his eyes. Tasha had smiled and said, "You look gorgeous," when she first saw him, but Data would have felt more comfortable in his dress uniform. He wondered what had happened to Tasha's.

The entire small group adjourned to Rikan's parlor after dinner. Pris Shenkley sat down next to Data and struck up a conversation.

"Why do you not work for the Federation?" he asked her.

"Because they would take control of my work away from me," she replied. "It is true that the Federation now builds only defensive weapons, and eschews aggression. However, I prefer to use my talent where I can control who uses my weapons."

Data told her about the recent visit of the *Enterprise* to the planet Minos, and the weapon which had turned upon and destroyed its creators.

"Yes," she said, "I fear precisely that mentality. It is too easy to build better and better weapons, for no reason other than that one can do so. For Dare, I build precisely what is needed for a particular assignment, not doomsday machines that compete only with themselves."

"And will you build something for this plot to replace the Riatine?"

"No; everyone is already equipped with a variety of weapons they are familiar with. I designed the defenses for Rikan's castle, however."

He tilted his head. "Did you design the net used to capture me?"

She blushed faintly. "Not design, exactly—but I suggested that you would probably not expect something so . . . primitive. The net is actually a snare for a large Trevan animal. I thought it would be strong enough to hold you." She smiled. "I underestimated you. I didn't think it was possible to tear the strands of a quoghart net. If our people hadn't arrived quickly, you would have escaped."

She took one of his hands, turning it to study back and palm. "You are so strong . . . and yet so gentle. Have you any idea how attractive that is?"

He almost said yes, as it seemed every woman he had ever been intimate with had made the same observation, but *that* observation reminded him to access his flirtation files, just in time. "That is . . . my nature."

"Mmmm." She studied the palm of his hand. "You have fingerprints."

"Yes. And yes, they are unique, or at least not copied from those of anyone in Federation records."

"That's as it should be," she said softly. "You are unique."

Data was surprised to find Pris flirting with him, but had to access only the main directory of his flirtation files to keep up. She obviously had no desire to go beyond a pleasant verbal give-and-take, not surprising on one day's acquaintance.

Besides, Data discovered, he did not want to go further. He pondered that. He understood why he wished to interact with Nalavia as little and as impersonally as possible: the woman was evil. But Pris, like the rest of Adin's gang, had no criminal record that he had ever come across. Why should he be reluctant to function intimately with her, should she desire it? He was, after all, designed to function in a wide variety of capacities. Pris was nothing like Nalavia; she showed no deviousness or cynicism.

At the thought, his attention strayed to Darryl Adin, who tonight sat beside Tasha on the settee. Tasha seemed to spend all her time with Adin now. The man was obviously attempting to reawaken feelings Tasha had once had for him, to overwhelm her reason and devotion to duty with memories of a past that could never be recaptured.

Adin leaned closer to Tasha, and Data accessed his directional microphone to hear him murmur, "Let's go out onto the balcony." They excused themselves to Rikan, and went out into the moonlit night. Data could still see them through the glass doors, leaning against the balustrade and looking out over the night-black chasm. Adin put his arm around Tasha's bare shoulders, and she leaned against him, nothing more.

During all of this, Data had let his flirtation file entertain Pris—until she chuckled. "You are cleverer at talking nonsense than any man I've ever met! Where did you learn it?"

Data checked the file he had been accessing. "A modern adaptation of techniques detailed in the works of Jane Austen," he replied honestly.

Pris laughed aloud. "Well, it is utterly charming, and if I didn't have to be up early tomorrow morning I might ask you just what other techniques you happen to know. But then, you won't be leaving us for a while. I hope we will have the chance to get to know one another better."

"That would please me as well," he replied, but did not volunteer the answer to the question she had not quite asked.

The parlor was clearing out now, in deference, it appeared, to Rikan. Data noticed the old warlord's slightly stiffened posture as he forced himself to sit up straight.

When Data looked back at the balcony, Tasha and Adin were gone. In moments he would be alone with Rikan . . . forgotten.

Data had nothing to do for the night. There was no library computer, no science lab to visit to feed his voracious curiosity.

He would go down to the strategy room, he decided. Someone would certainly be there, and perhaps he would be allowed to explore what else was in that very fine computer.

But when he went to bid goodnight to Rikan, the old man asked, "Do you sleep, Mr. Data?"

"No, sir."

"Then will you do me a favor?"

"Certainly, sir, if I can."

"I am an old man. I don't suppose old age is something you will ever experience—but then neither will you have the pleasure of people indulging your whims simply because you are old." Rikan looked up at him, eyes still clear and sharp. "How old are you, Mr. Data?"

"Twenty-six Federation Standard Years, sir."

The warlord's eyes widened. "So young! Then you are just at the beginning of life's experience. But you have been many places among the stars, done more in those twenty-six years than I have in my long life."

"That may be true, sir, especially as I was . . . created . . . as an adult. On the other hand, I never had the experience of being a child."

"That is sad," said Rikan. "Childhood is the happiest of all times—or ought to be. But I am becoming forgetful. The favor I would ask is that you come to my room after Trell has helped me to bed. Although my body is tired, age robs me of the ability to sleep easily or well. Will you come and talk with me?"

"Gladly, sir."

So when Trell informed him Rikan was ready, Data went to the warlord's room, keeping in mind the servant's caution, "Please do not stay late. My lord needs to rest, for he will be up at dawn, no matter how few hours of sleep he has had."

Ensconced in the large bed, Rikan seemed smaller and frailer than in his usual stiff clothing. He was propped up against the pillows. "More wine?" he asked, pouring himself a glass and offering to do so for Data.

"No, thank you, sir. Alcohol has no effect on my metabolism. I have tasted your wines only to add to my experience of bouquets and flavors."

The warlord smiled. "You spend your life gathering data?"

"It is what I was designed for."

"Not only that, surely," said Rikan. "You said *experience* a moment ago. I can see that you have feelings, that you are concerned about your colleague Natasha, and about your duty to the organization you serve."

"You read my concerns very well," Data admitted.

"I have many years' experience over you," said Rikan. "I

was surprised to find out how short a time you have been . . . alive?"

"Conscious," Data supplied.

"Is not the organic part of your makeup alive?"

"In a sense; it does require nutrients, and replenishes itself. That part of me, however, existed in stasis for an unknown length of time before my consciousness was awakened."

"Ah," said Rikan, "how intriguing. Can you remember being brought to consciousness? Or are you like a person, who cannot remember the moment of birth?"

Birth. Tasha had called it that, "Then this very spot was your birthplace," when she saw his home.

"It is the first event I can remember. My mind was not a *tabula rasa;* I was already programmed with language, a great deal of basic knowledge, and information gathered by four hundred colonists on my home planet."

"I wonder," Rikan mused, "whether that would be a greater or a lesser shock than birth. I suppose no one will ever know, as no one can experience both."

"No, sir," Data responded automatically—and then realized the implied question. "Not at current levels of technology. And if it should ever become possible to transfer human consciousness into an android body . . . I do not know if, having once been human, a person could adapt."

Rikan studied him. "Do you feel less than human, Data?"

"I am . . . *other* than human. I am stronger and faster than any fully-organic humanoid. I have more information at my immediate disposal, and can manipulate it more efficiently. Still, I am capable of learning and growing—not merely increasing my information files."

"Obviously," Rikan told him with a smile. "I have never felt impelled to have a conversation like this one with the very clever computer system Adrian installed here. You are clearly a person, Data."

"Yes. Still, I would be human if I could. I look at you, sir, for example, and while I know that with experience I am learning judgment, I wonder if it is possible for me to acquire wisdom."

The smile broadened. "Ah, Data—do you not see that your question is its own answer?"

Data did not. "Sir?" he asked with a puzzled frown.

"Never mind," said Rikan. "You will outgrow that quandary—and discover others. Do you age physically?"

"Apparently not, sir. However, I have existed for too short a time for conclusive estimates as to how long I may continue. As Tasha frequently reminds me, I am not indestructible, but unless I suffer irreparable damage, Starfleet scientists believe this body will last several centuries."

"You may not suffer the physical indignities of age, but long life has other cruelties, far worse than loss of strength and keenness of the senses. Survivors are considered fortunate, Data—and the irony is that those who envy us our longevity either do not live long enough to know the cruel fate in store for us . . . or else they live to share it."

"Sir?"

Rikan stared past Data, at nothing. "I had a wife once, and a beautiful daughter. I had good friends and colleagues, who shared the same experiences I did. They are all gone now—including many who were younger than I. My child, gone before me. My wife, following within the year. My friends, the companions of my young manhood—all are gone now."

The warlord's eyes refocused on Data. "Did your designers realize what they would subject you to, when they gave you both sapience and sentience, and then condemned you to outlive everyone you love?"

"I do not know whether I am capable of love, sir."

"How can you not know, when I know upon one day's acquaintance?"

"I cannot procreate," Data explained. "There is no reason for me to be designed with the capacity for—"

Rikan laughed. "Ah, Data, how very young—and how very human—you are in that respect! To confuse the mating drive with the love born of fellowship is utterly typical of young people. No, no—I am speaking of love for one's friends and colleagues, which you display in abundance."

The laughter faded once more into ineffable sadness. "And that cause of greatest joy is also the source of greatest pain."

"I understand," said Data.

Rikan gave him a sad smile. "No, you do not, but you will . . . and perhaps sooner than you think. Data, you were created as what Adrian calls a 'survivor.' Jevsithian says that Adrian is a survivor, whether by fate or doom or simply strength of will. You heard the seer's prophecy?"

"Such prophecies cannot be scientifically tested," Data pointed out.

"But if it should come true, what do you think it means?"

"To win and yet lose? To win the battle, but die, I should think."

"Possibly," said Rikan. "We organic people are also capable of logic, Data. The first moment you saw Adrian you attempted to arrest him. I do not think you can shirk that duty, and the charges you named—murder, conspiracy, treason—are surely punishable by death."

"The Federation has no death penalty," Data explained.

Rikan closed his eyes with a shudder. "I feared as much. Incarceration, then, for the rest of his life."

"Confinement to a rehabilitation colony," Data said, "and only until he is cured of his aberration."

"The name makes no difference. You do not know Adrian well yet. To lose his freedom would be far worse than death to such a man. And that, I think, is why the seer said he would first win all—which augurs well for Treva—and then lose."

The brilliant old eyes opened again, looking at Data with a question in their depths. "Lord Rikan," the android said, "please do not ask that of me. For all the good he may have done since, Darryl Adin did once turn traitor to everything he purported to believe in. If I neglected the opportunity to return him to Federation justice . . . I would be doing exactly the same thing."

Tasha Yar spent the next two days with Darryl Adin, their old camaraderie reawakened as they plotted to substitute barrels of a placebo for the Riatine being carried to Treva's cities. With the routes and schedules Data supplied, it was a simple operation: when each truck stopped and the operators left it to have a meal, it was surrounded by similar vehicles, shielding it from surveillance as its cargo was rapidly removed and replaced by placebo in identical containers. The operators of those other vehicles—all Trevans from Rikan's territory—distracted their fellows of the road while the exchange was accomplished. Sdan, Poet, Aurora, and Pris provided means of disabling or fooling the vehicles' sensors. Child's play, as Data had put it, with their information, equipment, and expertise.

By dinnertime on the second day, all was accomplished without incident, everyone was back at Rikan's castle, and good cheer reigned.

Yar and Data, of course, had not been allowed to go along. As Yar waited for Dare to return, she knew she had made a decision: he had outwitted her and Data both, and certainly had a plan devised for his own escape when his mission here was over. While she could not in good conscience just let him go, she would do nothing to anticipate his escape. She would simply trust him to plan something as unique as his trap for Data.

The android, meanwhile, was far quieter than usual. With the strategy room nearly empty, she missed the friendly talk they had shared on the way here. *He suspects,* she thought grimly. *I wonder if he thinks I would actually aid Dare to escape?* But she couldn't ask; better to let Data worry about her loyalties than plot to prevent Dare's escape.

After dinner, everyone crowded into Rikan's parlor to continue the celebration. Thus it was easy for Dare and Yar to slip out to the balcony, and thence away from the noise to Rikan's music room, where they had come before. Like the rest of the castle, it retained its ancient atmosphere and furnishings, while modern technology produced exquisite sound at the press of buttons hidden inside a small enamelled box on one of the tables.

Dare programmed up something soft and unobtrusive,

and they sat talking quietly for a time. Finally, Dare said, "I want you with me, Tasha."

"What?" she asked, startled, fearing he meant to ask her to run away with him.

"When we strike, three days from now—when the effects of the drug wear off, and we organize the uprising against Nalavia. I want you at my side."

"I can't," she said tightly. "The Prime Directive—"

"Tasha, this planet called for Starfleet help! *Give* it!"

"We were called to fight *you.*"

"That will change as soon as people's heads are clear. If we stay here and monitor, will you come with me as soon as the people move against Nalavia?"

"Do you really think one person will make that much difference, Dare?"

He put his hands on her shoulders and looked into her eyes. "You will to me," he said softly . . . and kissed her, this time very gently, tenderly, waiting for her response.

Which she could not hold back. Desperately, she put her arms about his strong torso and hugged him close. "It can't last, Dare," she whispered fiercely.

"I know," he replied softly, stroking her hair. "Tasha, I know you. It would be wrong to ask you to leave the life you have made for the hit-or-miss existence of an outlaw. I shan't ask you that, I promise. But I will ask you one question: do you still believe I am guilty? Do you still think I betrayed you?"

"No," she answered. "I never completely believed it, Dare. I don't know how there could have been all that evidence against you—but I've known all along that the man I love could never do such a thing."

She felt him relax in relief beneath her touch. Then he kissed her again, just as tenderly, and murmured, "We may never see one another again."

"I know. But let's not think about that now. We have three days, Dare—some people never have even that long."

He smiled, the wonderful, warm sweet smile that she remembered so well, and stood, extending his hand to her.

She took it, determined to take what she could have, now, and let tomorrow take care of itself.

If life was bliss, albeit only temporarily, for Tasha Yar, it was painful confusion for Lieutenant Commander Data. His discussion with the warlord Rikan left him questioning the feelings the old man claimed he had. Did his concern over Tasha's behavior stem from that noble form of brotherly love Rikan wanted to credit him with?

Or in his search to comprehend the human spirit had he stumbled into the dark and self-defeating emotion of jealousy?

Data knew textbook definitions for all these terms, but they were little help, as he so often found when faced with human reality. He noticed Tasha disappear with Adin a second evening—and this time they came to breakfast together the next morning, perfectly groomed and perfectly relaxed . . . and just a little too perfectly content.

Doubt about his own motives kept Data silent for most of the day; besides, Tasha was constantly at Adin's side, and what he wanted to say to her should be said in private.

Finally, though, as people began leaving to dress for dinner, Data managed, "Tasha, may I speak with you?"

"Of course, Data. Come along to my room."

When they entered, Tasha closed the door and took off the light jacket of the outfit she was wearing, hanging it on the peg rail.

For one horrified moment, Data thought she meant to change clothes in front of him, a way of saying, "You mean no more than any piece of machinery that might be in my quarters." But she did not. Instead, she waved him to the single chair, then sat down on the bed. "I think I know what you're concerned about, Data—and you needn't be. I won't let my feelings for Dare get in the way of my duty."

"That is, indeed, my concern," he said, grateful that she had broached the awkward subject. "However, in your plans to monitor the expected uprising against Nalavia, I wonder if you have considered what will happen when it is over and peace has been restored."

"Data," she said in her favorite tone of utter reasonableness, "I have no plans to turn outlaw and join the band of the Silver Paladin."

"I did not think you had," he replied. "I meant our immediate duty once we are back in contact with Starfleet."

She chuckled. "If you think you can succeed in arresting Dare, you go right ahead and try."

Data had never before faced such a situation. "Are you saying you will not?"

"I'm saying that I don't think either you or I will ever get the chance, Data. Dare won't stay around that long."

"But if he does?" Data persisted.

"He won't," Tasha said firmly, and got up as if to dismiss him.

Data also got to his feet. "I am asking for fact, not opinion, Lieutenant. If you have the opportunity to arrest Darryl Adin and return him to the Federation, will you do so?"

Her eyes flashed and her jaw set. "Are you pulling rank on me . . . *Commander?*"

"Do I have to . . . Tasha?"

She stood firm for a moment, staring eye to eye with him. Then her mouth trembled, and he saw a tear start at the corner of her eye. "You shouldn't have to ask me, Data. Yes, damn you—if it comes to that, I will do my duty. But I know it won't come to that—Dare will never let it."

Data left her then, relieved. Tasha's word was good. Why, then, did he feel a peculiar guilt at making as certain as he could the arrest of her lover?

The day had gone to making plans for taking over the radio and video broadcasts once Nalavia's people had the hypnotic drug out of their systems, and for countering Nalavia's move to institute martial law. Yar began putting on makeup, preparing to don a diaphanous blue and lavender gown Pris had lent her in place of the gold for tonight.

Rikan's formal dinners were such a lovely quaint old custom, she thought, a delightful contrast to the high-tech work of the day. She brushed her short hair, bending over to fluff it out. At the moment Dare's hair was longer than hers, but he had never minded her short style. Since childhood, she had always kept it cut too short for an assailant to find much to grab onto, and Dare, bless him, had never once "wondered what it would look like if . . ." as had every other man she had been intimately acquainted with. Except Data, of course.

Poor Data. He was genuinely worried that she would ruin her life over Dare. Not that she was not tempted, but she knew her love accepted her decision.

If only there were some way to prove his innocence. But there was not. She remembered his court-martial as if it were yesterday; there was just too much incontrovertible evidence to disprove, especially at this late date.

So she would do what both life and a career in Starfleet security had taught her: plan for tomorrow; live for today. Tonight she and Dare could escape to his quarters again, and pretend there was nothing more to life than love and laughter.

Yar looked into the mirror and was pleased with what she saw. She couldn't be objective; she *felt* beautiful, no matter what the mundane world might see. Now all she had to do was get that unfamiliar dress on—

"Alert! Alert! Incoming flyers! All hands to battle stations!"

At the announcement ringing through the halls, Yar dropped the froth of blue and lavender and skinned back into the plain tunic and trousers she had worn all day. Only when she was out in the corridor did she realize she didn't *have* a battle station.

A few doors down, Data emerged from his room, wearing his Starfleet uniform. "The strategy room," he said, and together they ran downstairs into highly organized chaos.

Cupboards which had remained closed before now stood open. Poet and Pris were issuing formidable looking weapons to the members of Rikan's household. Sdan was at the computer console, and the viewscreen showed a schematic of the castle and its surroundings.

Two force screens glowed softly, one around the castle itself, one several miles away. "Shields?" Yar asked. They couldn't be anything like a starship's shields, unless a matter/antimatter generator was hidden beneath the cliff-side.

"The inner one," Sdan replied. "Outer one's a static generator that'll knock a flyer's controls haywire. Good pilot can fly on visual, but the inboard computer won't work. They'll have to fire their weapons on manual."

"But you've actually got a shield around the castle?"

Pris handed out the last of the weapons and came over. "A weak one," she replied. "It's battery-powered, and will last about half an hour against the sort of weapons these flyers can carry. We'll try to drive them off before it goes." She handed Yar and Data each a phaser rifle of heavy design. "If the outer defenses work, you don't have to get involved. But if they fail, and some of Nalavia's flyers get through the shield, you'd better be prepared to defend your own lives!"

Chapter Ten

Lieutenant Commander Data saw that Pris Shenkley was correct. "Where do you need us?" he asked.

"Join Dare on the upper ramparts," she replied. "Those guns will bring down a standard military flyer—provided it doesn't get you first."

"Is the instrument scrambling in effect everywhere inside the outer defenses?" Tasha asked.

"Yes. Our own computer's shielded, of course. Our anti-aircraft installations should take out most of the flyers—"

"Pris!" from Sdan.

They all turned to the viewscreen—which showed something that was definitely not a flyer zipping through the outer defenses. "Missile!" exclaimed Pris. "Launch counter-attack!"

"Launched and running," Sdan replied, as another point of light shot out of the chasm below the castle, met the incoming missile—seconds after the screen showed the explosion when they met, the castle rocked with the sound of the blast.

"Nalavia's fooled us," said Poet. "The best-laid plans—"

"You didn't consider the possibility of an attack?" Data interrupted.

"An attack, yes," said Pris. "But if she's using missiles,

she doesn't care if she kills everyone in the castle. That includes the investigating team from Starfleet!"

Aurora joined them. "Missiles! Nalavia's insane. How do we plot strategy against a madwoman?"

"But you *have* counter-weapons," Tasha pointed out.

"Certainly; we are prepared for all-out war. But we didn't expect that with you here," said Aurora. "We thought Nalavia would try to take you back, not kill you!"

"It's my message to the *Enterprise*," said Tasha. "Dare said it would pinpoint our location—but obviously, to send it so steadily we had to have your cooperation. Nalavia must think we've gone over to your side." Her knuckles went white as she clutched the weapon she carried. "Damn! We should have sent it once only—we might have sneaked that through."

"Too late to worry about it now," said Sdan. "Once that shield goes we'll be up to the armpits in Nalavia's troops." So the castle's force shield was not up to all-out assault.

"Has Nalavia communicated with you?" Data asked. "Has she made demands for surrender?"

Sdan hit the communications board. "Nothing. But— she's stopped jamming Starfleet frequencies. Sure—she needs all power to push voice communications to her own troops through *our* scrambling."

Tasha jumped at that. Leaning over Sdan, she quickly programmed in the Starfleet emergency frequency. The Vulcanoid made no attempt to prevent her.

"This is Lieutenant Tasha Yar, on Treva, to any Starfleet vessel. Lieutenant Commander Data and I are under attack, at these coordinates. Emergency priority—repeat, Starfleet investigating team under attack. Any Starfleet vessel, please respond!"

There was no answer—but it could take from minutes to hours for the message to reach the nearest Starfleet vessel to Treva.

There were more explosions as missiles met anti-missiles, and then a flash of white burnout lit the strategy room as one got through and took out the shield.

"We should go up to the ramparts," Data said. "They will need every hand."

"And if there's an answer from Starfleet, we won't get it now," said Tasha, tuning out the burst of static as jamming resumed on Starfleet channels.

Adin, Barb, and the Tellarites were on the ramparts already, armed with guns like those Pris had given Data and Tasha. The first of the flyers approached, guns blazing.

Anti-aircraft fire lit the twilight and the first few went down before reaching the final defenses.

Then one got through. Adin took aim—one quick burst, and it exploded in flame and fell into the chasm.

But more came, wave after wave, locating the guns in the chasm by the bursts of light, bombing and strafing them. Each wave brought more flyers closer to the castle.

The six on the ramparts lay on their stomachs, protected from anything approaching from below. They hoped to shoot down flyers before they could get above the castle.

A troop carrier suddenly emerged from a cloud of flyers, guns blasting outward as from its bottom armored troopers dropped onto the lower ramparts!

"We are outnumbered," Data said, although he never ceased firing, taking down two troopers even as he spoke.

"Not once the locals are mobilized!" Barb told him, disposing of three more with equal efficiency.

Adin tapped his badge. "Sound retreat! Make your way back inside till—"

"Dare!" Barb yelled.

Adin rolled onto his back just in time to put his shots next to Barb's in a silent antigrav flyer that had circled while they were busy with the troop carrier. It sailed in over them, weapons blasting.

All six guns fired at the looming shadow—it spit sparks, but kept coming!

"Run!" Barb shouted.

They had destroyed the craft's steering controls.

Data could see the panicked face of the pilot through the windscreen as the flyer sailed out of control, on a collision course with the castle ramparts!

The Tellarites scrambled for the narrow stairs. Data reached for Tasha, who did not argue, but let him toss her after them, executing a perfect running landing at the top of the stairwell.

Data turned back just as Adin dropped his gun and grasped Barb around the waist, hauling her bodily out of the line of fire of the craft's port gunner, still firing impassively on his way to death.

Beneath the sound of those guns, though—

Data whirled, firing at another flyer on a strafing run at the three people left on the ramparts!

He jumped aside then, turning in midair, and dived for the other two in a flying tackle, to knock them out of the line of death patterning across the rooftop.

Hitting Adin with his full weight, he knocked the breath from the man—but there was no time for finesse. Adin's fall took Barb down. She rolled and came up shooting—

As the crippled flyer hit, behind her.

The world exploded. Data heaved the half-conscious Adin toward the stairs and turned for Barb—

She was propelled into his arms, her life's blood splattering him as debris from the flyer tore her to shreds.

The ramparts were collapsing as the dead flyer settled.

Data turned, found Adin struggling to his knees, Tasha climbing out of the stairwell to help him.

"Tasha! Get back!" Data shouted, letting Barb's body fall and grasping Adin by the arm as he ran for the stairs, forcing the man to turn with him. He shoved him toward Tasha, who hauled him by the other arm as the three of them fled down the narrow, winding stairs, the noise of the exploding flyer pursuing them.

The stairs shook. Dust and debris poured down on them. The two humans were coughing and choking by the time they emerged into a stone corridor. Tuuk and Gerva were waiting. "Where's Barb?" asked Gerva.

"Dead," said Tasha. "Hurry—the roof's collapsing!"

The retreat signal ringing in their ears, they found more stairs leading down—with five of Nalavia's armored troopers at the bottom. Only the Tellarites were armed, but they needed no help. Weapons designed to pierce a flyer's hull sliced as easily through the troopers' armor as through bread. They also, incidentally, destroyed a heavy wooden table behind the troopers and made a rather large hole in the wall. Fortunately, no structural supports were harmed.

Data and Tasha followed the Tellarites, for the Starfleet personnel did not know the designated retreat area for Rikan's castle. Darryl Adin said nothing, merely moved with Tasha, leaving Data to bring up the rear.

In the strategy room, though, Adin went straight to the viewscreen, where Aurora was studying the schematic. "Report," he said.

Pris came in from another direction, took one look at Data, and blanched. "You're hurt!"

He looked down, and saw the green-gold of his uniform stained with the burgundy of human blood. "No," he said, and remembered that Adin's people were at least as close to one another as the *Enterprise* bridge crew. "I am sorry—it is Barb's blood. She was killed on the ramparts."

Adin turned from the screen. "So should I have been, but for you, Data." He added, "Barb died fighting; she would have asked no more. Now, let's make certain she didn't die in vain. Where's Rikan?"

"Here," came the warlord's voice. Like the rest of them, he had been caught dressing for dinner. He wore an elegant lace-trimmed shirt and perfectly-cut trousers, but no tunic or jacket. One shoulder of his shirt was torn, drops of blood spattered its pristine whiteness, and a bruise darkened the warlord's cheek. But, like Data, he was marked with the blood of somebody else. The knife thrust through his belt, wiped off but not properly cleaned of clinging stains, testified to how he had come by it.

"Jevsithian?" Adin asked.

"I am here." The seer was seated in a far corner, untouched by the activity.

"Poet?"

"Bloody, but unbowed." The man was seated on the edge of a back table, cleaning his glasses while someone treated a cut on his forehead.

His remaining people and their charge accounted for, Adin requested Rikan to check his people, and turned back to the viewscreen.

Suddenly Sdan said, "Here they come!"

Everyone surged toward the viewscreens as the schematic of the castle shrank to include the surrounding countryside.

From three directions, Rikan's people were on the move, on foot, in ground vehicles, and in flyers. They might live in the country, but these were no primitive farmers armed with pitchforks and pruning hooks. Soft glows indicated the power packs of phasers, disruptors, percussion guns.

"Where did they get all those weapons?" Tasha asked.

"It's rather that they managed to keep them," Rikan replied. "Nalavia attempted to disarm Treva's citizenry, but the country folk would have none of it. The reason for their delay is that to keep her troops from finding them they have kept their weapons disassembled, the parts separate and mingled with tools and machinery."

"Your idea, Dare?" Tasha asked.

"Not that one," Adin replied. "One of the reasons I was willing to take this job is that these people are ready to fight their own battles—all they need is some expert guidance."

"Not that we can give them much at this moment," said Aurora. Data heard the frustration in her voice.

"We can give them leadership," said Rikan, and started for the door.

"Where do you think you're going?" Adin demanded. "You hired us to protect you."

The warlord stopped, turned, and looked down at the man from his imposing height. "No, sir, I did not. I hired you to help us fight Nalavia." Rikan might be old, but he had lost none of his noble bearing. "A Trevan warlord does not hide while other people fight his battles."

"And if Nalavia succeeds in killing you—who will be the rallying point for those who oppose her?" Adin threw back at him.

"Not a coward, you may be certain," Rikan replied with dignity.

"Rikan is right," Jevsithian suddenly spoke up. "He is the

213

last of the warlords—and his crest will be adopted as the sign of Treva's true freedom."

Rikan's man, Trell, turned on the seer. "What are you saying? That my lord will win? Or that he will be made a martyr?"

But the Grokarian replied only, "I see what I see: Rikan's crest as the emblem of freedom, side by side with the sign of the Silver Paladin."

Rikan put a hand on Trell's shoulder. "I must lead my people. Trell, if I die, it is my time. I fought in my youth on the field of battle, but in recent years only in the halls of politics. This is my last battle—I know it in my blood!"

Rikan went to arm himself, as Sdan reported, "The rebel flyers are engaging Nalavia's—and her infantry are being diverted to fight Rikan's ground troops. They're pulling away from the castle—now's the time to reclaim it!"

So Adin's gang, Data, Tasha, and Rikan's personnel began working their way up through the castle, clearing out Nalavia's soldiers. Someone had adjusted Tasha's combadge to the frequencies Adin used. Data stopped and adjusted his own, so that he was able to follow more of the battle than what was happening in his own vicinity.

Sdan left communications to Aurora, and joined in the fight to reclaim the castle. It was slow work, even with the aid of the security system, for once they had spread out it was necessary to check just *who* a life form reading was before attacking, lest they end up fighting themselves.

But finally the castle was secure. One tower and part of the upper floor were in ruins where the antigrav flyer had hit, but most of the huge old structure was still standing in the first faint gray of dawn.

Forty-three of Nalavia's troops had managed to enter the castle. Sixteen of them were now dead—one by Rikan's dagger at the opening of the fray—and the rest imprisoned in the kind of cells Data had suspected had to be here: ancient rooms dug out of the solid rock of the cliff, but now protected with force fields that would, indeed, hold even an android prisoner.

Barb was the only casualty among Adin's gang, but seven of Rikan's people had died fighting, and a number of others were too badly injured to continue,

Everyone else, though, gathered in the courtyard as daylight brightened and Rikan prepared to go into battle.

The warlord was resplendent in tough but lightweight body armor, carrying the helmet that bore his crest. His people cheered as he entered his waiting flyer—a vehicle also decorated with the symbols of his ancient lineage. There would be no doubt as to who was in that well-armed flyer . . . either to Rikan's people, or to Nalavia's.

The battle was on the other side of the chasm now, flyers and ground troops alike engaged in a struggle to the death.

But how could Rikan and Adin hope to win, Data wondered. Nalavia could throw fresh troops at them long after their own were exhausted.

Nothing he had seen in Adin's armory was the kind of weapon that could destroy a city—not that such weapons were ever supposed to be in private hands, but he had no doubt at all that only moral scruples kept this strange band of mercenaries from building them.

So there was no way to defeat Nalavia by numbers; it had to be done with skill, cleverness, and the desperation of Rikan's people fighting for their lives, homes, and families.

When Rikan had gone, Adin and Poet took one small, sleek fighting flyer, the Tellarites another, Sdan and Pris a third, and sailed off to escort him. Data turned to Tasha, who stood watching them leave with a look of yearning.

Of course—while she espoused Starfleet's teaching that to be forced to fight was in itself a defeat, once battle was engaged it called to her blood. Data looked after the flyers sailing toward the battlefront. "There are no more vehicles."

"There's our shuttle," said Tasha.

"It is not designed for fighting," he reminded her. The craft was unarmed, and because it was built for deep-space voyaging one could not open the ports to shoot conventional weapons.

But then Data remembered, "There is the flyer I stole to get here. It is probably still where I hid it."

Tasha looked at him in amused surprise. "You *stole* a flyer?"

"It was too far to walk," he said honestly, and was once more puzzled when something he said in all seriousness caused a human to break into laughter.

But Tasha gave him no time to ponder the vagaries of humor. "Let's go find it!" she said, but she ran back toward the castle instead of the road.

"Where are you—?"

"Weapons!"

The light phaser rifles they had been issued for searching the castle were indeed inappropriate for midair combat.

But the heavy-duty guns were just inside, cleaned and reloaded after the night's activity. They each took one, and extra charges. No one questioned them as they set off on foot down the road.

Data could not ask Tasha to climb down the cliffside the way he had come up, so they had a long journey to the hidden flyer. It was almost two hours later that they finally soared across the chasm, toward a battle that showed no signs of slacking.

Tasha Yar let Data do the piloting, trusting his android senses to keep them from hitting trees, hills, or other flyers as they swung beneath one of the military craft so she could get off a shot at its vulnerable thrusters.

She took out the left one, and the flyer spun wildly.

"Got 'em!" she exclaimed as Data took them up and away from the crash.

They whipped over the top of a slow troop carrier, and pulled up beside a sleek fighter, Data somehow holding the clumsy civilian craft in tandem while Yar took out both the startled pilot and gunner.

As they sailed away, g-force pressing her into her seat, Yar laughed with glee. "Data—you were born for this! The only man I ever want piloting me in a dogfight."

"Inquiry: 'dogfight'?"

"One-on-one air battle—I never thought I'd see it outside simulator training! Look! There's Rikan—get around to starboard—take out the flyers homing in on him!"

"Tasha—are you all right?" Data asked.

"Of course I'm all right. We're doing great! Let's get that big one over there—I don't like those torpedo ports."

"Aim at the thrusters or rudders, please," said the android. "There is no need to take lives if—"

"Dammit, Data, they were shooting at *us!*" Yar told him, annoyed at his lack of enthusiasm. It was too long since she had been in action, and the fact that Nalavia's forces had attacked first made theirs a defensive action. So Starfleet taught that it was a defeat to have to fight at all—well, they had *tried* to let the Trevans decide for themselves. It wasn't her fault that Nalavia had launched her attack before the drug worked its way out of her people's systems.

The large flyer was aiming a rocket bomb at Rikan's craft—if it hit, it would be the end of the warlord.

Two of Dare's sleek fighters were moving to intercept— Yar could not see if one of them held the Silver Paladin himself.

She and Data swung around to starboard, and a yell of triumph rose in Yar's throat as under Data's inhuman skill they maneuvered as neatly as any craft built for fighting.

The flyer had no inertial control; Yar was thrown against her harness as they rose and whirled, increasing her exhilaration. It was a long time since she had felt such an adrenalin high. She blasted at the craft attempting to reach Rikan's flagship.

Rikan was firing too, as were Dare's flyers, darting about and keeping the gunners too busy to dog Rikan's movements. The warlord's pilot was good, Yar noted peripherally, changing course often to avoid presenting a target.

The radio was open, but it was such a jumble that Yar paid it little attention until slowly a wave of excited exclamations began piercing the tight-voiced orders. "They're retreating!"

Who was retreating?

The thought was lost in a blast of rocket fire that came close to taking out their windscreen.

Data banked sharply in a groan of protesting metal, and they ducked a rocket sizzling from a different craft.

The radio squawked, "Ground troops pulling out!"

"We've got 'em running!"

But Yar's attention was on the second heavily-armed flyer trying to beat the small fighter craft off its sister ship so the two could go after Rikan.

"Rikan—pull back!" Dare's voice.

Data whipped around and straight back into the confrontation, but—

"We are losing rudder control," he said.

At the same moment one of the heavy flyers got a rocket off toward Rikan—homing right on target!

Yar and Data were close enough to see the thrusters blast as the pilot tried to maneuver out of its path, but the flagship did not have the speed of one of the little craft.

The rocket caught the flagship portside, ripping a hole in the fuselage and setting it spinning in a downward spiral.

"Rikan's hit!" came Poet's voice on the radio.

Instantly, aircraft converged and a free-for-all erupted, Nalavia's flyers seeking to deal the death blow, Rikan's trying to protect the falling craft.

"Tasha," Data said, his voice loud enough to carry over the noise of battle but unaffected by tension, "I have overstressed this craft—two minutes to systems failure."

"Follow Rikan down!" she instructed, then punched the radio. "This is Yar. Data and I will follow Rikan and protect him on the ground. Our craft is damaged."

"Tasha?!" Dare's voice.

"Yes. We're not hurt."

Data fought the controls as their flyer bucked and yawed, but somehow he kept in sight of the spinning flagship, which finally hit ground, wobbled up onto its side, and crunched through a stand of trees to come to a shuddering halt. He aimed for the path it had cleared, and with sheer android strength held them on course as he set down, hard but safe.

They untangled themselves from their harness, grabbed their weapons, and ran for the flagship.

A military flyer sailed down on a strafing run.

Yar and Data dropped and fired—one of their shots must have hit the power generator, for the flyer exploded, showering them with fiery debris.

Data threw himself over Yar.

A flaming piece struck the android's back, pushing his full weight down onto Yar. The way he moved, she forgot how heavy he was until times like now, when she thought her ribs would break—and might have, except that he scrambled up at once, throwing the debris aside.

His uniform was on fire!

"Roll!" Yar told him before he had realized it himself.

He didn't question her—must have felt the continuing heat by then—and in seconds the fire was out.

Yar touched him. The material was scorched but, "It did not harm my skin," he said.

"You won't object if I check for myself later?"

"No. But now we must get to Rikan."

Above them, the air battle continued. Yar let Data help her over the broken trees. Data, Worf, Vulcans she worked with—their physical strength was so much greater than hers that objections to such aid were absurd. Her human male colleagues had learned, though, not to offer unless she asked.

By the time they reached the downed flagship, two of its occupants had crawled out—neither one the warlord.

"Where's Rikan?" Yar asked.

"Inside," said one of the men. "He is injured, but not mortally. Trell can care for him."

"I'll go in," she said.

The craft had landed on its side, one door inaccessible, the other now on top. Yar climbed up slippery aerodynamic planes not meant to be walked on, and slid into the tip-tilted cabin.

The lighting worked, but the control console was buckled inward and dead.

Rikan lay on what had been the side of the ship but was now floor, Trell bending over him.

"Rikan?" Yar asked. "How badly are you hurt?"

His helmet had been removed, and his companion was easing the armor away from his left leg.

Although he was pale, the warlord essayed a smile. "Natasha. It is nothing, a broken leg. In a long life, how many broken bones does a warrior suffer? It will heal."

Trell cut away Rikan's trouser leg. Yar saw no blood. It would be difficult to get him out of here, though.

Shots erupted outside. The shadow of another attacker sailed over them.

Yar turned, hitting her combadge. "Data?"

"A small flyer. I do not think it will come back against four guns—but there will be others."

"We must get Rikan away from the ship," she said. "It's too easy a target."

"I will help you."

It took little effort for Data to get into the flyer, but he saw the problem immediately. "I can carry you out, sir," he said to Rikan, "but not without risk of compounding that fracture. The break appears clean. I am programmed with all standard first aid techniques, and I have the strength to set it, but the pain—"

"I can stand the pain. Do it, Data, and then you can splint it by strapping the armor tight."

Trell and Tasha held the old man's shoulders. There was no way to ease his pain, but at least Data could make it quick. Rikan groaned and broke into cold sweat, but then lay panting. The unnatural bulge was gone, the leg in normal alignment. "Good job, Data," Tasha said.

Trell and Data then put the armor back around the injured leg, strapping it with webbing from the seat restraints.

Rikan was so much taller than Data that the android could not carry the old man without his injured leg dangling painfully. Trell and Tasha helped to support it as they struggled to lift the warlord toward the door overhead.

Tasha's combadge chirped, and she tapped it. "What's going on down there?" came Adin's voice.

"Rikan is injured. We're trying to get him out," she replied.

"I'll have one of the larger flyers come down. We'll escort it in."

Leaving communication open, they heard angry exclamations as more of Nalavia's flyers converged on Rikan's downed flagship, coming in for the kill. But Rikan's people were also there to protect their fallen leader. Battle raged above them.

Data said, "I will have to climb out, and then lift Rikan. Can you hold him?"

Trell nodded, and he and Tasha supported the warlord while Data got above them, balanced carefully on the slippery deck, then reached down and took the warlord under the arms to lift him out and lay him gently on the hull. Then he turned to give Trell a hand while Tasha scrambled out on her own.

Another flyer swooped toward them—Data slid Rikan under the slight protection of the open door while Tasha jumped down, picked up the discarded guns, and tossed one to Data. She blasted at the flyer—but its return fire chopped the ground in a straight line toward her!

One of Adin's small craft was right behind, peppering the determined attacker. Trailing smoke, still it kept to its course, blasting away at the small group on the flagship.

Tasha leaped up onto the flagship, and Data grasped her hand to haul her into what shelter there was, while he put more shots into the oncoming kamikaze. There was no stopping it—even if all systems were out, inertia would carry it straight over the flagship.

"Tasha! Take cover!" came Adin's voice over both their combadges—but it was not in Tasha to abandon the injured man she was protecting. She and Data remained between Rikan and the oncoming craft, Trell pulling a sidearm and joining them.

The door sheltered them for a few seconds, shots thudding into it without penetrating. Then the flyer was beyond it. The tail gunner saw them, fired—

Trell slumped, knocking Tasha into Data.

Tasha gave a yelp as her feet were knocked out from under her on the slippery hull. Data caught her before she fell over the edge.

The flyer continued on its helpless course and crashed into the trees with a terrific explosion.

"Tasha? Tasha—I'm coming to help!" came Adin's voice.

His flyer made a difficult landing on a section of the plowed-down trees, even as Tasha was saying, "I'm all right. It's Trell."

There were no flyers coming at them just then, so Data turned . . . and saw that Trell had fallen across Rikan's chest. The old man felt for a pulse at Trell's throat, but the gouts of blood where projectiles had emerged from the servant's back told clearly that there could be none. Gently, Data lifted the body away.

Rikan looked up at him, not a man to cry, but his voice was hoarse as he said, "Trell was my man for twenty years, and his father before him. Good men, loyal and true. And now I have outlived them both."

By this time Adin and Poet were climbing up onto the flagship. For once, Poet had no handy quotation; perhaps he recognized that all cliches about death were meaningless in the face of the thing itself.

"Dare!" Sdan's voice on their combadges.

"We're all right. Get a flyer down here that's capable of carrying an injured man."

"One of Rikan's is trying to set down—bad terrain there."

"Just do it!"

The larger flyer came in sight, escorted by the neat little fighter craft. It circled first, but finally managed to put down not far from where Data and Tasha had landed. Data, Adin, and Poet eased Rikan down from the flagship and began the tortuous journey over the broken trees, trying not to jolt the old man.

Tasha and Rikan's two remaining men escorted them, guns at the ready, but—

"What's going on?" Tasha asked suspiciously. "Why aren't more flyers coming after us?"

Adin hit his combadge. "Gerva, Tuuk, report! What's happening?"

Even as he spoke, several military craft sailed high above them, moving at top speed toward the capital city.

"Nalavia's called them in!" came Gerva's voice. "First the ground troops, now the flyers."

"Dare!" said Tasha excitedly. "That means she's got troubles at home. Our plan worked—the hypnotic drug's worn off, and her own people are rebelling!"

Adin grinned. "That must be it. Rikan—we're going to win!"

The warlord grinned in return. "I think you're right, Adrian. Please get me home so—"

"Commander Data! Lieutenant Yar!"

The voice over their combadges was totally familiar, but totally unexpected: that of Jean-Luc Picard.

"We are here, Captain, safe and well," Data replied. "Where are you, Sir?"

"In standard orbit. Prepare to beam up."

"We have one of Treva's leaders, injured," Tasha said. "It's not serious, but he could be healed much more quickly in sickbay than here."

"I accept your judgment, Lieutenant. Transporter—" he turned them over to the operator.

"Three to beam up," said Tasha. "These co—"

"*Four* to beam up," Data corrected.

Tasha looked at him, puzzled, and then suddenly went so pale he thought she might pass out.

But Tasha Yar was not a woman to faint. "Oh, my God," she murmured, staring at Adin, whose face lost all expression.

"Is that three or four to beam up?" the transporter operator wanted to know.

"Just one moment," said Data. He watched Tasha watching Adin . . . and he waited. She was Chief Security Officer; the duty was hers. But she had to know that if she did not perform it, Data would. Would she force him to—?

Swallowing hard, Tasha turned the gun she still carried on Adin.

Poet made a move for his sidearm, but Adin waved him back.

He continued to look calmly into Tasha's eyes. Data made no claims to intuition, but he was virtually certain Adin expected her to let him go.

But, although her lips were bloodless, while two spots of fever glowed in her cheeks, Tasha choked out the words: "Darryl Adin, by my authority as an officer of Starfleet Security, I arrest you on the charges of unlawful flight to avoid incarceration, for treason, and for murder."

Chapter Eleven

TOO NUMB even to curse fate, Tasha Yar trained her weapon on the man she loved. The familiar sensation of the transporter took them, and they materialized in the same position aboard ship.

Dr. Crusher, just entering the transporter room, stopped dead at the tableau.

Yar didn't move. Dare remained expressionless as she ordered, "Security team to transporter room, on the double. We have a dangerous fugitive in custody."

Dr. Crusher said to the medics who had followed her in, "Get the patient," and they moved carefully around Yar and her prisoner to lift Rikan onto a gurney. Out of the corner of her eye Yar saw Data bend to help, and Crusher stare at the android's bloodstained, disheveled appearance.

"I am quite all right, Doctor," Data assured her.

"Let me be the judge of that. I'm ordering you to sickbay, too."

Then they were gone—the doors hardly shut behind them before they whooshed open again to admit Worf and one of the other Security personnel, Lieutenant Carl Anderson.

Never taking her eyes or her gun off Dare, Yar said, "This is Darryl Adin, a fugitive convicted of murder and treason. I know him to be extremely dangerous."

225

Worf said, "We can handle him," in his booming voice. He and Anderson stepped forward, phasers drawn. Dare seemed suddenly small and vulnerable before the towering Klingon.

"Take him to the brig," Yar instructed. Then, remembering a recent lapse of security with renegade Klingons, she added, "He is probably carrying concealed weapons—and he is Starfleet Security trained." Which meant he had the ability to turn almost anything into a weapon.

For the first time, Dare let an expression cross his features: his lips curled back in a snarl. He was again that bitter and dangerous man she had met only days ago on Treva.

When Worf and Anderson had escorted the prisoner out, Yar felt her knees weaken. She wanted nothing more than to sit down on the edge of the transporter platform and cry.

But that was not the behavior of a Starfleet officer. She squared her shoulders, held her head high, and proceeded to the bridge to report to the Captain.

Lieutenant Commander Data was released from sickbay as soon as the medics checked him over. In the antiseptic atmosphere, he became conscious of being filthy and reeking—but a few seconds in the sickbay's sonic shower put both himself and his uniform to rights, except for the scorch mark on the back. He decided it was more important to report to Captain Picard than go to his quarters to change.

Tasha had made the same decision; she was with Picard and Riker in the Captain's ready room, still wearing the civilian clothes she had beamed up in.

Until that moment Data had avoided wondering if Tasha were angry at him. She did not act angry. Rather she was pale and slightly stiff. Data had seen humans in that state before; it meant they were weakened by illness, shock, or injury, but determined to carry on.

He knew he would never understand the emotional blow Tasha had taken in being forced to arrest the man she loved, but her reaction gave him another clue to add to his study of human behavior.

A clue he wished he didn't have.

On the one hand, he admired Tasha for doing her duty. On the other, although it was illogical for her to blame him for her pain, he feared she would.

Data added his report to Tasha's. When they reached this morning's battle, and the unexpected arrival of the *Enterprise*, he concluded, "We assumed Nalavia withdrew her forces because she needed them to control the people in the cities—that the suggestibility drug had worn off."

"I think you're right," said Riker. "There seems to be a civil war going on down there. You were not sent to Treva to start a war, but to prevent one."

Tasha said nothing. Data considered before he spoke. "Starfleet's aid was requested by the apparent legitimate government. However, we found that due process had been subverted. Nalavia ignores Treva's constitution, and enforces her power with acts of terrorism. I accessed the evidence from her own computer."

"So you took it upon yourselves to join the rebellion against her," said Picard.

Data opened his mouth to protest, and closed it again. From the moment Nalavia's troops attacked Rikan's castle, there was no denying he and Tasha had done exactly that. So he said simply, "Yes, sir."

"Lieutenant Yar?" asked the Captain.

"Yes, sir. Nalavia meant to use us as hostages to force you to destroy Rikan's stronghold."

"She must have known Starfleet would do no such thing," said Picard.

Tasha looked at Data, then back to Picard. "Suppose her plan had worked, sir. Suppose Dare—Adin—had not kidnapped me, Data not escaped. If she had imprisoned us and attempted to coerce you?"

"We would've done everything in our power to get you out," Riker answered without waiting for Picard's response.

"Everything?" asked Tasha.

Riker began, "You don't think we would abandon—"

"Just a moment," the Captain interrupted him. "Lieutenant, are you suggesting—?"

"I don't think Nalavia will be content with a single planet, especially not one with such a small population as Treva's. I think she's out to gain power here on the edge of the Federation—make other worlds hesitant to apply for Federation membership by making us look like hypocrites."

Data nodded in sudden comprehension. "Nalavia tried to arrange matters so that either way, she would win. If you had used the ship's weapons to destroy Rikan, or if you had attacked Nalavia to rescue us, either could be interpreted as a violation of the Prime Directive."

"But she didn't count on Data's ability to access her computer, or his escape," said Tasha. "And she certainly could not have expected her enemies to kidnap me."

"Had that not happened," Data agreed, "it would have taken me longer to become suspicious. Since I thought that it was Nalavia keeping Tasha and me apart, I felt no compunction about breaching her security. It was my duty toward a colleague in jeopardy."

"All that will be included in the final report," Picard said. "You operated under standard procedures . . . until you became involved in the fighting."

"We were under attack, Captain," said Tasha.

"That is true," Data agreed. "Nalavia attacked Rikan because she knew we were in his castle."

"We knew too much," said Tasha. "I am certain she meant us to be casualties of an insurrection."

"Mmm," said Picard, rubbing his chin. "You are probably correct, but how do we prove it? A piece is missing from the puzzle of Treva. And until we find it, I intend to stay in orbit here."

"Why did you come here?" asked Tasha. "We sent a distress signal, but what was the *Enterprise* doing in this vicinity?"

Riker laughed. "When we got your earlier message, repeating on a non-Starfleet frequency, we didn't know what to think."

"Wesley thought it was code, but he couldn't break it," said Picard. "Worf thought it was sent by someone else to make us think you were safe when you were really in trouble, and Deanna . . . she just had a bad feeling about it." He shrugged. "I was outnumbered. Since it turned out that you really were in trouble, I was right to rely on the suspicions of my bridge crew."

"What are you going to do now, Captain?" asked Tasha.

"Data," said Picard, "I want you to look at the reports of all recorded activity in this sector for . . . how long has Nalavia been in power?"

"Five Trevan years, sir."

"Very well—for that time plus several years before. Look for anything odd."

". . . odd, sir?"

Picard sighed. "Data, I don't know exactly what to tell you to look for. An unexpected pattern—or else something that doesn't fit an expected one. It's a hunch. You're the only one who can help me play it."

Confused again over human feelings, Data nonetheless settled himself at the computer terminal in his quarters and began the search. It took an hour.

When Data called the Captain to report, Picard said, "Meet me in my ready room."

Riker was there again, and in moments Tasha joined them. She had said nothing directly to Data since they had beamed up from Treva, and she said nothing now. She was back in uniform, self-possessed, but still pale.

"Report, Mr. Data," Picard instructed when they were all assembled.

"What I have found in this sector over the past ten years is a steadily increasing number of references to Orions."

Tasha's eyes widened. "Orions? Why Orions?"

"I do not know," Data replied. "I found large banking transactions involving conversion of Orion currency; Orion trading vessels docking at ports in nearby systems; Orion communications and data management technology spreading across a number of worlds in this sector. There is your unexpected pattern, Captain. As to exceptions to the expected pattern, despite widespread Orion activity, I did *not* find any mention of slave trading."

"Interesting," said Picard. "The one thing that would have brought the Federation in. Anything else?"

"Yes, sir. In the center of all this Orion activity lies Treva—with not so much as the purchase of a flyer or a weapon from the Orions."

Riker frowned. "From what you've told us, Nalavia doesn't seem the type to care who she deals with. If everyone else in this sector is trading with the Orions, why isn't she?"

Suddenly Tasha said, "Captain! Do you remember how you chose the away team for this mission? A woman and an android?"

A slight smile tugged at Picard's mouth. "So you figured that out, did you?"

Riker, attempting to conceal annoyance, asked, "Figured what out?"

Data replied, "The Captain sent an away team who are immune to Nalavia's sensuality."

Riker responded with his congratulatory smile. "Of course. Very appropriate, Captain."

Picard began, "But what has Nalavia's sensuality to do with—?" Then the proverbial "light dawned." "Tasha— you think Nalavia is actually an Orion?"

Data frowned, accessing the information he had drawn from the Trevan President's computer. "Nalavia's records indicate that she was born on Treva . . . on a farm in a remote area almost at the limit of their developed territory. Nine years ago she was elected to the Legislative Council, where she soon became a popular leader, and eventually was elected President."

"Those early records," said Picard. "Could they be faked?"

Data considered. "There is no way to tell from the information in my memory banks. However, I can access the palace computer via the ship's computer, as I put a frequency code and recognition signal into its programming so I could transfer its data without having to remain physically in the computer room. There was . . . the danger of being caught," he explained at Picard's stare.

"You said you accessed the computer. You did not say you sneaked about the Presidential palace—"

"Yes, Captain," replied Data, "I . . . 'snooped, sneaked, proceeded by stealth.' Most intriguing. It appears I was wrong when I said it was a form of human behavior I was not designed to emulate. When the occasion required, I discovered that I can emulate it extremely well."

"But if you already have all the information from Nalavia's computer in your memory banks," asked Riker, "what more is there?"

"I have a *copy* of the data. There is no way to tell from it whether any of that information has been changed. But that computer is more than nine years old, and uses a long-outdated system of data storage. It is physical, not virtual memory, and thus will contain all original data, even if it has been altered and written over. If Nalavia's records are falsified, I will be able to trace it."

Picard said, "Mr. Data, you had an opportunity to observe Nalavia closely. Do you think she could be an Orion?"

"Yes, sir," he replied honestly. "There are certainly Orions operating in this sector, but by refraining from slave trading they avoid attracting the Federation's attention. It is probable that Nalavia is not Trevan. Orions have been surgically altered before to pass as other species, in order to infiltrate the Federation. Nalavia is trying to prevent Treva from joining the Federation, while the Orions establish a foothold in this sector. The pattern fits . . . and explains both Nalavia's sensuality and the artificial appearance of her eyes. Even with the natural green of her skin bleached out, the vivid blue eyes of Orion females might give rise to suspicion. But coloring them makes them appear unnatural."

"Yes," said Tasha. "Data is right. I'm sure Nalavia is an Orion."

Data added, "She wanted no one on Treva—or Federation visitors—to find a clue to her origins. Hence no trade with the Orions, and no upgrading of equipment like the palace computer, which appears to be a very old Ferengi model."

"If Nalavia is Orion," said Picard, "we can certainly act to prevent a planet which has applied for Federation membership from being taken over by enemies of the Federation! Mr. Data, I want that evidence. Use the terminal here, and get on with it. We have a war to stop!"

"Yes, sir," Data replied, sitting down at the Captain's terminal as the others left the ready room.

But Tasha lingered after Picard and Riker had gone out to the bridge. "Data?" she said softly.

He looked up.

"I should have said it earlier. I . . . want to thank you," she said.

"Thank me?"

"For making me arrest Dare. You were right. It was my duty, not yours, although I know you'd have done it if I hadn't."

"You are—" He stopped the automatic response midstream. "No. You are not welcome to the pain I caused you. Tasha, I hope I never again have to cause a friend such pain, but I am glad you understand I had no choice."

"I understand," she replied, and left him.

Data found the falsified entries easily: inserting a birth record required rearranging the file on all births that day; falsifying school records meant shifting names to insert Nalavia's. Once Data retrieved the original files, which showed no trace of Nalavia's existence, Starfleet Command quickly gave the go-ahead for interruption of all Trevan broadcasts with the information. From that point on, events on Treva became a mere "cleanup operation."

At first people didn't want to believe they had elected an alien to their highest office, but as they were thinking for themselves now, it didn't take long for them to accept that the reason for Nalavia's increasing cruelty could be that she was not one of them. She surrendered to Starfleet when

Treva's people stormed the Presidential palace. In sickbay, her identity as an Orion was quickly verified.

It appeared, once the storm had settled, that the Trevans were ready to appoint Rikan their new President—even make him king—but he insisted that they follow the constitution and set up elections. He left the *Enterprise* glowing with health and happiness, and Data was sure he would indeed be elected President—and serve Treva well as it completed its application for Federation membership.

Data and Tasha beamed down with Rikan to his castle, where he accepted the congratulations of his people before the waiting media. He did not speak long, but ended by saying, "I could not have held out against Nalavia alone. Treva owes its freedom not only to Starfleet, but to the man known as the Silver Paladin. He will be remembered and honored always on our planet."

Data heard Tasha's soft gasp, saw her stiffen and fight back tears. He also saw Adin's people watching them from one side of the courtyard, silently accusing. When the interview was over, Rikan tried to lead Data and Tasha over to them, but the seven turned their backs as one, and walked away.

"Let them go," said Tasha. "I don't expect them to forgive me. I can't forgive myself."

"I have always thought Adrian incapable of the charges laid against him." Rikan said.

"I'm sure of it," Tasha replied. "But there is no way to prove it, no way at all."

"Not even with the help of your very clever and talented friends?" asked Rikan, looking at Data.

Data started to protest, but thought better of it. It was better to say nothing, as there was nothing he could do for Darryl Adin.

The strange thing was, despite all logic that said Adin had been proved guilty beyond any doubt, reasonable or unreasonable, he also had what he could only describe as a . . . feeling . . . that the man was innocent.

On that uncomfortable note, they bade farewell to Rikan, and beamed back to the *Enterprise*.

Data went back to the bridge, but all during his shift, with nothing to do but routine checks, his primary consciousness kept focusing on the two prisoners in the *Enterprise* brig. They were now headed to Starbase 68, where both Nalavia and Darryl Adin would be handed over into Starfleet custody.

Nalavia would probably be confined in comfort if not luxury for a time, until the Orions arranged some kind of exchange—probably for Federation citizens taken on a slaving expedition. Of course he had no way of knowing what punishment might await the woman among her own people, since she had failed at her mission. He hoped it was severe.

Data was startled at the thought. Vindictiveness? So soon after jealousy? What was happening to him? In his wish to be human, he had never considered such emotions. Unlike anger, which he had often observed to give people strength to change their lives, these feelings had only negative value. He decided to delete them from his programming.

But . . . he could not.

They were entwined with too many other bits of memory; he could not delete his jealousy over Tasha's feelings for Darryl Adin without also removing parts of his respect and friendship for her, as well as numerous concrete facts about their mission to Treva. It was the same with his antipathy toward Nalavia.

He had no choice but to do what humans did with negative feelings: contain them, refuse to dwell on them, and most important, refuse to act on them.

Or . . . refuse to let them prevent him from acting.

Suddenly Data realized that he had been repressing one area of his programming ever since Rikan had suggested he might do something to prove Darryl Adin innocent. He didn't know if it could be done . . . but once he had acknowledged even the remote possibility, he knew he had to try.

Data didn't know why he thought such evidence existed. He had been over those records; there were no time/entry discrepancies. But then . . . an expert with such a computer would know how to avoid those. He would.

He was an android; he was not capable of intuition, or what Captain Picard called a "hunch." Yet despite all evidence to the contrary he was certain Adin could not have committed the crimes he was convicted of.

He accessed information about intuition and hunches. They were explained as the organic mind determining a pattern from various disconnected facts, some of which might not be consciously remembered.

But Data remembered everything; he could not be reacting to forgotten information.

Still . . . it was something like his anticipation, opinion, and gestalt programs. Consciously, he let his search function examine the data that formed his opinion that Adin was innocent. The man's actions. His activities as the Silver Paladin. His Starfleet record before the *Starbound* incident—

On his last mission before the training cruise of the *Starbound,* the defeat of the Orions at Conquiido had been led by Assistant Security Chief Darryl Adin of the U.S.S. *Seeker.* In recognition, he had been promoted to Commander, and sent to the Academy to update his training prior to posting aboard one of the larger starships.

When the *Starbound* was assigned to transport dilithium, how could the Orions miss the opportunity to steal such a treasure, and at the same time destroy the man who had dealt that hard and recent blow to their plans of conquest? The prosecution charged that the Orions had not missed it—that they had worked on Darryl Adin's greed to lure him into conspiring with them, and then let him "take the fall."

But what if they had *not* found such a weakness in his character? What if the tenuous evidence linking Adin to the Orions were forged? If the man were innocent, he must be set free.

Even if when he left the *Enterprise* he took Tasha with him.

The moment he was off duty, Data went straight to his quarters and instructed the ship's computer to link directly with the main computer at Starbase 36.

"That is not necessary for the files you are seeking," the female voice told him. "All data from those files is in the ship's computer."

"I must have access to the memory in which that data was originally stored."

"You are creating an unnecessary overload on ship's communications," the computer objected.

"Just do it," said Data. "That is an order."

As he expected, the memory of the main computer at Starbase 36 was a Standard Unlimited Virtual. What he had done with Nalavia's computer was impossible, for there was no physical storage to retain discarded information.

Yet . . . Data's own brain was a highly-advanced adaptation of the same concept, and he remembered every experience. Even given the instruction, "It never happened," he did not forget; he simply inserted a new command not to act on that information. He placed a similar safeguard on information requiring a security clearance, so that he would neither divulge it upon a routine request for information nor speak or act in such a way as to reveal that the secured information existed.

Data had used computers with unlimited virtual memory all his life, but never before questioned what happened to information deleted from them. Was it truly erased, or did it simply become inaccessible? There was supposed to be no way to retrieve it.

No human way.

But suppose he could access the memory of the Starbase 36 computer directly, using his own mind to manage the data? Intriguing! Whether he accomplished his goal or not, it would be a unique experience—

—and a potentially dangerous one. He was almost certain he could make the connection. But . . . would he be able to disconnect? Was his personal consciousness strong enough, differentiated enough from that of a sophisticated computer, to allow him to maintain his identity?

There was only one way to find out. Cautiously, Data tapped into the link the ship's computer had provided, trying to remain conscious of his own body seated at his terminal while his mind reached out—

The starbase computer had no personality, no self-awareness to object to his intrusion. He found he could impose his own order on the chaotic mass of information: just think about the stardates he wanted, and he had access to the comlink data, hotel registrations, everything. It all matched the evidence provided at Darryl Adin's court-martial.

But had it been changed, tampered with in any way?

As Data formulated the question, he . . . felt something. In its information processing mechanism, the computer's brain had similarities to his own—and he sensed familiar patterns associated with that particular set of data. Frightening patterns.

Frightening?

The starbase computer could not be frightened. It was Data's fear—a memory from his past.

Priam IV!

It was the most terrifying thing he had had to do in order to become a candidate for graduation from Starfleet Academy. All cadets had to pass the test, but there was no way to fool an android into believing the situation was real . . . except to alter his perceptions.

There had been no projections in a holodeck for Data, no Starfleet test personnel acting roles in his psychodrama. Rather, he had permitted, in fact aided, Starfleet's most skilled computer experts to block his awareness of where he truly was, and place the Priam IV scenario directly into his personal consciousness. His most vivid memories of the test did not stem from the scenario itself, although it had certainly been frustrating enough while he thought himself living it. No, the horrifying parts for Data had come before and after the test, when he felt his mental control taken from him, albeit with his permission and cooperation, and later, unexpectedly, when his consciousness was restored.

It had taken him days to reconcile the true and false

memories occupying the same space and time in his awareness. It was not only illogical, it was a flat impossibility, something the mind of a sentient android was not designed to accept. He knew *why* his mind contained the two sets of memories—himself lying still in a Starfleet laboratory while technicians monitored his body to be certain nothing malfunctioned, and himself on Priam IV coping with the Prime Directive in a no-win scenario. However, knowing why did not make it easier to live with the sense of paradox.

As it was the Priam IV scenario he was intended to remember, he finally put an access-denial command on his true condition during that time, and it stopped surfacing to disturb him. Still, like everything else he had ever experienced, the memories were available should he lift the prohibition.

What he felt in the Starbase 36 computer was similar: two conflicting sets of memories occupying the same space-time, one set resident, the other restrained by an access-denial command. The starbase computer had no consciousness to be disturbed by the paradox. It was also incapable of removing the command, even though it had created it when the operator who had changed the files "deleted" the originals.

Data tried various utilities, but whoever had done this piece of programming knew every method for covering his tracks. Not surprisingly, the android could not lift the prohibition by any means available to purely organic programmers. He would have to interface directly with the starbase computer's memory.

Determinedly, Data let his consciousness merge with the computer memory, and reached to access the hidden files. Paradox awakened fear, but he set it firmly aside, seeking, seeking—

The prohibition held. He was perceived as an outside force, like any user of the computer. What was deleted was not accessible to him.

Unless he could persuade the computer he was part of it.

He had begun this search for Tasha's sake, but now his own curiosity was aroused. He *knew* that the information had been tampered with. If he could just maintain his self-awareness, he should be able to access the hidden files and emerge unharmed. Letting go all but the most tenuous link with his body on board the *Enterprise,* Data became one with the non-sentient mass of—

Conflicting information!

Not merely the memories he was seeking, but everything ever entered or deleted from the Starbase 36 computer bombarded him. With no judgment to assert priorities, the files in the virtual memory free-associated in over-whelming abundance, overpowering Data's own memories, assaulting his consciousness! Drowning in paradox, he fought for control, struggled to impose the order of his self-awareness on the uncaring chaos dragging him toward annihilation.

Weak-kneed and fighting back tears, Tasha Yar approached the brig for the first time since she had forced Darryl Adin to beam aboard.

He was wearing a gold standard-issue coverall. The force field glowed across the front of his cell, and two armed guards stood alert before it.

Sound traveled perfectly well through the force field. At her footsteps, Dare looked up from where he was sitting on the platform that served as seat or bunk, then stood to face her, again completely expressionless.

Yar carried a bundle of clothing. She stopped, facing Dare, and said, "Guards, you are dismissed."

"We can move off so you can talk privately—" Anderson suggested.

"I *said* you are dismissed." she repeated firmly. The two men looked at one another, but turned and walked away.

Yar waited until they were around the curve in the corridor before she palmed the switch and the force field died.

Still Dare stared at her, neither moving nor speaking.

She stepped forward, holding out the bundle of clothes, the black jacket he had beamed up in on top, displaying the Silver Paladin combadge. "You are free, Dare," she said. "Here—you can call your friends. I'm sure they're following the *Enterprise,* even if they can't match our speed."

Finally he spoke. "Tasha." It was a harsh whisper. "What are you doing?"

The tears spilled even as she smiled. "I told you—you're free. Dare . . . you've been exonerated."

His mouth opened as he took a sharp, disbelieving breath. "What?"

"It's true! You were framed—the Orions set up the attack on *Starbound* to get that consignment of dilithium and discredit you at the same time. They altered the records in the Starbase 36 computer. You were never notified of the Security meeting, but they changed the records to show that you were there—the evidence of their tampering was in the computer, once Data dug it out."

"Data!"

"Yes," she explained. "No one else could have done it. No human could have gone into a modern Starbase computer and traced long-erased records, but Data got the idea after doing something similar with Nalavia's old computer to find out who she really was."

"Another bloody Orion," Dare snarled.

"Yes. But Dare—that's what made the connection for Data: the Orions you defeated at Conquiidor, then your supposed deal with them at Starbase 36. We all knew that made no sense, but only Data was able to prove it—at the risk of his life."

"What?" sharply.

"Geordi—Lieutenant LaForge—found him unconscious. Data doesn't black out, you know. I don't really understand—I don't think any of us can—but Data somehow connected himself with the Starbase 36 computer, and got inside its memory to locate the tampering. He almost couldn't get out again."

"Is he all right?" Dare asked, genuinely concerned.

"Yes. Apparently Geordi was able to call him back. They're good friends."

"I think your Mr. Data has a very large number of good friends, including me. But after all that, will Starfleet accept evidence that is really just his word?"

"They already have!" she told him gleefully. "Dare, there is no questioning evidence from Data. And besides, it's been corroborated. Captain Picard sent the information to Starfleet Command, they ordered an investigation of Starbase 36—and found the Orions' mole still in place. The owner of a club frequented by Starfleet personnel on shore leave."

"Another Orion?" Dare asked.

"Yes—altered to appear human. Not being Starfleet, he was not subject to medical examinations. But when the authorities set up a scan of civilians, he gave himself away by trying to run."

"A publican," said Dare. "Who knows what a clever spy could make of the babbling of drunken crewmen? But is it enough, Tasha? Even if I'm cleared of the original charges, there is still escaping from custody—"

"In light of circumstances, they've dropped those charges, since you didn't kill or injure anyone in your escape. And"—she grinned—"apparently embarrassed some highly experienced Security personnel."

"I had equal experience, and I was fighting for my life. Tasha—I find it difficult to believe there's a chance. Even with the evidence that I was set up at the starbase—what about the sabotage aboard the *Starbound?* I know I didn't do it, so who did?"

"It looks as if it was Nichols," said Yar.

"The Chief Engineer? But why, Tasha? He was ready to retire after an honorable career. Why would he do such a thing?" Dare asked.

"His records show he had no income besides his pension, and no plans for the rest of his life. He was retiring because he couldn't do his job anymore; no company would take him on with that recommendation. Dare, I don't fully understand, but Data uncovered communications between Nichols and the Orion agents. I really don't think he knew they were using him to set you up; he probably thought they just wanted the dilithium. He . . . he used the Starbase 36 computer to study businesses for sale. There is no way he could have afforded a business of his own on just his pension."

Dare nodded. "As Chief Engineer, Nichols had access to the entire ship; it would have been no trouble to install that circuit breaker." He shook his head. "I can't even feel anger at him. The Orions used him, and then they killed him. He was just a foolish man who was only ever good at one thing, and when he lost that he didn't know what to do with himself."

Yar smiled, relieved that Dare was not vengeful. "At least it's all over now."

"Not quite," said Dare. "I don't know if I can face a hearing—"

"You don't have to," she explained. "Captain Picard has good friends among the admiralty. Starfleet Command organized an emergency board of inquiry, and the results came not five minutes ago. You are a free man . . . and"— she turned the pile of clothing she carried over to reveal the garment on the bottom—"if you want it, you can be reinstated in Starfleet Security at the rank of commander."

He reached hesitantly as if to touch the green-gold and black of the uniform she offered. But then he put out both hands, took the entire pile of clothing from her, and tossed it onto the bunk. He pulled her into his arms, murmuring into her hair, "Thank you! Oh, God—thank you, Tasha!" And he kissed her. Only to break off to ask, "Why didn't you tell me all this was going on?"

"Because I didn't know. Data confided only in Captain Picard, and he contacted Starfleet Command." She sighed. "They didn't know if it would be enough to clear you, so they decided not to get my hopes up. And when Starfleet

Security arrested the spy . . . he said he was your contact. It was Data's evidence against his word—but in the end Starfleet believed Data. It's all over, Dare."

"Thanks to you," he said. Then his beautiful smile. "And Data. What does one do for an android who has just saved much more than one's life?"

"Your thanks will be sufficient," she assured him. Then she went to the pile of clothing and located his silver combadge. "I do think you should let your followers know at once, before they do something stupid. They followed us when we left Treva; we tracked them on the sensors until our speed left them behind. They must know we're headed for Starbase 68. Why don't you tell them it's only Nalavia we'll be dropping off there? I don't think they'll be much interested in mounting a prison break to rescue *her*."

"Tasha," Dare chided, "you can't think my gang would have tried to break me out of a Federation Rehabilitation Facility."

"Think it? I *know* it. And I wouldn't have been surprised if they'd succeeded. I'm just glad that now they won't have to."

She left him to make his call and change clothes, accepting his assurance that "I can still find the bridge of a starship."

But when he found it a short time later, not long after his non-standard communication had lighted a tell-tale on Yar's board, he was in his civilian clothes, not the uniform she had offered. He thanked Picard, and Data, then asked, "Can you arrange for me to wait in an unsecured area at Starbase 68? My people will pick me up there."

Picard frowned. "Of course, if that is what you want. But surely Tasha told you—"

"That Starfleet would take me back. Yes, she did, and I appreciate the gesture. But I have other obligations now. And . . . I'm afraid I've lost my taste for rules and regulations." He turned to Yar, who was gripping the edge of her console in the effort to hold back her disappointment. "Tasha, when you have the chance, we must talk."

"Go," said Picard. "But Mr. Adin," he warned as both Dare and Yar moved toward the turbolift, "understand that I have no intention of losing my Chief of Security."

Dare's smile was wolfish again, although not sinister this time. "That, I believe, is up to Tasha."

They went to Yar's quarters, where she learned that the Captain had guessed quite accurately what Dare would offer her. "We've always wanted to work together. I respect the fact that you must serve out your tour of duty. But then—" He put his hands on her shoulders, looking into her eyes and shaking his head with a smile. "What a pleasure it is just to know we can communicate! I will let you know where I go, and it's never difficult to follow the *Enterprise* with all the chatter amongst the spacelanes."

"You've known all along what I was doing?" she asked.

"Not always, but the occasional reference. Once you were aboard *Enterprise* it became easy. But I don't want you light-years away, Tasha. I want you at my side."

"Then why not accept Starfleet's offer? Dare, after admitting its mistake, Starfleet Command would probably give you any posting you wanted. You could serve here, aboard the *Enterprise!*"

"Where *you,* my little kitten, are Chief of Security. I love you, Tasha, but I'm not ready to take orders from you."

"Especially as you would far outrank me," she agreed. "But I can't step—"

"Don't even say it! Tasha, I would never suggest such a thing; you have worked too long and too hard to get where you are. No, love, the only way you and I can work together now is as equals, and face it, that cannot happen in Starfleet. Join me, and learn what it is to be bound by no rules but your own conscience."

"Dare, I can't—"

"Don't say it," he repeated, placing a finger over her lips. "There's no need to decide today, Tasha. Believe me, I do understand how important Starfleet is to you. But I also believe you will outgrow it. I will still be there, love. We're survivors, you and I." He replaced the finger with his lips, and Yar relaxed into his embrace.

He was right. She didn't have to decide today—couldn't, really. Her current enlistment had a long time to run . . . and Dare understood that she must serve it out. But he was free now. They would see one another again, as often as possible.

And one day, perhaps . . .

Chapter Twelve

THE *ENTERPRISE* was in routine flight. There were no clues that it was to be the most difficult day so far of Lieutenant Commander Data's life.

He was at his usual post. Worf, on the upper bridge, reported no obstacles or vessels, then turned to Tasha and began to discuss the ship's martial arts competition. Data heard the pleasure in Tasha's voice as she realized that Worf had bet on her to win.

Tasha seemed happy, even though Darryl Adin had not accepted Starfleet's offer of reinstatement. Data was pleased that he had found the evidence to clear Adin—for it was now obvious that Tasha's reunion with the man she loved had made no difference at all in her friendship with Data, Worf, Deanna, and others.

Rikan was right: Data had confused two very different kinds of . . . love. He was still uncomfortable using that word, for as the warlord had suggested, humans also got its many meanings confused. Possibly Data had done so because he had been programmed by humans. Whatever the reason, he was secure now that the friendships he had formed aboard the *Enterprise* could only be enhanced by the addition of others to the circle.

Data's consciousness was drawn from his personal musings when the mission suddenly ceased to be routine. Deanna Troi's shuttle crashed on Vagra II, and Data, Riker, Tasha, and Dr. Crusher beamed down to rescue her and her pilot. But the away team was prevented from reaching the shuttle by the peculiar creature called Armus.

Even then, there was no warning, no apprehension. While strange life forms were nothing new to the crew of the *Enterprise,* none of them could take a talking tar pit very seriously. No one tried to stop Tasha when she attempted to walk brusquely past it, worried about her close friend Deanna trapped in the shuttle.

How they underestimated Armus!

When the thing struck Tasha, Data and Riker turned their phasers on it, while Dr. Crusher rushed to the fallen Security Chief. The attention of the men was on the fact that their weapons were ineffective; neither of them realized that Tasha was seriously injured, let alone—

"She's dead," Dr. Crusher reported to the Captain. Data heard not surprise, but total lack of belief in her voice, saw the same in Riker's face.

They transported aboard, and Dr. Crusher folded Tasha's limp body into Data's arms. Operating on standard procedures, he carried her to sickbay, placed her on the treatment couch, and started for the bridge to report to Captain Picard.

But the Captain was emerging from the turbolift into the corridor outside sickbay. "How is she?"

"I do not know," Data replied. "Surely Dr. Crusher can revive her." It was not a kind lie; he assumed Tasha had suffered cardiac arrest from an electrical shock, an easily-corrected condition.

"Come on, then, Data," said Picard. At the android's raised eyebrows he added, "We may not be able to do anything, but I, for one, do not intend to wait on the bridge for a report."

So Data followed Picard back into sickbay, realizing that he, too, wanted to know Tasha's fate first-hand.

Data went to stand beside Riker, feeling helpless. As one effort after another failed to revive Tasha, Picard joined them, knowing as surely as Data did that Dr. Crusher continued her efforts long after all hope was gone. Data looked from one man to the other, seeing in their strained looks a refusal to accept the death of a friend until Dr. Crusher finally announced, "She's gone."

"Gone?" Picard asked as if he still could not believe it, forcing Dr. Crusher to explain further, her voice tight with unshed tears.

Data said nothing. He was uncomfortable with human grief . . . and his own feelings were a tumult such as he had never experienced before. He continued in that state until the strategy meeting called by Captain Picard.

Data remained silent, while the humans all began to speak at once. He felt alien among them . . . until Picard broke into the babble. "Lieutenant Yar's death is very painful for all of us. We will have to deal with it as best we can, for now. Until the shuttle crew is safely beamed aboard this ship, our feelings will have to wait. Is that understood?"

There was silence—and then, when Picard began asking for suggestions, Data was heartened to see his crewmates do exactly what he did: put all else aside, and concentrate on the effort to bring Deanna Troi and her pilot safely home to the *Enterprise*. He was no more automaton than they; all understood that sorrow for the dead must wait while they sought to save the living.

On returning to the planet, Data had his first direct experience with sadism. Armus was a textbook case—but with its combination of power and hostages, it was invulnerable to textbook solutions.

And it seemed fascinated with Data. Although it viciously exercised its power against Dr. Crusher, Geordi, Riker, each time it involved Data in the torture. Then Captain Picard joined them—and provided the solution.

"I want to see my people in the shuttle," Picard demanded.

"Entertain me," Armus answered—

—and Picard merely shook his head and murmured a negative.

From that point on, Data knew how to deal with Armus, and so did Dr. Crusher. Armus might be able to control them physically, but they did not have to allow it to control their feelings.

The creature must have known it had met its match from its first confrontation with the Captain, for after testing Data and Dr. Crusher it ignored Geordi and released Riker, allowing the four of them to beam up to the *Enterprise* so it could take on the Captain, one on one.

Hearing the Captain's report of that confrontation later, though, at the final debriefing, Data found once again that he did not understand. "Sir," he said, "it appears that you did to Armus what Armus attempted to do to us: you controlled it by frustrating it. You implied that you would help it to leave its planet—and then you refused to do so. Its futile rage weakened it so that we were able to beam you and the shuttle passengers aboard."

"That is correct, Data," said Picard.

Data frowned. "I do not understand. If such emotional manipulation was wrong for Armus—"

"Data!" Geordi gasped.

At the same time Dr. Crusher said angrily, "You can't accuse the Captain of—"

"Let him speak!" Picard overrode their protests. "That is a valid question, Mr. Data."

Data explained, "It is not the act of leaving Armus behind I question, but the method. An act in and of itself has no moral value, positive or negative. We have all fired our phasers to injure or kill, for example. In self-defense or in defense of our colleagues, such acts are justified."

As Data paused, searching for the words to explain his disquiet, Picard anticipated him. "What you are asking, Data, is whether I acted in revenge, with the same sadism as Armus."

Data felt the others staring at him, but although he would not have couched it in such harsh terms, that was in essence his question. "Yes, sir," he admitted.

Picard gave a slight sad smile. "I cannot answer that, Mr. Data."

"What!" gasped Riker. "Sir, we all know you would never—!"

"No, Number One," Picard said calmly, "you don't know that because I do not. That is the greatest danger in confronting evil: it is contagious. I have no doubt I did what was necessary. *Why* I did it—whether I achieved the superhuman feat of feeling no thrill of revenge for Tasha's death or the pain Armus put the rest of you through—I will probably question for the rest of my life."

"I am sorry, sir," said Data. "I should not have asked."

"Oh, yes, Data," the Captain replied, "you should have. I have more years of experience than the rest of you, but that doesn't make such decisions any easier. Sooner or later we all face the no-win situation. One of the hardest lessons of life is that there are times when the best we can hope for is a draw. When the battle is with one's own conscience, that is the most difficult of all."

With that, the debriefing ended—but the long, tense day was not yet over. At last there was time to confront their grief over Tasha's death. First there was the public funeral service, open to anyone aboard the ship. Data had attended many such services in his years in Starfleet; today he heard familiar words of comfort and consolation, but did not find either.

He had lost colleagues before. This was the first time he had lost a friend.

Off duty, Data returned to his quarters after the service— only to have his introspection interrupted within minutes by the Captain on the intercom. "Please come to the holodeck, Mr. Data."

"The holodeck, sir?"

"You are named among those for whom Tasha left a farewell message."

"Yes, sir," Data responded automatically—but there was nothing automatic about his internal response. He knew of the Starfleet tradition, of course . . . but no one else had ever included him in it.

The whole bridge crew were there, including Wesley Crusher. Dr. Beverly Crusher also joined them.

Data stood back, a little behind the rest, not knowing what to expect. When Tasha's image appeared, he saw Wesley look to his mother, and felt an affinity for the boy.

When Tasha had made the recording, she had guessed right about dying quickly in the line of duty. She spoke of her love for her friends, her gratitude to Starfleet, and her personal feelings for each of them.

When it came to Data, she called him her friend, and added, "You see things with the wonder of a child, and that makes you more human than any of us."

As Tasha's image faded, only Captain Picard responded, "*Au revoir,* Natasha." Then he added, "This gathering is concluded," and people began filing off the holodeck.

Data, though, walked forward, staring at the cloud images, trying to understand what had just happened. Again he felt isolated. Picard joined him, but waited for Data to speak first.

"Sir," said Data, "the purpose of this gathering . . . confuses me."

"Oh? How so?"

"My thoughts are not for Tasha," Data explained, "but for myself. I keep thinking how empty it will be without her presence. Did I miss the point?"

"No, you didn't, Data," the Captain assured him. "You got it," and he left the android to his contemplation.

For a time Data simply stood there, wishing . . . wishing he could talk to Tasha just once more, wishing he understood how humans coped with such loss.

As Tasha's image had said, he had his memories. He supposed some would think him fortunate because he could recall every detail of every moment he had spent with Tasha, and it would not fade with time as human memory did. They could probably not understand that it only meant he would remember more clearly exactly what was now gone from them.

Then he recalled something the warlord Rikan had said. "Survivors are considered fortunate, Data—and the irony is that those who envy us our longevity either do not live long enough to know the cruel fate in store for us . . . or else they live to share it."

So this was what the warlord had meant. Data wished he could talk with Rikan—actually considered for a moment using some of his unused accumulation of personal subspace radio time to do so.

And then he remembered Captain Picard saying in the debriefing, "I have more years of experience than any of you."

Jean-Luc Picard was also a survivor. But like the legendary Captain James T. Kirk, Picard functioned best among the stars, not behind a desk—and having learned its lesson with that same Captain Kirk, Starfleet would allow him to do so for as long as he continued both capable and willing.

After the long, difficult day, the entire bridge crew were off duty. Certainly the Captain would want to rest.

But when Data returned to his quarters, there was a message on his console to contact Picard.

"Oh, yes, Data—there is one more matter concerning Tasha on which I need your advice. Would you mind coming to my quarters?"

"I will be right there, sir."

The "matter" was one final holographic message. Picard was seated at his desk, turning the cartridge over in his hands. Data had no doubt for whom it was intended.

Picard looked up. "Sit down, Data. I think you know what this is."

"Tasha's farewell message for Darryl Adin."

The Captain stared at the cartridge again. "That's right. Do you know where he is?"

Picard could have asked the computer. Data did not say so. "He is still on Treva, sir, aiding President Rikan in setting up his new government."

"Then shall we transmit this to him there?"

"Yes, s—" Data broke off. "No, sir. If you please, Captain, I have a great deal of personal leave time accumulated. With your permission, I will take Tasha's message to

Mr. Adin. I do not think it should be delivered by a—" Data gasped in amazement at what he had almost said.

Picard looked up at him with a small smile. "By someone who did not know Tasha," he suggested. "Permission granted." He handed over the cartridge. "It is the first time you must do this, Data, but it will not be the last." Data was almost certain he was remembering delivering the news of her husband's death, and probably a similar message cartridge, to Dr. Crusher. Or perhaps it was a sequence of many such events that put the shadows in the Captain's eyes.

"It is the price we pay," said Data, "for being survivors."

Picard blinked at him in surprise. Then he nodded. "I hadn't thought of it that way, but you are right, Data. And thank you for volunteering. You know Darryl Adin better than I do, but I would have gone myself rather than coldly transmit the information."

"Starfleet policy is to make every effort to send such messages in the care of someone who knows both parties," said Data.

"And Starfleet policy has nothing whatsoever to do with your offer," the Captain told him.

"No, sir," Data admitted.

"Well, then, go and see about rearranging the duty schedule to allow for your absence. And Mr. Data," he said as the android turned to go.

Data turned back. "Yes, sir?"

"I said before that you understood the purpose of Starfleet farewells. However, I note that you have no farewell message on file."

Data looked down at the table, frowning slightly, then back at Picard. "You are correct, sir. I will remedy that situation immediately. It never seemed . . . appropriate before."

"But it does now?"

"Yes, sir."

Picard nodded. "I was right, then. Mr. Data, you very definitely have got the point."

THE
STAR TREK
PHENOMENON

_____ **ENTROPY EFFECT**
66499/$3.95

_____ **KLINGON GAMBIT**
66342/$3.95

_____ **PROMETHEUS DESIGN**
67435/$3.95

_____ **ABODE OF LIFE**
66149/$3.95

_____ **BLACK FIRE**
65747/$3.95

_____ **TRIANGLE**
66251/$3.95

_____ **WEB OF THE ROMULANS**
66501/$3.95

_____ **YESTERDAY'S SON**
66110/$3.95

_____ **WOUNDED SKY**
66735/$3.95

_____ **CORONA**
66341/$3.95

_____ **MY ENEMY, MY ALLY**
65866/$3.95

_____ **VULCAN ACADEMY MURDERS**
64744/$3.95

_____ **UHURA'S SONG**
65227/$3.95

_____ **SHADOW LORD**
66087/$3.95

_____ **ISHMAEL**
66089/$3.95

_____ **KILLING TIME**
65921/$3.95

_____ **DWELLERS IN THE CRUCIBLE**
66088/$3.95

_____ **PAWNS AND SYMBOLS**
66497/$3.95

_____ **THE FINAL REFLECTION**
67075/$3.95

_____ **MINDSHADOW**
66090/$3.95

_____ **CRISIS ON CENTAURUS**
65753/$3.95

_____ **DREADNOUGHT**
66500/$3.95

_____ **DEMONS**
66150/$3.95

_____ **BATTLESTATIONS!**
66201/$3.95

_____ **CHAIN OF ATTACK**
66658/$3.95

_____ **DEEP DOMAIN**
67077/$3.95

_____ **DREAMS OF THE RAVEN**
67794/$3.95

_____ **ROMULAN WAY**
68085/$3.95

_____ **HOW MUCH FOR JUST THE PLANET?**
62998/$3.95

_____ **BLOODTHIRST**
64489/$3.95

_____ **ENTERPRISE**
65912/$4.50

_____ **STRANGERS FROM THE SKY**
65241/$3.95

_____ **FINAL FRONTIER**
64752/$4.50

_____ **IDIC EPIDEMIC**
63574/$3.95

_____ **THE TEARS OF THE SINGERS**
67076/$3.95

_____ **THE COVENANT OF THE CROWN**
67072/$3.95

_____ **MUTINY ON THE ENTERPRISE**
67073/$3.95

_____ **THE TRELLISANE CONFRONTATION**
67074/$3.95

THE

STAR TREK

PHENOMENON